The Last Will
And Testament
Of Atticus
Wainwright III

Leigh Fenty

Copyright © 2121 Leigh Fenty

All rights reserved

The characters and events portrayed in this book are fictitious. Any similarity to real persons, living or dead, is coincidental and not intended by the author.

No part of this book may be reproduced, or stored in a retrieval system, or transmitted in any form or by any means, electronic, mechanical, photocopying, recording, or otherwise, without express written permission of the publisher.

Printed in the United States of America

To my son James. I won't be leaving you a huge family fortune, but hopefully I'll leave you with the memory of a mom who did her best and loved you without judgement.

Table of Contents

Chapter One	11
Chapter Two	15
Chapter Three	19
Chapter Four	22
Chapter Five	29
Chapter Six	38
Chapter Seven	42
Chapter Eight	47
Chapter Nine	53
Chapter Ten	64
Chapter Eleven	73
Chapter Twelve	81
Chapter Thirteen	91
Chapter Fourteen	99
Chapter Fifteen	110
Chapter Sixteen	119
Chapter Seventeen	126
Chapter Eighteen	135
Chapter Nineteen	142
Chapter Twenty	148
Chapter Twenty-One	154
Chapter Twenty-Two	164
Chapter Twenty-three	171
Chapter Twenty-Four	180
Chapter Twenty-Five	190
Chapter Twenty-Six	196
Chapter Twenty-Seven	203
Chapter Twenty-Eight	209
Chapter Twenty-Nine	214
Chapter Thirty	223
Chapter Thirty-One	228
Chapter Thirty-Two	236
Chapter Thirty-Three	244

Chapter Thirty-Four	253
Chapter Thirty-Five	258
Chapter Thirty-Six	263
Chapter Thirty-Seven	268
Chapter Thirty-Eight	276
Chapter Thirty-Nine	281
Chapter Forty	290
Chapter Forty-One	294

Chapter One

Noah opened his eyes as the bed moved next to him. Missy Steinberger sat up and wrapped a blanket around her shoulders. Her delicate features and her perfect physical form, defied the fact she'd been twenty-nine and holding for at least a decade. She had an advantage though. As the wife of a wealthy man, she had nothing better to do with her time than spend it at the yoga studio or at the gym with her personal trainer. Her new hobby was tennis and spending quality time with the club's pro, aka Noah.

"Do you mind if I use your shower?"

He shrugged. "Go for it."

Missy headed for the bathroom, then stopped and returned to the bed with a smile. "Unless we have time for another match."

Noah glanced at his watch, then smiled at her. "Don't you have a husband to get home to?"

Missy shook her dark curly locks as she climbed onto the bed. She ran her hand through his blond hair, then patted his muscular chest. "Mr. Steinberger is in Philadelphia until Monday." She was married to a man at least twenty years her senior, which seemed to be the case of many of the women Noah gave tennis lessons to. That made it easier for him to justify the extra-curricular activities he engaged in with some of his more persistent clients.

"Well, you may not have a busy day, but I do." When his phone rang, he picked it up and shrugged. "Sorry, it's my brother. Got to take it." He swung his legs over the side of the bed and sat up. "Hey, Marcus." He glanced over his shoulder to catch Missy heading for the bathroom. She dropped her blanket and glanced over her shoulder at him before she disappeared into the room.

"You working?" Marcus asked.

Noah glanced at the bathroom door. "Um, not exactly."

"I didn't catch you in mid-coitus, did I?"

"Why are you calling?"

"Did you get it?"

Noah picked his shorts up from the floor. "Hang on." He set the phone down and slipped them on, then retrieved the phone. "Get what?"

"The summons from the old man."

"I haven't gotten anything from him. What does he want?"

"When was the last time you checked your mail?"

Noah stood up and searched the room for his shirt. "Last week." He picked up a discarded shirt from the floor and smelled it. He frowned as he dropped it onto a chair and pulled another one off of a hanger in the closet.

"Go check your mail. But get dressed first."

"I'm dressed. I may occasionally go sans clothing in my condo. But I don't go check the mail buck naked."

"That would certainly make your neighbor's day."

"Yeah, but not her husband's. He'd probably come out shooting.

"So go look and don't hang up. Take me with you. I want to hear your reaction when you read it."

Noah sighed as he left the bedroom and headed for the front door. When he stepped outside, he got a wave from his neighbor, Diana. They had an ongoing flirtatious relationship, but never crossed the line. Sleeping with the married women from the tennis club was one thing. Overstepping with the neighbor's wife was quite another. He waved at her as he walked down the sidewalk toward the mailbox. Since he paid his bills online, he rarely checked the contents. He hoped by ignoring it, the mail carrier would give up and stop filling it with junk mail.

He opened the box and pulled out a three inch stack of mail. Most of it was advertisements and solicitations, as he expected. But he continued to shuffle through it in search of a correspondence from his father.

The letter was near the bottom of the pile, an ivory linen envelope with his name and address written by someone other than his father. He knew his father's bold hand. This was dainty and flowery. The new wife obviously wrote it. He tucked the stack of mail under his arm and kept the envelope out. "Okay, got it." He headed for the house.

"Open it."

Noah entered the house and set the stack of mail on the kitchen table. He put his phone on speaker and set it next to the pile.

"So the old man couldn't be bothered to address it himself?"

"Just read it."

Noah slid a finger under the flap of the envelope and ripped it open, then took a moment to read the note, which was written in his father's handwriting.

"No, not going."

"It's mandatory."

"Don't care." As he dropped the note on the table, Missy came into the kitchen. Noah picked up his phone and took it off speaker. "I'll call you back." He said, then hung up on his brother, not even giving him the chance to object.

Missy came up to him and put her arms around his neck. "I swear you have the best shower I've ever been in."

"It's the on demand water heater."

"Whatever it is, it's fantastic. I really wish you'd join me in there some time. It's big enough for two."

It was true. The shower was the only thing that was unexpectedly large, in his otherwise compact, one bedroom condo. "Maybe next time."

Noah had to promise a shared shower on her next visit, before he was able to get Missy out the door. He then made himself a sandwich and grabbed a bottle of beer, before he headed to the deck on the back of his condo. Though the living space was small, the complex was exclusive and he was on the waiting list for over a year before he got in. Part of the appeal was its close proximity to the club, close enough to ride his bike when he wanted to, and the weather was cooperating. He sat down on a cedar chair and propped up his feet on the matching foot stool, then took a bite of his BLT before calling Marcus back.

Marcus answered on the second ring. "What the hell, man?"

"Sorry, had some business to attend to." He took a sip of beer. "Like I said, I'm not going."

"It's the reading of the will. You need to go."

"He's not dead yet."

"It's just his way to get in one last power play. There's no fun in screwing everyone if he can't see their faces when he does it."

"I really don't want to see all of those people."

"You mean your family?"

"You're the only family I have. And Mom, sometimes. Dad's various and sundry ex-wives are not my family."

"What about Libby and Dell? They're our half-sisters."

"Libby is fine, for now. Her crazy mother hasn't ruined her yet. Dell, no. I don't accept her as family."

"Okay, whatever. Regardless of all that. You need to go. If for no other reason than to give me a sane person to hang out with."

"You could bring Roberto."

"I wouldn't do that to him. I love him too much."

"Then we could both not go."

"Noah. I don't know why you're fighting it. You know, in the end, you'll go. If for no other reason than curiosity."

Chapter Two

Noah watched the tennis ball soar over his head. He couldn't help but compare it to his life, out of control and at the complete mercy of an individual whose interests lie in a realm separate and unrelated to his own. He was still fighting the inevitable, a weekend with the Wainwright family.

Mrs. Simpson waited patiently for Noah to retrieve the ball and join her at the net. "Why does it always do that?" Her words came out as a whine, which was a distinct contradiction to her outward appearance.

She was representative of most of Noah's clients, well past her prime, with her true age probably only known to her physician. Ash blonde hair, streaked ever so strategically, framed her medically preserved face. The tennis whites she wore bore the name of a top designer, and though the skirt was a bit on the short side, she still had the body to pull it off, thanks to a personal trainer and an in-house dietitian. She had money to burn and had no qualms about letting the world know.

Noah jogged across the court in his daily business attire, a navy shirt with the club logo over the pocket and white shorts. Having spent most of his twenty-nine years in one athletic endeavor or another, he was in peak condition, though he seemed to tire a bit more quickly the last couple of years. Perhaps it had something to do with the cigarettes he just couldn't quite give up.

He smiled at Mrs. Simpson, causing her to tremble demurely. Thanks to the two years he spent in braces during middle school, his smile was worth at least $10,000.00 a year in tips.

"It's all a matter of control. You're doing fine." He stuffed the ball into the pocket of his shorts before looking at his watch.

"It's not that time already, is it?" She set a well-manicured hand on the top of the net.

"I'm afraid so."

"Let me buy you lunch." The hand moved from the net to Noah's tanned forearm.

He took a step back and studied the strings on his racket. "You know I can't do that, Mrs. Simpson."

She pouted. "Consider it a tip."

Noah smiled at her. "You don't want me to get fired now, do you?"

The hand moved to her chest and patted the lightly freckled skin. "Oh my, no. Of course not."

He backed up a few more steps. "I'll see you next week then."

Noah had some special clients, like Missy Steinberger, but Mrs. Simpson wasn't one of them, nor would she ever be. She was about ten years past the acceptable age. Lately, it seemed like all of them were past the acceptable age. The older he got, the more selective he became, and lately, Missy was the only woman he spent time with off the court. Even her after hour visits happened only a couple times a month.

He wasn't sure when he started falling into this lifestyle, but lately he'd begun to fall out of it. He assumed it was a good thing.

After he showered and dressed, Noah was putting on his shoes when Tom, one of the other pros, sauntered in. Tom was dark and handsome in an Italian mobster sort of way, and a few years younger than Noah. Tom's brooding looks, was quite a contrast to Noah's sun bleached hair and deep blue eyes. His charming arrogance was a big hit with the ladies, but Noah found it boring and condescending. A little of Tom went a long way.

Tired and sweaty, Tom tossed his racket into his locker, then smiled at Noah.

"Tough match?" Noah asked, not really interested, but feeling like he should make some conversation.

"Gruesome. Where does that guy get the energy? He's got to be at least sixty and he barely broke a sweat."

"Oysters."

Tom stripped off his shirt and dropped it to the ground. "Come again?"

"Stamina. Sports and sex. Not all that different."

As he peered over the top of the locker door, Tom grinned at Noah. "Who the hell have you been having sex with?" Noah chose not to answer as he put on his other shoe.

Tom went on. "Who'd you shut down today?" He removed his shorts and wrapped a towel around his waist.

"Mrs. Simpson."

Tom headed for the showers. "Widowed three years ago. Majority stock holder at Simpson Paper Products. No heirs. She's worth about $25,000,000.00."

Noah stood up and grabbed his jacket. "How do you know this stuff?"

Tom glanced over his shoulder. "Research, my friend. Research." He disappeared around the white tile partition and turned on the water. His head appeared over the wall. "Do you think I still want to be a tennis pro when I'm thirty?"

Noah tried not to let Tom's question bother him as he slammed his locker door closed and left the room. Since his last client, Mrs. R.T. Weston of the Boston Weston's, had cancelled, he was leaving early and would miss the rush hour traffic.

He opted to ride his bike today, since the days were still not too hot. He peddled the five miles to his condo, through the light afternoon traffic. When he arrived at his small front yard, he dismounted and hoisted the bike up onto his shoulder as he dug for his keys. Diana came out her front door and smiled at him.

"Afternoon, Diana."

"Noah, glad I caught you. Dean and I are having a BBQ this weekend. We'd love to have you join us."

Noah knew Dean wouldn't be overjoyed with the invitation. Dean knew how his wife was, and he knew she spent a lot of time watering her yard, especially when Noah was on his patio.

"I've got a family thing this weekend. But thank you."

"Maybe next time," she said with a tiny pout, not knowing that Noah was immune to pouts of any kind.

Noah nodded as he unlocked his door and headed inside. He hung his bike from two hooks in his ceiling, then sunk down on the couch. Marcus was right. His curiosity had won out. Thursday morning he would leave the city to spend the weekend with the very definition of a dysfunctional family.

Chapter Three

The Wainwright family home was nestled in the foothills outside of the city. It was a twenty-minute drive on the freeway followed by fifteen minutes on a winding road that made it seem like you were farther away from civilization than you were. The house sat on five acres of manicured lawns and gardens, with a tennis court, a pool, and a freestanding garage that housed six cars. Four of the vehicles were vintage models worth a small fortune.

The house itself was decadently oversized with eight bedrooms, ten bathrooms, a library, and a formal dining room. There was even a room off the library that held nothing other than a white grand piano. Nobody in the family played the piano, but his father decided at some point he needed to own one. So, there it sat in a room no one ever entered.

Noah spent his first three years in the house, but when his parents divorced, his mother moved them across the country to California. His mother left the marriage with a large settlement and trust funds for the sons when they turned eighteen. On the surface the payout seemed generous, but the defrayal was a fraction of what the old man was worth, and in the end barely sustained the boys through a few years of college.

Visits were infrequent and grew fewer and farther apart as the brothers neared adulthood and became old enough to decide for themselves. The last required visit was twelve years ago, the summer before Noah turned eighteen.

He and his brother returned to the east coast for college and their mother followed a few years later. As a young adult, visits to his father became infrequent. They talked on the phone occasionally, and had dinner together five years ago, but Noah hadn't seen him since.

Atticus wainwright still had a hold on them, along with the rest of the family, as proven by the reunion now in progress. He still had the power to convince his four children and his three ex-wives to drop what they were doing and spend a weekend together at the family estate with no explanation of why or what to expect. He lured them all by mentioning the will, knowing they wouldn't be able to resist.

Noah turned off the freeway and drove along Apple Blossom Lane, so named for the fruit trees that lined the road winding through the neighborhood. The houses got progressively nicer along the route, with the home of Atticus Wainwright being the number one perfect example of unapologetic opulence all the neighbors strived for.

Noah turned onto Wainwright Dr. and drove under the arch with his family name spelled out in two foot metal letters. He sighed as he felt the familiar ache in the pit of his stomach. It would be with him until he escaped on Monday morning.

When he came to the iron gate crossing the road, he pulled up to the video surveillance camera and shifted the car into park, to wait for Simms, the Wainwright butler, to answer the call.

Sooner than expected, Simms' voice crackled over the speaker. "Master Noah."

"Simms, how's it hanging?"

Without a response from Simms, the gate slowly opened in front of Noah. He pushed the talk button again and said, "Simms, you're no fun," before he pulled through the gate and followed the circular drive.

An array of cars dotted the driveway, and Noah tried to match them to his step-mothers. Black Jag, Dakota. White Mercedes had to be Laura's, because he knew Dell drove the red BMW, and his mother's car was the vintage Mustang. The only car missing was Marcus'.

"Dammit. Where the hell are you?" Noah pulled in behind the black Jaguar and turned off his engine. He settled back in his seat with no intention of going inside without his brother.

The double front doors opened, and he saw Simms step out onto the front entryway. Noah got out of his car and waved at him.

"I'm waiting for Marcus," he yelled across the red brick drive.

Simms nodded, then disappeared into the house.

Simms had been with the family since before Noah was born. He was in charge of everything dealing with the running of the house. When the boys were small and making their obligatory summer visits, Simms was in charge of them, as well.

Chapter Four

Dell Wainwright Albright circled the mahogany dining table like a shark around a lone surfer. The table designed to seat twenty was set-up for nine. A small name card accompanied each array of fine china and sterling silverware.

The leopard print blouse she wore was a few sizes too small and barely contained her ample bosom. She held a half-full martini glass in her manicured hand; the bright red nail polish was the same shade as her short, cropped hair. She was born blonde as were her half-brothers and sister, but had been a redhead since high school. Her exotic attire along with her extreme hair and makeup made her look older than her twenty-five years.

Buddy came up behind his wife. "What do you think, sugarplum?" He stuck his hands in the pockets of his khaki dockers and rocked up onto his toes to peer over her shoulder. Buddy and Dell were the same height, so with the heels she always wore, she was taller than him. He was a non-descript little man who, at thirty, was slightly overweight. He had a full head of naturally curly strawberry blond hair that he tried to tame by wearing it short. His red Hawaiian shirt with white hyacinths was quite a contrast to the animal theme his wife had going on.

Dell drained her glass and handed it to Buddy. "Should've made it a double." She started circling the table again. "A Wainwright family reunion. How wonderful." She made it all the way around the table and nodded at the empty glass Buddy still held in his hand. "Do you want me to beg?"

He glanced at the glass, then smiled. "Coming right up, my sweet." He went to the bar in the corner of the room and poured vodka into a large glass shaker, then dribbled in some vermouth. He used a long glass mixing wand with the head of a lion on the end to swirl the alcohol around a few times. He sucked the end of the stick before he put it aside, then poured the martini into two glasses. He picked up both and brought one to Dell.

"Is your mother coming?"

"The whole family, Buddy. That means the second Mrs. Wainwright, too."

"The darling of the Grand Ol' Opry."

"Right." She looked at the glass in her hand, then handed it back to Buddy. "Olives."

"Of course, my dove." He returned to the bar and picked up a red plastic sword. He stabbed three olives and dropped them into the glass, then brought it to her.

She took a sip as the double doors to the dining room swooshed open and Dakota Wainwright made her appearance. She floated into the room like a hot summer breeze and stopped inside the doors as though she was expecting a round of applause. She was moderately successful for a few years in Nashville and had been milking the notoriety ever since. Even though she was a well-preserved forty-six, a younger hipper generation of country singers swooped in and changed the face of country music. Her old-school, Patsy Cline inspired style, was no longer popular.

She went to Dell and air kissed her on each cheek. "Hello, darlin'." Though she was born and raised in New York, she adopted a southern drawl to go along with her country star persona.

"Mother." Dell took two steps back away from her.

Dakota wagged a finger at her. "Haven't we talked about you using that derogatory word?"

"Right, *Dakota*. How're you?"

Dakota removed the baby blue cowboy hat she wore and ran a hand through her red hair. The shade was less extreme than Dells, but still a jarring scarlet. The hat matched the blue boots she wore, along with her tight denim jeans and white western shirt.

She looked at Buddy as though she just noticed him. "Buddy."

"*Mom.*"

Dell looked at the glass in her hand, then at Buddy. "Keep them coming. I need to get fortified if I'm going to make it through the day."

"Shouldn't take more than a couple, sweet pea, after that lunch you drank."

"Fix one for Dakota, too."

Dakota circled the table. She picked up a name card, frowned at it, then exchanged it with another.

"I'll be damned if I'm going to sit next to that child bride of his."

Buddy filled the shaker again and took a third glass off the shelf behind the bar. After dropping three olives in each glass, he handed a martini to each of the women, replacing Dell's empty glass.

"I guess the old man still has it," he said.

Dell glared at him. "The only thing he has is fifty million dollars."

The double doors opened again and Laura Wainwright entered with her daughter Libby. The girl was a beautiful seventeen-year-old who resembled her mother, though her light hair was a contrast to Laura's dark coloring. But Laura's beauty faded after five years as the third Mrs. Wainwright, and thirteen years as an ex-Mrs. Wainwright. She hadn't handled it as well as the first and the second wives had, and she looked every bit of her forty-three years. She was dressed in a somber ensemble of black pants and a dark purple blouse. In contrast, Libby wore a bright yellow sundress.

Laura nodded at her predecessor. "Dakota."

Dakota rushed to Laura and kissed the air in the vicinity of her left cheek, then turned her attention to Libby. "This can't be little Libby. Look at you, you're all grown up. Atticus would be so proud." She brushed a stray blonde hair away from the girl's blue eyes. "If he wasn't such a selfish bastard."

Laura gave a slight smile to Dell and nodded at Buddy. "Dell, Buddy. Nice to see you again."

Dell smiled back. "Buddy's pouring, what'll you have?"

Laura shook her head. "Nothing for me." She started circling the table and picked up the name card Dakota just moved.

Dakota came up to her and took it away from her. "Don't even think about it." The two women stared at each other for a long moment, before Laura took a step back and continued around the table.

Buddy called out to Libby. "How about a Coke?"

Libby glanced at her mother and got a nod, before she went to the bar and perched on the edge of a black and chrome barstool.

Buddy pointed at her mouth. "Got rid of the hardware, huh?" He opened a can of Coke and poured it over some ice, then handed it to her.

She took a sip. "Three years ago." She smiled a thank you before heading to the small buffet table set up with hors d'oeuvres, unaware of the unseemly assessment her brother-in-law was giving her.

But Dell was all too aware of the look in Buddy's eye and the thoughts behind it. She went to him and blocked his view.

"Down boy."

"What?"

"She's my sister. And seventeen will get you twenty."

"Just admiring nature's handiwork, darling."

Dell pulled a flower from a vase on the bar. "Here, admire this."

Buddy put the flower to his nose but dropped it when the doors opened again and Tiffany Wainwright entered the room.

Dell looked at her husband anticipating his reaction to the beautiful, young, and fourth Mrs. Wainwright, but after his initial reaction he looked down, and was busy rearranging glasses on the bar and barely looked up at her.

Nature truly blessed Tiffany and she walked with the assurance of knowing conversations ceased and all eyes gravitated towards her whenever she entered a room. This day was no different, as she smiled demurely at her guests. "You must think I'm a terrible hostess. I'm Tiffany, Atticus' wife." She pushed her highlighted blonde hair off her tanned shoulders and smiled brightly.

Buddy seemed to notice her finally, and he brushed past Dell and rushed to Tiffany with an extended hand. "The lovely number four." When she put her hand in his, he kissed the back of it.

Dell stepped up and forcefully removed Buddy's grip on Tiffany. "I'm Dell, and this insensitive letch is my husband."

"Buddy," he added.

"How nice to meet you both."

Dakota joined them and looked Tiffany up and down. "You must be the reason Atticus is in such poor health."

Buddy nodded towards Dakota. "The second Mrs. Wainwright."

Laura approached with Libby by her side.

Buddy smiled. "Laura, the third—"

Laura glared at him. "Shut up, Buddy."

"Excuse me," Dell said through tight jaws. "I believe I'm the only one who can tell him that." She looked at her husband. "Shut up, Buddy."

Laura offered a hand to Tiffany. "Hello." She put a hand on Libby's shoulder. "This is my daughter, Libby."

Tiffany smiled. "Oh, yes. The baby of the family. Atticus has told me so much about you."

Laura frowned. "Atticus hasn't laid eyes on her in over a year." She apparently reached the limit of her polite benevolence and took Libby's arm, then led her daughter away from her replacement.

Buddy, still smiling, said, "I seem to be the appointed bartender. Can I pour you a martini?"

Tiffany returned his smile. "It seems to be a bit stuffy in here." She took his arm. "I prefer wine. Would you escort me to the wine cellar?"

"Umm, sure. I'd be delighted."

Dakota went to Dell and the two of them watched the doors close behind Buddy and Tiffany. "You need to keep a leash on that boy."

Dell shrugged. "I really don't care what he does."

Dell went to the bar and refilled her glass. She and Buddy had been married for five long years. She often considered leaving him, but always come to the same conclusion. It'd be too much of an effort. She'd molded him into a compliant little puppy who did her bidding, and she didn't want to start over with someone new. The fact he had a wandering eye wasn't too concerning. It's not like any of the women he ogled would have the least bit of interest in accepting his awkward advances.

Dakota watched her for a moment then turned to Laura and Libby who joined them at the bar. "So, what do you think?"

"She's what? Twenty-five?" Laura asked.

"Still, you have to be at least a little impressed," Dakota said.

Laura sniffed. "Atticus' bank account is the only reason she's in this house."

"Honey, that's the only reason any of us are in this house." Dakota headed for the door. "I'm going to go poke around. Libby, you want to come with me?"

Libby glanced at her mother before saying, "Sure." She followed Dakota out of the room.

Laura glanced at Dell, who was behind the bar. "Your mother is such a colorful character."

Dell headed for the door. "Yes, isn't she though?" She left the room, leaving Laura alone.

*****

Dell headed across the black-and-white marble floor of the foyer. When Simms appeared from out of nowhere, she stopped and looked at him. In other families, he might've been considered to be more than just an employee after such long faithful service. But this was the Wainwright's and the line between classes was dark and impenetrable.

Simms cleared his throat quietly and bowed slightly. "Mistress Delilah."

She stepped around him and looked up the staircase that wound gracefully to the second floor. "Is he up there?"

"Yes, Miss."

As she continued on her way, she opened the two glass doors at the entrance to the library and went inside. The thick carpeting silenced her heels on the floor as she crossed the room and went behind the bar.

Simms appeared at the doorway. "May I assist you?"

Dell poured a healthy shot of brandy into a snifter. "I got it covered, Simms." She took a swallow as she waved a painted finger at him. "You may go do whatever it is you do."

After giving another slight bow, Simms left her to her brandy and went back out into the foyer just in time to meet Buddy coming from the wine cellar.

"Where's that precious wife of mine, Simms?"

"In the library, sir."

As Buddy left in pursuit of his wife, Simms watched him enter the library.

Until two months ago when the new missus moved in, life had been quiet. Now the house was swarming with Wainwrights. He sighed as he headed off to make sure the housekeeper had done her job and the bedrooms were in order.

Chapter Five

Laura surveyed the place cards again and debated on whether it was worth Dakota's rath to switch them, when the doors opened again and Tiffany walked in with a glass of wine in her hand.

"I see you found that wine you were after."

Tiffany smiled as she came up to Laura. "Perhaps you can help me. I'm trying to keep everyone straight. You were Atticus' last wife?"

Laura ran her eyes over Tiffany starting at her tanned legs and ending with her frosted locks. "From the looks of things, I believe you'll be Atticus' last wife. Which works out pretty nicely for you, doesn't it?"

"I know what you think, but I love, Atticus."

"Of course, we all did."

"I'm sorry things didn't work out for you, Laura, but you shouldn't blame me. You were the one who walked out on your marriage."

Laura smiled. "Is that what he told you? I left because Atticus made it impossible for me to stay. You see, once a Wainwright bride hits thirty, she's loses all of her appeal." Laura was thirty, when Atticus's eye started roaming. She stayed another year, but finally took her daughter and left, leaving behind a fortune and an unfaithful husband.

Tiffany headed for the door. "I hoped we could be friends, but..."

Laura called out after her. " You don't need to worry, though, he'll be dead before your next birthday. Hell, he may be dead before the weekend."

Tiffany pushed open the doors. "I'll see you at dinner."

Laura pulled out a chair and sat down. "I hoped we could be friends, *pu-leeze*."

The door opened again. This time Ruth came through the door. She was the first Mrs. Wainwright and mother to Noah and Marcus. She was dressed casually in linen slacks and a silk shirt.

If you had to pick out one ex-Mrs. Wainwright to be the 'sane one', it'd be Ruth, even though she had her troubles over the years, including a second failed marriage.

Now in her mid-fifties, she found peace in being alone and tried to spend the last few years making up for lost time with her two sons. She spent a fair amount of time leaving them to fend for themselves while they were growing up, and was surprised, but happy they turned out okay, regardless of her inattention and the lack of a dependable father.

She went around the table and looked at the place cards. "Was that the adolescent Mrs. Wainwright I just saw stalk out of here?" All of the women had been twenty-five or younger when they married Atticus. A pattern he followed again, even at the age of seventy.

"Yes, isn't she just divine?"

"Now, now let's keep those claws retracted, at least until dinner." Ruth counted the place settings. "The old coot's not joining us for dinner."

Laura stood up. "Apparently he's too ill, and hasn't left his bed in weeks." She went to the terrace doors and looked out at the manicured grounds. The ornate gazebo, next to the koi pond, was her contribution. She looked at dozens of them before making a final decision. By the time they delivered and assembled it, she was six months away from leaving. She wondered how many women passed through the house between her and Tiffany, and sat on the matching chaises she painstakingly chose the fabric for.

Ruth pulled out a chair and sat down. "Just like Atticus to hang on. Frankly, I'm surprised. He's always been a robust man. Even convinced a twenty-five year old woman to marry him."

Laura turned away from the door. "She married the money, not the man."

"Do you think she's going to get it all?"

"For her two months of marriage?"

"If we're basing the inheritance on time served, I should get the majority of it. I was married to him the longest," Ruth said.

"Seven years, was it?" Laura shook her head. "Don't know how you did it."

"Seven years, two months and twenty-some odd days. Two days after I left with my boys, Dakota moved in."

"Well, you may have survived life with Atticus the longest, but I take the prize for the messiest divorce."

"Well, yes. I'll give you that one."

"Thank God I had my career. I don't know how Libby and I would've survived on that piddling little settlement I got from him." Laura always prided herself on her success in the business world. Had she not spent five years as Mrs. Wainwright, she'd be a CEO by now. At least that's what she told anyone who listened.

Ruth straightened the silverware of the place setting in front of her. "So, how's life at the top of the corporate ladder?"

"Not quite at the top yet, still clawing my way up, I'm afraid."

"One junior partner at a time?"

Laura headed for the door. "On that note…"

"Don't get me wrong. I don't blame you. One does what one needs to do to get ahead. A motto followed by most of the members of the Wainwright family."

Laura opened the doors. "I'm going to go find Libby and rest up before this charade commences."

*****

Ruth stood up and went to the bar. She contemplated on whether or not to pour herself a drink, as she looked in the mirror and ran her fingers through her hair. She started to go gray a few years ago, so made the decision to embrace it. It was now a lovely shade of silver, thanks to her hairdresser.

She addressed the empty room. "So, Atticus, you old bastard, what do you have up your sleeve? Wouldn't surprise me at all to find out you're leaving it all to your cat. Wouldn't that just show us all." She went behind the bar. "You can snub all us wives, I could hardly blame you, we all got settlements when we left, but you damn well better take care of your children." She looked at the alcoholic options available in the bar. "Well, maybe not Dell. Not sure she deserves anything, but…"

Deciding against alcohol, she came out from behind the bar, then turned towards the door as Noah and Marcus came into the room. She smiled at them as she held out her arms. "My two handsome boys."

Noah went to Ruth and embraced her. "Mom, great to see you." He kissed her on the cheek.

Marcus waited his turn a few feet behind Noah, then hugged Ruth when his brother stepped away. "You look wonderful, Mom. Love that blouse."

Ruth held him out at arm's length. "No Roberto?" Marcus shook his head. "Well, you can't blame him," she said.

Noah smiled. "Yeah, I wouldn't be here if I didn't have to be." When Ruth looked at him, he added, "Would you?" She shook her head. "So, where is everybody?" he asked.

"Oh, they're around. You're the last to arrive."

Marcus glanced at his watch. "So dinner's at, what 7:00 ish?

"7:00 exactly." Ruth corrected her son. "There is no ish at the Wainwright manor."

Marcus headed for the door. "Well, I'm going to go wash off some of this travel grime."

Noah watched him go. "Yeah, that thirty minute drive out of the city was gruesome."

Marcus glanced over his shoulder and said, "Forty-five, thank you very much." Before he left the room.

Noah called out after him. "Only because you drive like an old lady."

Marcus was the older of the two sons by fifteen months. He was a Matre d' at an upscale restaurant in the city, and lived in a converted apartment above it. He and his partner, Roberto, spent a small fortune renovating the space, which was now the envy of all their friends.

Ruth put a hand on Noah's chest. "So how's America's number one bachelor doing?"

"Fighting to stay on top."

"Any new women I should know about? Someone from the club, perhaps."

Noah picked up a slice of ham from the buffet table. "Mom, the average age of my clients at the club is fifty. Trust me, there's no one new."

"So being a tennis pro has no perks at all?"

"Well, thanks to the guy I work with, I know the financial status of every member. He's made it his mission in life to find a sugar mama before he reaches thirty."

She smiled at her son, who, aside from his longer hair, and lack of a mustache, looked exactly like his father at the same age. "And what's your mission in life?"

"To make it through the summer so I can hit the slopes in the winter."

Ruth put a hand on his cheek. "Your father would be so disturbed by that."

"Well, that's my ultimate goal." He stepped away from Ruth. "To disappoint the old man. And I must say, I've been doing a damn good job." He patted his shirt pocket. "You wouldn't have a cigarette on you would you?"

Ruth opened her purse and dug around. "I thought you quit."

"I did. I do. Daily."

Ruth handed him a cigarette and a lighter. "You need to go outside. Strict orders from the nurse. Oxygen or some nonsense."

Noah took the cigarettes and went out on the terrace as Ruth headed for the door.

She called out to him. "I'll see you at dinner."

*****

Noah lit his cigarette as he looked out at the manicured garden and the tennis court beyond it. He learned to play tennis on the court at the hands of a retired professional. His name was Sergio, and he had high hopes for his young protégé. Noah sighed. Just another one of the many people in his life who he disappointed.

Marcus came out onto the terrace and sidestepped the cloud of smoke Noah exhaled. "I thought you quit."

Noah nodded and dropped the cigarette onto the flagstone path that led from the deck and meandered through the garden on its way to the tennis courts, then stepped on it.

Marcus looked at the flattened stub. "You're seriously going to leave that there?"

Noah shrugged. "Isn't that what the groundskeepers are for? To keep the grounds?"

"Pick it up."

Noah sighed, but picked up his trash before he followed Marcus inside and deposited it in a trash can beside the door.

Marcus circled the table and studied the name cards. "So I just met her."

"The newest Mrs. Wainwright?"

Marcus nodded. "No wonder the old man's on his death bed."

Noah checked the time on the grandfather clock in the corner of the room. At night, when the house was quiet, you could hear the hourly chime, even upstairs. "We still have time to make a run for it."

"Tempting but no. My curiosity is superseding my survival instinct."

"You know what they say about curiosity?"

"Well, if I was a cat, I'd be worried." Marcus' cell phone rang and he pulled it out of his pocket, then smiled when he saw the number and headed for the door. "Oh, hey hon."

Noah went to the hors d'oeuvres table and picked up another piece of ham. He hated that he caved and decided to come. He was ready to go home, and he hadn't even talked to any of the others yet.

Tiffany came into the room and said, "Don't ruin your dinner. We've got seven courses tonight."

Noah turned and smiled at her. "I guess I'll need to pace myself."

Tiffany crossed the room and offered her hand to Noah. "I'm Tiffany. You must be Noah." She was everything Noah expected her to be, young, beautiful, and… He couldn't quite put his finger on the third thing.

He shook her hand. "Yes, your youngest stepson."

Lowering her blue eyes in the pretense of innocence, the fourth Mrs. Wainwright took a quick appraisal of her husband's second-born son. Uncomfortably aware of Tiffany's scrutiny, Noah took a few steps back from her.

"What're you doing in here all by yourself?" She seemed to like what she saw.

The third thing came to him. Inauthentic. "With this many Wainwrights around, alone is always your best bet."

"They do seem to be an odd bunch."

He noticed she didn't include herself in the odd bunch, even though she was married to a man forty-five years older than her and was younger than his two sons and the same age as his oldest daughter. He headed for the bar in an attempt to put some distance between himself and his newest stepmother. "You're being much too kind."

"So, I hear you're quite a tennis player." She followed him to the bar and sat on a stool in front of it.

"Do you play?"

"Play?" She asked, her presumption of virtue not quite believable.

"Tennis." He'd played this game of double entendres many times with the women at the club. He was good at it, and he made a good living because of it. But this wasn't a woman from the club. This was his father's wife.

"No, but I've always wanted to learn."

And there it was. *Walk away, while you still can.* "Maybe we could hit a few this weekend."

She fingered the gold chain at her neck. "Only if you promise to be gentle with me."

"I'll treat you like it's your first time." *Good God. Stop already.*

Tiffany fussed with the flowers in the crystal vase at the end of the bar, then looked at him. "Everyone else seems to hate me, but you, well you don't quite fit into the rest of the group."

"Oh, we all have our little quirks." He wasn't sure why he was standing behind the bar. He didn't want a drink, but it put a barrier between the two of them, so he stayed.

Tiffany took out a silver case and offered a cigarette to Noah.

He shook his head. "I'm trying to quit."

She took one out for herself, then stood up and stepped to the doors leading out to the terrace. They were oversized French doors set in a glass wall that spanned the full length of the dining room. "So, what are your quirks?" she asked as she opened one side and stepped out onto the red brick floor.

Noah sighed, then came out from behind the bar and took the lighter out of her hand to light her cigarette. "I talk in my sleep."

"What a coincidence. I listen in mine."

Noah took the cigarette from her and took a puff. "So, if the old man suddenly stopped breathing in the middle of the night, you'd be there to hear it"

Tiffany took the cigarette back. "I'm afraid Atticus and I don't share a room."

"Did you ever?"

Tiffany looked at him for a long moment. "Now, don't let me pull the step-mom card. I'm sure you don't really want to know the answer to that question." She stubbed out her cigarette with the toe of her Louboutin heels and went back into the room. "I love Atticus."

Noah glanced at the butt of her cigarette, then quelled the voice of Marcus in his head, as he resisted the urge to pick it up and followed her. "Oh, I'm sure you do. In fact, I can think of about 50 million reasons why you would."

"Is that what he's worth?"

"You do realize he's probably figured out a way to take it all with him?"

"Now that would be a shame. But then why did he send for his lawyer?"

"Did he?" This was unexpected news, though nothing his father did ever surprised him.

Tiffany headed for the door. "Ms. Schmidt will be here Sunday morning. She's bringing a revised copy of the will."

"Revised? When did that happen?"

"Right after we got back from the honeymoon. Now, if you'll excuse me, I've got to tend to the dinner preparations."

Noah watched her go. She was good. She wormed her way into Atticus' house and somehow convinced him to marry her, even though he'd been single for thirteen years. And now, suddenly and unexpectedly, Atticus was on his deathbed. The timing seemed suspect. Or was she just that lucky?

Chapter Six

Noah entered the room he'd share with Marcus for the weekend. It was the same room they shared as children, but it had since been redecorated in a classic guest room blandness. The furnishings were expensive but generic and boring in shades of green and brown.

As a child Noah's bed cover were Star Wars themed. A few years later he went through a Superhero phase. Now, the bedspreads were brown with green stripes. Very uninspired.

Marcus was sitting on one of the twin beds, tapping a message into his phone. He looked up at Noah and nodded. "You should get dressed for dinner. It's after six."

Noah looked at his attire, jeans and a black polo shirt. "I thought I was dressed."

Marcus dropped his phone on the bed. "Put on some slacks and a better shirt."

Noah looked at his reflection in the full-sized mirror that hung on the door to the bathroom. "I didn't bring slacks. I don't own a pair of slacks."

Marcus got up and went to the closet. His clothes were unpacked and hanging neatly in an organized rainbow of color coordination. He took out a pair of brown pants and a rust colored long-sleeved shirt and held them out to Noah.

"I'm not going to wear your clothes, man."

Marcus continued to hold them out at arm's length.

Noah rolled his eyes, then took the offered clothes. "What's wrong with my shirt?"

"What isn't wrong with your shirt? Just because it's black doesn't mean it's formal."

Noah sighed as he went into the bathroom to change. He and Marcus were the same height, but Marcus lacked the muscular build Noah spent most of his life achieving. When he came out, he looked at his reflection again in the mirror. As usual, Marcus was right.

They were close growing up and remained so as adults, even though their lives took very different paths. Marcus' job required him to wear a suit, while Noah spent his days in shorts, the club polo, and tennis shoes.

He went to his overnight bag and pulled out a crumpled pack of cigarettes. There was one left, and he stuck it between his lips and looked at Marcus. "Do you have a match, lighter, two sticks to rub together?"

Marcus shook his head. "I won't enable your disgusting habit."

Noah removed the cigarette and slid it back into the package, then dropped it into the overnight bag. "So, the lovely Tiffany and I had a conversation."

"Don't even think about it, brother."

"What? Oh, no. I'd never."

Marcus tilted his head at him. "Really? The stud of Misty Glen?"

"She's our step-mother, sort of."

"Do you suppose she and the old man…"

"Oh, God, stop. Now that's all I'll see when I look at her."

Marcus smiled. "Good." He checked his phone then set it on the table next to the bed as he took a seat. "So, what are the chances of him leaving us some serious money?"

"Zero." Noah sat on the other bed across from Marcus. "Apparently, there's a new will. The lawyer is bringing it Sunday morning."

"Damn Tiffany." Marcus shrugged. "I wasn't really expecting anything, anyway. Seeing as I'm the…black sheep of the family."

"Bastard that he is, maybe he called us all here to tell us he's not leaving any of us a cent."

Marcus thought about it for a moment. "Maybe he's mellowed out with death staring him in the face and all. You never know."

Noah shook his head. "No way."

"He has to do something with his money. He's not going to leave it up to fate or his lawyers to decide." Marcus crossed one leg over the other and smoothed out a wrinkle in his gray slacks. "Although, I can envision him looking down on us and getting quite a kick out of watching the fight that would ensue."

"He won't be looking down from anywhere. He's much more likely to be looking up through the fiery depths of hell. After taking it over, of course, firing all the Devil's employees and selling off bits and pieces of purgatory to the highest bidder."

"But hypothetically, let's pretend he's not a bastard, what would you do with say, ten million?"

Noah thought for a moment. "I'd buy a chalet in Vale and a bungalow in Hawaii."

"So, skiing and tennis? Really, nothing more industrious? Or different? Or interesting?"

"What would you do with ten million?"

Marcus smiled. "I'd buy a house in the Hamptons and become a famous author."

"An author?"

"Yes. I'd write Spicy Gay Romance novels."

"Wow, okay. You know, you could do that now."

"I realize that. But, if I did it now, I'd be writing in the closet in the middle of the night after working all day. That's no fun." He stood up and took a turn around the room. "Do you want to hear some titles I've come up with?"

Noah shook his head. "No, I really don't."

Marcus went to Noah and pulled him to his feet, then dragged him to the mirror. He studied Noah's reflection. "You could be a model for the cover of my first book."

Noah backed away from him. "I don't want to be the model for your gay porn."

Marcus put a hand to his chest. "It's not porn. Romance novels aren't porn."

"What's the difference?"

"One is classy, and the other isn't."

"So they'll be spicy in a classy sort of way."

"Yes. Now, since you're mocking my dream, let's change the subject." Marcus sat on the bed. "Who do you think will be the first ex-wife to get drunk and say something outrageous to Tiffany?"

"Dakota," They said in unison.

Chapter Seven

Dinner was as unpleasant as Noah expected it would be. The Wainwright women had a talent for acerbic deprecation and they were all at the top of their game while they suffered through all seven courses. During the third course, which was stuffed mushrooms in a red wine sauce, Dell stuck two fingers into her empty martini glass and fished out the olives. After pulling them off the sword, she fed them to her husband, then patted him on the head. He smiled appreciatively and moved in for a kiss, but managed only to peck her red hair right above her diamond studded earlobe.

At that point, Noah tuned them all out.

That ended when Tiffany tapped the rim of her glass to gain everyone's attention. They all paused in various stages of eating and looked at her.

"I know you're all curious why Atticus asked you here." The obvious statement drew only silence from the group. "Well, I'm afraid I don't have an answer for you." The silence continued. "But I'll venture to guess it has something to do with the will."

Dakota broke the silence. "Honey, do you really think anything else would've gotten us all here?"

Once the truth on everyone's minds was so succinctly stated by Dakota, the uneasiness in the room abated and the eating resumed.

Noah once more tuned out.

The woman serving, who Tiffany called Charlotte, caught his attention though. She seemed familiar to him, but he couldn't place her. She appeared to be his age, though it was hard to tell in the starched gray uniform she wore, and with her dark hair pulled back tightly into a neat French braid that ended a few inches below her collar. She went about her business in the invisible way hired help seemed to master, but there was an underlying attitude. Was it disdain? That too, he was having trouble identifying.

When she caught him watching her, she gave him a nod. She had light blue eyes that would've been pretty if there was something besides contempt in them. He smiled at her and she looked away.

"Noah. Noah, dear."

He looked at his mother. "Sorry."

"Where were you?"

"Lost in these mushrooms."

"Laura asked you a question."

Noah looked at Laura who pushed her unfinished plate of mushrooms toward the middle of the table. "I was wondering if you'd have the time to give Libby some tennis lessons this summer." She glanced at her daughter. "Don't slouch dear."

Libby, who was sitting perfectly straight in the high-backed chair, pulled herself up a few more inches as she stole a look at Noah. He winked and gave her a small smile.

"Sure. I'll be in town until the end of October."

"Wonderful. I'll contact you next week. She doesn't go back to school until September first."

Noah looked at Libby again, who looked less than thrilled at the prospect of taking tennis lessons from her half-brother. He nodded at her and got a small smile in response. He wondered if she was always so intimidated by her mother. He never really had a one-on-one conversation with her. The little time they spent together over the years, was always in the presence of Laura. He supposed he'd find out, when and if the tennis lessons started. Unless of course, Laura would accompany her daughter.

Noah tried to avoid further eye contact with the women, but wasn't quick enough, and Dakota smiled at him.

"So, why didn't you bring some attractive young admirer with you this weekend? We wouldn't have minded."

"I'm afraid I'm in-between admirers at the moment." The woman in the gray uniform looked up from her serving tray and glanced at Noah. He gave her a small smile, but she looked away again.

Laura glanced at Tiffany then smiled at Noah. "I see how bringing a date might be a risky proposition with your father's fondness for little bits of fluff."

With steel in her eyes, Tiffany smiled sweetly at Laura. "You can't blame a man for wanting a little cheesecake after a diet of—"

"Ladies, please," Marcus said. "Let's take off the gloves, at least until dinner's over."

*****

After dinner Noah wandered into the kitchen hoping to run into, and figure out who, the woman behind the blue eyes was. She was at the sink savagely scrubbing a large aluminum pot. When he cleared his throat behind her, she glanced over her shoulder.

"Are you lost?"

"No, just in search of a beer."

A young man came in through the doors carrying and impressive stack of dirty dishes. Noah stepped out of the way, and the dishes were deposited in the sink with a clatter.

Charlotte frowned at the man who mumbled an apology as he took over at the dish washing. She dried her hands as she looked at Noah, then nodded toward the refrigerator.

"Have you forgotten where the refrigerator is?"

Noah went to the oak panel appliance and opened the door. He grabbed a bottle of imported beer, then turned and held it up to her. "I guess not." He studied her for a moment. Here in a less formal setting, she was even more familiar. "Do I know you?"

She cocked her head. "I don't know, Noah, do you?"

He pointed a finger at her and smiled, but it still wasn't coming to him. When Marcus came into the kitchen, they both turned to look at him.

He smiled at Charlotte and said, "Hey Charlie," and gave her a hug.

"What the...?" Now Noah was more confused than ever.

Marcus looked at Noah as he pointed at her. "Charlie."

It suddenly dawned on him. He and Marcus were forced to spend two months with Atticus the summer they were seventeen and eighteen, respectively. Ruth was going through her second divorce and needed some time to sort things out. Charlie was spending the summer helping her father in the kitchen. He was the on-call cook for special occasions, but that summer he was there full-time.

"Charlie from that last miserable summer we spent here."

She frowned at him. "Um, thanks."

"Oh, no, not you. You weren't the miserable part. You were the only thing that made it bearable."

Marcus smiled. "That's not much better, Noah."

"You know what I mean." He took a breath. "Let's start over." He held out his hand. "Hi, Charlie, nice to see you again."

She took his hand. "Noah, how are you?"

"What're you doing working for my father?"

She dropped his hand. "Just trying to make a little extra money this summer, and he pays well."

"Seriously?"

"Yes. But if you two don't leave me alone to get my work done, I'll get fired, so…"

"Right, of course." Noah took a few steps towards the door. "Are you going to be here all weekend?"

"Yes."

"Great, I'll see you around, then." He and Marcus headed for the door.

Marcus stopped and looked at her. "How's little Seraphina?"

"Oh, she's great."

The men left the kitchen and headed down the hall toward the stairway that led to the second floor.

"Seraphina?" Noah asked. "She has a kid?"

Marcus laughed. "No, Seraphina is her cat."

"Oh. And how do you know that?"

"We're Facebook friends."

*****

After the men left, Charlie sat down at the butcher block island in the center of the kitchen. She hoped he'd be coming this weekend. It's why she took the job. But now, that she saw him, she wished she hadn't. He was cute at seventeen, but now he was a full-blown hunk. *And he didn't even remember who you were.* "Sounds about right."

Richard glanced over his shoulder. "Huh?"

She shook her head. "Nothing." She stood up and resumed her work, trying not to think about the smile that still made her heart stop.

Chapter Eight

It was still early and Noah wasn't yet ready to retire for the night, so he left Marcus in the room and headed for the stairs. As he passed his father's room, his curiosity got the best of him and he stopped outside the door and put his ear to it. He took a step back as he realized he didn't want to know what was going on behind the door.

He headed down the stairs, passed through the now empty dining room, and went out the doors to the veranda to get some air. As he circled the pool, he paused a moment and looked up at the star filled sky. Doing so brought back fond memories of nights spent out camping on the grounds with Marcus.

The fact that he had happy memories surprised him. But none of them had to do with his father. Since Atticus had very little interest in them, he put Simms in charge of the young boys. Even then, Simms was past his prime and his authority was of little consequence to them. They had free run of the entire estate to do as they pleased, and they took full advantage of it. Noah still remembered every foot of the place, right down to the grove of trees where he almost kissed Charlie.

He stared at the reflection of the moon on the pool. *How'd I forget about that?* They were waiting for Marcus in the small grove of apple trees. Even though Simms told them to come in before dark, they were still out an hour past the sun going down. They were standing under a large tree on the edge of the grove and he was about to lean in and kiss her, when Marcus came up to them. He wondered now if she'd been aware of his intentions that night.

Noah left the pool and headed for the garden. When he saw the glow of a cigarette in the far corner by the roses, he decided to investigate.

Halfway there he recognized the figure as Libby, and when he approached her, she put the cigarette behind her back.

He gave her a little smile. "Hey, what're you doing out here all alone?"

Libby shrugged.

He nodded toward the arm behind her back. "Do you have another one of those?"

She feigned innocence, then sighed and held it out to him. He took it and looked at it for a moment. "You know, these things will kill you." He took a long drag before he handed it back to her.

"Are you going to tell my mother?"

He considered the question for a moment. He started smoking at nineteen while in college. She was still in high school. "I'll make you a deal. You promise me that's your last one for a few years, and I won't tell your mom."

She looked at the cigarette for a moment, then dropped it and stepped on it. "Deal." She sat on a bench and glanced at him, before looking at the ground in front of her. "They're kind of disgusting, anyway."

Noah studied her for a moment. "So, do you really want to take tennis lessons?"

She shrugged. "I guess."

"That's not very convincing."

"It was Mom's idea. But it's better than some things she's made me try. She's trying to find something for me to excel at."

"You're seventeen. You have lots of time to find your thing."

"Tell that to my mom." She looked at him, then smiled and looked away.

"What?"

"She says she doesn't want me to end up like you."

Noah laughed. "Well, I guess that's good advice. I'm a twenty-nine-year-old tennis bum, after all."

She looked at him. "You drive a nice car."

"Well, don't tell your mother this, but I probably make more money than she does. Or at least I would if I didn't take winters off. The ladies I teach to play tennis, are darn good tippers."

"That's so great. I love it, and she'd hate it."

"That's why you're not going to tell her." He sat down next to her. "So what would you do if you had a choice?"

"Dance." She lit up when she said it.

"Really? Like ballet?"

Libby smiled. "No, she'd probably like that. Hip Hop."

He looked at her. "Interesting. Didn't see that coming."

She lowered her voice as though her mother was lurking in the shadows and would hear her. "I've made some videos and posted them online."

"Cool, send me the link. I'd like to watch them."

She nodded and then was quiet for a few moments before she surprised Noah with her next question. "So, what's with our dad?"

"Um, how do you mean?"

"Is he really dying?"

Noah took a moment before answering. "That's what they say."

"Huh. It's weird. It should make me sad."

"But it doesn't. I get it. He's not the kind of man to be sad over. He's never done anything for me, and I assume he's never done anything for you, either."

"Sometimes, I feel like he's trying, but then it's like he catches himself and switches back into robot mode."

Noah laughed. "I know exactly what you mean." He stood up. "He's the tin man."

She smiled. "Before he got his heart."

Noah held a hand out to her. "You better get back to your room before your mother wakes up and finds you missing. I imagine she wouldn't be happy to see your bed without you in it."

Libby took his hand and stood up. "Thanks."

"For what?"

"For not treating me like I'm a kid."

"You're welcome."

They started walking towards the house. "So," Noah said. "No more cigarettes?"

"No more cigarettes."

"Promise."

She grabbed his hand and locked her pinky finger around his. "Pinky promise."

They returned to the house and Libby went upstairs, but Noah, still not tired, headed for the kitchen. He was surprised again to find someone unexpected. Tiffany was sitting on the butcher block counter in the middle of the kitchen, eating a piece of pie.

She smiled when she saw him. "Oh, you caught me."

"Isn't it past your bedtime, young lady?"

She pointed her fork at him. "I could say the same thing to you, stepson." She stuck her fork into a bite of cherry pie and held it out to him. "Care for a bite?"

Noah shook his head. "No thanks." He opened the refrigerator. "I'd rather drink my calories."

She slid off the counter and set her plate in the sink. "So, how incensed are the Wainwright ex-wives going to be when the new will arrives?"

Noah shrugged. "I suppose it depends on what it says." He studied her for a moment. "Do you know what it says?"

"I have no idea."

Noah had to admit. Whatever game Tiffany was playing, she was good at it. She almost sounded like she meant it.

"If he changed it, they'll all assume he changed it for me."

"Maybe he did."

"They'll all hate me. Will you hate me, too?"

"I don't care about the money, Tiffany. The rest of you can fight over it. I don't want any part of it."

She smiled. "That's a little hard to believe."

"Well, it's true, none the less." He headed for the door, but she called out after him.

"Do you play pool as well as you play tennis?"

Noah studied her for a moment. He had plenty of women flirt with him, but she was different. He wasn't sure if she was as available as she was trying to make him believe. Not that he was interested. He meant what he said to Marcus, but still he was intrigued. He wasn't sure what she wanted, but he was pretty sure it was a lot more complicated than a romantic interlude.

"I'm not bad."

She slid off the butcher block counter and headed for the door, taking his arm as she passed him. "Shall we?"

"Sure, why not?"

*****

Tiffany played quite well, and Noah's game was off, resulting in a victory for her the first game. She smiled at him across the table. "Maybe you should stick to tennis."

He leaned his cue against the table then set the balls up for another game.

He looked at her. "Who taught you to play?"

"Two older brothers."

Noah returned to his cue and motioned for her to break. "So, what do they think of your new husband?"

She leaned over the end of the table and took her first shot, then stood up and studied the position of the balls.

"They're happy for me, of course."

"Yeah, I bet."

She sunk two balls before missing, with the last shot bringing her within a few feet of Noah. She closed the gap and looked into his eyes.

"Why don't you like me?"

He took a few steps back away from her. "Now that's a question you don't really want to know the answer to." He sunk three balls in a row before he missed an easy shot and swore under his breath.

Tiffany laughed. "I believe I make you nervous, Noah."

He looked at her. "You could be right."

"Why?"

"Because I can usually figure people out, but you…"

"I'm not that complicated. Give it a try. I can take anything you have to say."

"I'm sure you can." He leaned on his cue and hesitated a moment before letting her have it from both barrels. "I think you married my father for his money. And I believe you couldn't care less that while we're down here playing games, he's upstairs on his deathbed. Also, I think you assume you're going to get the bulk of his inheritance when he dies."

"That's a pretty brutal assessment considering you just met me a few hours ago."

"Well, you have until Sunday to prove me wrong." He set his cue on the table and headed for the door. "I'm going to call it a night."

She called out to him. "And what if you're wrong?"

"Then I'll ask for your forgiveness."

As Noah left the room and headed for the stairs, he could hear Tiffany clearing the table.

Chapter Nine

Noah sat on the edge of his bed in the dark room, listening to Marcus' rhythmic snoring. It, like everything else about his brother, was neat, tidy, and predictable. The moon filtered through a gap in the curtains, cutting a swatch of blue light across the hardwood floor.

Getting to his feet, Noah undressed, then went to the window to close out the moonlight. Looking at the driveway below, he spotted Ruth standing by her car lighting a cigarette.

Noah slid the window open and called to her. "What're you still doing up?"

She looked up. "I could ask you the same question."

Noah filled his lungs with the night air. "I was getting acquainted with my new step-mother." Even though Ruth was fifteen feet below him, he could smell the smoke from her cigarette. He savored it for a moment, hoping it would satisfy his craving until morning. He'd been smoking for ten years and had been trying to quit for almost that long. The habit contradicted his healthy lifestyle, and the fact he couldn't quite kick it irritated him.

Ruth shook her head. "Don't get too chummy, she's trouble."

Marcus stirred. "Can you talk about this over breakfast tomorrow?" he asked through a yawn.

Noah glanced over his shoulder at him, then looked back down on Ruth. He lowered his voice a notch.

"I make it a rule to never get involved with the old man's women."

Marcus grunted from his bed. "What a distressing reflection on our family tree that such a directive exists."

"Good night, Mom," Noah said before closing the window and pulling the curtains together to block out the moonlight.

Marcus rolled onto his side and propped himself up onto an elbow. "So, were we right about her?"

Noah went to his bed and pulled back the bedspread, then laid down and stared up at the ceiling. "I sometimes wonder if Dad would've been a different man if he found just one woman who really loved him."

"You need to know how to love before you can be loved, brother."

Noah looked at Marcus. "Do you suppose it's a hereditary trait?"

"No, I think it's more a matter of not opening yourself up to getting hurt, trait."

"Are we still talking about the old man?"

"Good night, Noah."

It wasn't long before Marcus was snoring again, but Noah found slumber to be elusive as he stared into the darkness. When he was a child, the high ceilings with their ornately carved moldings laid the seeds of many a nightmare. And even now, as an adult, he had difficulty sleeping in this, or any other room of his father's cold and unfriendly house. He closed his eyes and tried willing himself to sleep. After a while, out of sheer boredom, he dozed off.

*****

Buddy was mixing mimosas at the bar as Dell waited impatiently and watched Charlie set up the breakfast buffet table. She snatched a bite-sized cinnamon roll off of a tray as Charlie walked by, then looked at the grandfather clock. They'd all be there in the next ten minutes.

Buddy came up behind her and handed her a glass. "Here you go, my little dumpling."

Dell sighed and took a drink. "You better make them stronger than this if you expect me to get through breakfast."

Buddy retrieved a bottle of champagne from the bar and topped off her glass as the door opened and Dakota and Ruth entered. Considering the fact Dakota was the affair that ended Ruth's marriage, the two women got along remarkably well. Perhaps it was because four years after she replaced Ruth,

Dakota found herself traded out and raising a three-year-old Dell by herself. Her replacement never made it to the alter though. Atticus spent a few years enjoying bachelor life before he married Laura.

Dakota air-kissed Dell and nodded at Buddy before checking out the buffet table.

Ruth joined her. "Well, isn't this an embarrassing display of greed and gluttony?"

"Looks good, though," Dakota said as she poured herself a cup of coffee.

Dell came up behind them. "We've got mimosas."

Dakota took a sip of coffee. "One poison at a time, dear. I need my caffeine first."

Ruth glanced towards the bar. "I think I'll go straight for the alcohol."

Dell followed her to the bar and got a refill. "So, where are those two handsome step-brothers of mine?"

"I'm sure they'll be along. I haven't known either of them to miss a meal yet."

*****

Noah groaned as Marcus shook him again. "I swear Marcus, if you do that one more time..."

Marcus stood over him with his hands on his hips. "What? What horrible thing will you do to me?" He sat on the edge of his bed. "You're going to make us late."

With a sigh, Noah sat up and rubbed his eyes. "Do I have time for a shower?"

"No, you have five minutes. There's no *ish* in the Wainwright family, remember?"

"Sort of-ish." Noah smiled. "All right, I'm getting up." He picked his jeans up off the floor. "And don't tell me to wear slacks."

Marcus held up his hands. "Wear whatever, just get dressed."

Noah put on his pants and pulled a navy polo shirt out of his bag.

"Not that shirt, though."

Noah looked at him. "Are you kidding me?"

Marcus smiled. "Yes, I am. Blue is your color. But tuck it in."

"I'm not tucking. I don't tuck." He went to the bathroom to run a comb through his hair. Both brothers were blond, a trait all the Wainwright children got from their father, but years in the sun had made Noah's hair lighter than Marcus'. His hair was also much longer than Marcus' short styled haircut. Noah's appearance was best described by an enamored client who said he looked like he just walked out of the ocean with a surf board under his arm. Whether that was true or not, it certainly helped when it came time for his female clients to tip at the end of a lesson.

Marcus called out to his brother. "Where were you last night? I don't know what time you came in, but it was late."

Noah came out of the bathroom. "I couldn't sleep. Had a little chat with Libby. She's pretty cool when you get her away from Laura." He grabbed his wallet and phone. "And then I ran into Tiffany in the kitchen."

"Uh oh."

"I told you, I'd never go there."

"Okay, whatever. You said you'd never go there with Roberto's cousin either." He opened the door and let Noah go through.

"Roberto's cousin isn't married to our father. Besides, I tried to stay away from Rosita, but she was very persuasive."

"Hmm, poor little tennis pro, always getting taken advantage of by women."

They headed down the hallway towards the stairs. "I'm starting to get bored with it."

Marcus looked at him for a moment. "Seriously? Is my little brother finally growing up? Is he ready to find a Mrs. Tennis Pro and settle down?"

"Hold on. That's not what I said. I just might be ready to scale back and take some me time."

Marcus laughed. "Me time? Your whole life is me time."

Noah stopped at the top of the stairs and looked at him. "Are you calling me selfish?"

"Not selfish. More self-absorbed."

"Pretty sure that's the same thing."

The men walked into the dining room as the women were all milling around the table playing musical chairs. The loser would have to sit next to Tiffany. Noah made it easy for them and took the dreaded seat.

Ruth smiled at her son, then pointed a finger at him. "Behave."

He shrugged. "Why does everyone assume I'm a lothario?"

Dakota, who was sitting next to him, kissed him on the cheek then wiped off the lipstick she left behind. "Hey if the shoe fits, honey, buy a second pair."

"I don't even know what that means."

"Don't you worry about it. You're an angel. If your father was half the man you've turned out to be...well, he's not, never was, never could be."

Noah laughed. "I thought I was the underachiever of the group."

"According to who?" She looked around the table. "Don't you listen to them." She leaned in and whispered in his ear. "Laura, the corporate man-eater doesn't know what she's talking about."

Dell finished her drink, and Noah wondered how many had come before it. She set her glass down hard on the table. "Where's our gracious hostess, it's five past the hour?"

Marcus took a sip of his coffee. "Maybe she doesn't know about the *ish* rule."

At that moment, Tiffany came in with a flourish and stopped inside the door.

"Oh, you didn't need to wait for me. Please, help yourselves." She waved towards the buffet, then went to the table and took her seat next to Noah. "Good morning."

Noah nodded at her as everyone else got up and helped themselves to the buffet.

Tiffany smiled at him. "Not hungry?"

"Just waiting for the crowd to die down."

Marcus came up to him and squeezed his shoulder. "Come on, brother. Get it while it's hot."

Noah sighed and stood up. "Excuse me, Tiffany."

"Oh, by all means. Help yourself."

Noah followed Marcus to the buffet table and checked out the bountiful selection of food it offered, then he sighed and glanced around the room.

"No, not feeling this at all."

Marcus looked at him. "Just play the game."

Noah shook his head, patted Marcus on the shoulder, and headed for the door. He wasn't sure where he was going to go, but it didn't really matter. As he stepped out into the hall, Simms approached him.

"Did you need something, Sir? I can get the cook for you."

"Um, no. I'm just not hungry."

Simms studied him for a moment. "Perhaps Miss Charlotte can get you something more to your liking."

Noah smiled at him. "Good idea. Maybe I'll just pop in and say hi."

When he entered the kitchen, Charlie looked up from the serving plate she was filling with pastries.

"Are you lost again?" She handed the platter to Richard. The expert plate balancer was wearing a clean white jacket this morning and looked like he'd rather be anywhere but there.

"Just couldn't face breakfast with the Wainwright women."

She watched Richard leave the kitchen, then started filling another tray. "So, you left poor Marcus in there by himself?"

"My brother knows how to play the game. I just never wanted to learn. Besides, he has Buddy."

"I'm not sure Buddy counts as male companionship. What's with him, anyway?" She grabbed an empty plate from the cupboard and went to the pan of scrambled eggs on the stove.

"He's Dell's lap dog. I don't understand it, and really don't care enough to think about it, but they've been married for five years, so that's almost a family record."

"Who holds the record?"

"My mother. Seven years."

Charlie set the plate of scrambled eggs with three strips of bacon in front of Noah. "Here, you look hungry."

Noah picked up a fork and took a bite.

Charlie lifted the second pastry platter onto her shoulder. "I'll be right back."

Noah poured himself a cup of coffee and dragged a stool to the butcher block counter. He was half-way through his eggs when Charlie returned with Richard a few steps behind her.

She smiled. "I think they should be happy for a while." Richard busied himself at the sink while Charlie brought another stool over and sat across from Noah. "So, why haven't you found a sweet young thing to settle down with?"

"Because there's no such thing as happily ever after."

"Wow, you're jaded."

"I'm a realist. I've yet to see a successful relationship. My dad has three ex-wives. My mom's been married twice. And don't even get me started with the women at the club."

"What about the women at the club? Are they all sad lonely housewives looking for a little attention and maybe a fling with the hot tennis pro?"

"Pretty much, yeah." He smiled at her. "You think I'm hot?"

Charlie took his empty plate and carried it to the sink, then turned and looked at him. "So, how many of them have you flung?"

Noah shook his head. "You don't want to know."

"Actually, I really do."

Noah got up and refilled his coffee before returning to his seat. "So, that summer we spent together, I remember there being a spark or two."

"You're ignoring my question."

Noah nodded. "And I'll continue to do so."

"Okay, fine. Actually, you kind of broke my heart that summer."

"Sounds about right. How did I do that?"

"Whatever sparks there were, you quickly extinguished."

"Probably because I was trying to avoid breaking your heart."

Charlie grabbed a pastry left in the pan and took a bite. "Failed."

Noah looked at her for a moment. "So, what about you, why aren't you married with children?"

"Still looking for my Mr. Right." She cocked her head and smiled at him.

He stood up. "Don't be looking in my direction. I already broke your heart once."

She laughed. "Don't worry your pretty head about that. I have no interest in the guy who flings lonely housewives on a regular basis."

"You know, you can't really use that definition of fling as a verb."

Charlie shrugged. "Are you the grammar police?"

He took one last sip of coffee and set his cup down. "Yes, and I believe my work is done." He stepped back from the counter.

"Wait, one more thing." She glanced over her shoulder at Richard who wore earbuds, making him oblivious to their conversation. "So rumor has it, there's a new will."

"I wouldn't know anything about that."

She studied him for a minute, then smiled. "You're lying to me. You know something."

He shook his head. "What're you talking about? Why would I lie to you?"

"You're covering something up. I know when you're lying."

Noah sat back down. "You've spent less than an hour with me, yet you know when I'm lying to you?"

"Not from now, from before. We spent a summer together, remember?"

"And I spent the summer lying to you?"

"No, and that's not the point. You're lying to me now. What do you know?"

"First off, I'm not lying. Second, there's no way you could tell if I was."

Charlie leaned towards him. "Why don't you want me to know about the new will?"

Noah glanced at Richard, then whispered. "It's not you. It's them. I don't want that can of worms open until it's absolutely necessary."

"You think I'm going to go run and tell everyone?"

"No, of course not. Just the fewer people who know, the better. Nothing personal." He stood up again. "You wouldn't have a cigarette on you, would you?"

"No, but Richard does." She looked up at him. "You know everyone probably already knows."

"What?"

"How do you think I know?"

"Dammit." He went to Richard and tapped him on the shoulder.

A startled Richard, turned and said, "What the hell, man?"

"Sorry. Do you have a cigarette?"

Richard dug in his pocket and pulled out a crumpled pack. "Here's a couple."

"A light?"

Richard reached into a drawer, pulled out a book of matches, and handed it to Noah.

"Thanks."

He went back to Charlie. "Would you like to play some tennis later?"

"Sure, I guess. I have a few hours off between lunch and dinner."

"Okay, I'll see you after lunch."

He wandered out to the garden before he lit his cigarette. It was a beautiful space that took two full-time employees to keep in perfect condition. You'd be hard-pressed to find a weed or dying flower. At the center was the koi pond with a fountain in the middle depicting three children playing in the water. It sprayed up and tumbled over the edges, aerating the pond for the fish.

The statue of the three playing children was not something his father, or Atticus II would've picked out for the pond. Noah concluded long ago it must've been a contribution by one of the many wives that passed through over the last seventy-five years.

Marcus came up beside Noah and frowned at him. "Thanks for abandoning me."

Noah glanced at him. "It looks like you survived."

They sat on a brass bench with frogs on either end to hold it up instead of legs.

Marcus smiled. "Remember when we went fishing for koi?"

"Damn, that was one of my more awesome ideas."

"Until Mr. Kwan caught us and nearly murdered us for scaring his precious fish."

Noah leaned forward and rested his forearms on his knees. "The old man made me mow the front yard with a push mower."

"What is it, about an acre?"

"Seemed like ten at the time." He sat back up and looked at Marcus. "It took me two days."

"I'm sorry. I tried to tell him it was my idea, too."

"He knew better. You were the good son who was easily led astray by the bad son."

"Right, until I was nineteen, and I told him I was gay. After that, he only had one son." Marcus stood up and went to the edge of the pond. "Why am I even here? Did he summon me just so he could snub me one more time?"

"Yeah, the bastard. Let's leave. Right now. Go pack."

Marcus turned and looked at him and wagged a finger at him. "No, you don't. I won't be your excuse to leave this Wainwright family reunion. We're here until Sunday night."

"Damn, I thought I found a loophole."

Chapter Ten

Noah set the basket down and took out a tennis ball. He bounced it a few times, before serving it to the empty court across the net. He served two more, then checked his watch. They didn't set a definite time, and it was still early, but he was eager for Charlie to show up.

He turned to the green plywood wall at the back of the tennis court and hit a few volleys. Each time he returned the ball and hit it at the wall, he hit it a little harder. After thirty minutes of punishing the fuzzy green ball, he felt some tension from the past two days leave. When the wall finally got one past him, he stopped and took a moment to catch his breath. As he did so, he spotted Marcus watching him with a glass of wine in his hand.

"Feel better?" Marcus asked.

Noah nodded. "A little bit, yes. You up for a game?"

"With you, no." He glanced at his slacks and leather shoes. "Not quite dressed for the occasion, anyway." He pulled a handkerchief out of his pocket and wiped off the seat of a redwood deck chair before sitting on it. "Things are going well so far, don't you think?" He set his wineglass on the matching table.

"I suppose, for a Wainwright gathering."

"Nobody's killed anybody. We all made it through three meals now. Except for you, of course. Coward that you are." Marcus retrieved his wine and took a sip.

"I just don't see the point of being here. I could've driven up on Sunday. This whole family reunion thing is weird. And since I don't care about the money…"

"Oh, come on, Noah," Dakota said, as she appeared on the courts in cutoff jeans and a tight red t-shirt that said *Ride 'Em Hard*. "You really expect us to believe that?" She padded across the court in her baby blue tennis shoes, racket in hand. "Wouldn't you rather be spending your time traveling the semi-pro circuit instead of teaching little old ladies to play Sunday tennis?"

Noah refrained from mentioning that the little old ladies weren't much older than she was. "I'm too old."

"For what?"

"The semi-pro circuit."

"Nonsense." She went to the service line and assumed the ready position. "Now let's see some of that bedside manner that has those women all hot and bothered."

"You want to play tennis with me?"

She stood up straight. "Why the hell else would I be out here? I saw you playing all by yourself and felt sorry for you." She glanced at Marcus. "And Mr. Fancy Pants here, doesn't look like he's going to get out there with you."

"All right." Noah bounced the ball a few times with his racket.

"Now you take it easy on me."

They rallied back and forth for several minutes, with Noah doing his best to return Dakota's wild balls close to her. She wasn't a bad player, he had worse at the club, but she was by no means a good one. When a ball landed short in his court and bounced high, he couldn't resist the urge to smash it back. It flew within inches of Dakota's head and she threw up her arms and cowered as she let out a high-pitched yelp.

"Sorry." He ran up to the net. "You okay?"

"I'm fine, doll." She retrieved the ball. "Just watch the hair."

Marcus chuckled from the sidelines. "That's why I don't play with him."

Dell, hanging tight to Buddy's arm, came up beside Marcus. She was clearly inebriated, and she squinted in the afternoon sun. "Give her hell, Noah."

Marcus got to his feet and waved at his seat. With a nod, Buddy steered Dell towards it. "Here you go, lamb chop, let me pour you into this chair." She sat down heavily and glared at him, then looked up at Marcus and smiled. "Thank you. Next to Noah, you're my favorite brother."

"Ah, thanks."

"So," Dell said loudly, leaning forward in the chair. "Who thinks the old man got us here to drop some major bombshell?" She raised her hand and looked around. Getting no response, she went on. "And, who," She raised her hand again and waved it back and forth, "thinks the new Mrs. Wainwright—"

"Has come to join us," Buddy interrupted, as he spotted Tiffany coming onto the court.

"So, is this where everyone disappeared to?" She was dressed in very short shorts and a tank top.

Buddy looked at her, longer than he should have, then said, "Just watching my brother-in-law coddle my mother-in-law."

"Oh please, don't stop on my account."

Noah and Dakota rallied again, and he noticed that Tiffany's eyes never left his side of the court.

When Dell struggled to her feet, Buddy took her arm, as she said, "I think I need a nap before dinner." Buddy put an arm around her and steered her towards the house. She laid her head on his shoulder. "You're too good to me," she said, sounding like she meant it, but all who witnessed it knew she wouldn't remember saying it when she woke up from her nap.

He kissed the top of her head. "I know, baby doll, I know."

Marcus was the next to go when his phone rang. He took his empty glass and headed for the house.

Dakota missed an easy shot and turned to look at the ball, then headed for the net. Noah met her there. "Thank you for taking it easy on me," she said, slightly out of breath.

He leaned in close to her. "You sure you don't want to stay a little longer?"

Dakota glanced at Tiffany, then patted Noah's arm. "I'm pretty sure you can handle her."

"Eh, I think you're giving me way too much credit."

When they both spotted Charlie headed for the court, Dakota smiled at him. "Now her, you can handle. And you should."

"You think?"

Dakota gave him a wink then headed off the courts. She smiled at Charlie. "You just missed a great match. I almost had him there for a minute."

Tiffany looked over her shoulder at Charlie. "Shouldn't you be getting dinner ready?"

Charlie smiled at her. "Everything's prepared and ready to go."

Tiffany nodded. "Well, I guess I should go decide what to wear to dinner and check on your father."

"See you at dinner," Noah said.

Charlie came up to him. "Did I interrupt something?"

"Yes, thank God." He held out a racket. "You ready to play?"

She shook her head as she looked at the basket of tennis balls and the racket in his hand.

"After you left the kitchen, I realize there's no way I'm going to play tennis with you."

"Why not?"

"You play tennis for a living. I haven't played since that summer."

Noah twirled the racket in his hand. "Come on. We'll just hit some balls back and forth. We don't need to play an actual game."

She looked at the racket he held out to her but didn't take it. "I'm not going to embarrass myself."

Before he could prod her anymore, he saw Marcus returning.

"What's going on here?" He asked, as he came up beside Charlie.

"He wants me to play, but that's not going to happen."

Noah shook his head. "I'll hit to you both, Australian doubles. I'll use my left hand."

Charlie pointed a finger at him. "I remember you're ambidextrous. You play with both hands."

Noah shrugged. "But I'm better with my right. Come on. It'll be fun." He picked up another racket and held them both out.

Marcus grabbed a racket. "Fine. But play nice." He handed the racket to Charlie before taking the second one from Noah. "Come on, girl. We got this."

As he promised, Noah took it easy on them, and they had fun. They played for an hour before Marcus called it quits.

"Okay, I'm done." He approached the net and handed his racket to Noah, when he came up on the other side.

"You did good, big brother. And in slacks and street shoes, no less. I'm quite impressed."

"Well, Roberto and I have played a time or two."

Charlie joined them at the net. "I must admit, that was fun. Thank you for playing nice. Let's grab some water and go sit at our spot on the lawn."

Noah glanced at Marcus. "Our spot?"

Marcus smiled at Charlie. "I'll meet you there in five minutes. If he can't remember where it is, then…"

"I remember. Our spot on the lawn. I'll meet you there." Noah watched Marcus and Charlie head off as he tried to remember what they were talking about. It suddenly came to him. *The 4th of July.*

A few minutes later he found Marcus and Charlie waiting for him on the large expanse of lawn that gave them a clear view of the city twenty miles away. He sat next to Charlie and she smiled at him.

"You remembered."

"4th of July. We liberated a very expensive bottle of wine from the cellar and watched the fireworks."

Marcus nodded. "And what did we eat?"

Noah thought for a moment. "Popcorn and M&Ms."

"What else?" Charlie asked.

Noah shook his head. "Umm."

Marcus laid back on the grass. "Jerky. Peppered beef jerky."

Noah remembered. "Right, jerky. The combination sounds..."

Charlie laughed. "Awful." She was quiet for a moment, then asked, "Did you guys get in trouble for the wine?"

Noah shook his head. "I don't think so."

"We blamed the gardener for it," Marcus said as he covered his eyes to block the sun.

"That's right, we didn't like him much."

"Mr. Kwan?" Charlie asked.

"No, Kwan was the pond guy." Noah explained. "The other one. The tall lanky guy with the handlebar mustache."

"Oh, Mr. Canary. I liked him. Did he get fired?"

Noah laughed. "No, Dad was sleeping with his daughter, so he let it go."

"That girl with the freckles, she was only—"

"No, no. He's a bastard, but no. There was an older sister. Older than us."

"Not by much," Marcus added.

Charlie scooted around so that she was facing the men. "Okay, first off, that was mean of you guys. But enough about all that. I want the scoop."

Marcus sat up. "Scoop? What scoop?"

"The scoop that Ms. Schmidt is delivering a new will on Sunday. Noah, tell us what you know."

"Oh, right. I already knew about that," Marcus said as he leaned on one elbow.

Charlie frowned. "I told you everyone knew."

"I knew he knew. I told him."

"So is he going to leave it all to Tiffany, then?" Charlie asked.

"She thinks he is." Noah bent his knees and hugged them. "We're better off without it." He looked at Marcus. "All that money would ruin you."

Marcus shook his head while he considered Noah's assessment. "Maybe, but what a way to go."

Charlie looked at Noah for a moment. "What about you? Would you be able to handle a sudden influx of a lot of money?"

Noah smiled. "Fortunately, I won't have to find out. But I don't want any of it. I never have."

She cocked her head as she seemed to consider if he was telling her the truth. "You really mean that?"

"Yes, of course. I've got no use for his fifty million dollars."

Her eyes grew wide. "Wow, I didn't know it was that much. I should've charged more."

Marcus stood up and paced for a moment. "Okay, I get what you're saying about getting all of it. But I wouldn't mind a nice little chunk. Do you think he'd really leave it all to the new wife?"

"I don't know, but there are going to be a lot of angry women, if he does."

*****

As the dinner hour approached, Charlie excused herself to go back to work, and Marcus left soon after to make another call to Roberto.

Noah stayed on the lawn and contemplated the city in the distance. Even though he grew up in California, the east coast was where he belonged. He looked over his shoulder at the house. Not here, in this house, but in this city.

The last time he was at the house was five years ago. He lived thirty minutes away from his father and he hadn't seen him in five years. And he hadn't been around the whole family for even longer. He tried to distance himself from them while building a life for himself, away from the bickering and over-indulgence. He wasn't sure if there was actually a new will or not, but either way, things would change after this weekend. He'd be much better off being as far away from the Wainwright family implosion as possible. He stood up. "You need to get the hell out of here, Noah."

*****

Noah was stuffing things into his bag when Marcus walked into the room.

"What're you doing?"

Noah glanced up at him. "I'm leaving. I never should've come. I didn't want to come. I only came for you."

"Well, I'm still here. So why are you leaving?"

Noah zipped up his bag and dropped it onto the floor, then looked around the room. "If you were smart, you'd leave too."

"What's the rush, Noah?"

He sat on the edge of a bed. "The will, the new will, when the others find out…well, I don't want to be anywhere near here."

Marcus checked his watch. "It's almost time for dinner. If you stick it out through the meal, I'll pack up and leave with you afterwards."

Noah studied him for a moment. "I don't know that I can make it through another meal with the Wainwright women."

"I know, it's painful, but it'd give you a chance to say goodbye to Charlie, too. You can't leave without saying goodbye to her. That'd be a jerk move. Especially since she's not quite over her crush."

"What are you talking about? That was twelve years ago."

"Maybe so, but you never get over your first crush."

"I'm sure I wasn't her first crush or her last."

"Whatever. I had my first crush that summer. I'll never get over it."

Noah looked at him for a moment. "That kid from the gas station?"

"He didn't work at the gas station, he served ice cream at the place next door."

"Right. He was pretty good looking for a scrawny teenager. If he didn't have eyes only for you, I might've considered switching teams," Noah said with a smile.

Marcus took Noah by the arm and pulled him to his feet. "You, dear brother, would never be welcome on my team."

"Why not?"

"Because you're so…male." He checked out Noah's shirt. "Now, please, change the shirt."

"This morning you said blue was my color."

"That's true, but the point of what you said is, this morning. You put that shirt on twelve hours ago, played tennis in it, and…well twelve hours ago should be enough of a reason. Take it off and put on a clean shirt. My God, how do you get through life without me helping you get dressed?"

Noah frowned as he pulled off his shirt. "I manage, somehow." He sniffed the shirt. "I guess I'll go take a quick shower."

"Make it super quick. Dinner's in thirty."

Noah headed for the bathroom. "I know, seven-ish won't cut it."

Chapter Eleven

When Noah walked into the dining room, Dakota, Dell, and Laura were in the middle of a shouting match. If it weren't for Ruth waving him over, Noah would've turned right around, grabbed his bag, and left the Wainwright family home.

But instead, he smiled at his mother and went to her. She was standing by the bar watching Buddy mix a batch of martinis. Noah kissed her offered cheek and nodded at Buddy.

Buddy gave him a smile. "Looking sharp. Love that shirt."

Noah made a mental note to never wear the shirt again. "So what are they fighting about this time?" He waved off the martini Buddy offered him.

Ruth sighed. "I'm not sure anymore. I lost track several minutes ago."

"So, where's my brother? He left the bedroom before I did."

"He got a call from Roberto, he's out on the terrace." She put a hand on his cheek. "He says you two are leaving after dinner."

Noah nodded. "I can't..." He glanced at the still arguing women. "Do this anymore."

"You'll miss the reading of the will. Which was the whole purpose of coming in the first place."

"Yeah, well, I'm not so sure that's going to go like everyone thinks it's going to go." He turned to Buddy. "You got a beer back there?"

"What do you know?" Ruth asked.

"I don't know anything." He took the beer from Buddy and twisted off the cap.

"I'm your mother, I know when you're hiding something."

He took a drink. "I'm not hiding anything." He spotted Marcus coming in through the terrace door. "I'm going to go say hi to my brother, now." He walked away. *Why does everyone think they can read me?*

Noah crossed the room to Marcus. "I believe you talk to Roberto more while you're away than you do when you're home."

"When I'm home, there's no need for talking."

Noah thought about that for a moment. "Okay, I don't want to know the hidden meaning behind that statement."

Marcus smiled at him and took his arm. "Let's go sit and watch the show."

Noah watched the women for a moment. "Ten bucks says Laura leaves before they serve the main course."

"You're on."

They took a seat as Charlie and Richard came through the door with trays of soup and salad. They set one of each in front of everyone, which ended the current round of arguments.

The soup was clam chowder, one of Noah's favorites, and he was anxious to taste Charlie's version of it. As he picked up his spoon to take a bite, Simms came into the dining room.

Tiffany turned to him. "What is it, Simms?"

Simms bowed slightly, before he looked at Noah. "I have a message for Master Noah."

"Well, what is it?" She didn't hide her annoyance of having the meal interrupted by the help.

"It's for him, Mrs. Wainwright."

She sighed and looked at Noah, who set his spoon down and stood up. With everyone staring at him, including Charlie, he circled the table and followed Simms out the doors.

"Your father would like to see you, Master Noah."

"What?"

"Your father would like to see you."

"Me?" Upon seeing Simms' masked frustration, he asked, "Why?"

"I wouldn't know, Sir."

"Right, of course." Noah took a moment to examine the wooden floor. "Would you have an educated guess?"

"Master Noah."

"Sorry. So, when?"

"Now, Sir."

Noah refrained from repeating the word *now*, and instead asked, "After dinner?"

"Now, Sir."

"Like right now?" He rubbed the back of his neck. "Sorry, Simms, my father hasn't asked to talk to me since…I dropped out of college. And as you can imagine, that didn't go too well."

Simms started walking towards the staircase and Noah followed him. Simms stopped at the bottom and looked at Noah.

"Do I need to escort you all the way up, Sir?"

"No, I'm going. No escort necessary."

Simms nodded, but waited to leave until Noah started up the steps. He took twice as long as he should've for a healthy man in excellent physical condition. And once he got to the second floor, he stood for several moments before going down the hall to the door on the end.

Noah stood in front of his father's room for another five minutes, pacing in front of the door, while various scenarios ran through his mind. He finally knocked softly, then opened the door and peeked in.

"Dad?" he said into the darkness. When he got no response, he thought about retreating, but instead he stepped into the room and once more said, "Dad?"

"Come in, come in," came the grumbled response. "And close the damn door."

Noah closed the door behind him, then walked gingerly across the room. It was too dark to see any obstacles that might be between the door and the massive bed against the far wall. He headed for the shadow of the canopy and the blinking lights of the machines, and hoped for the best.

Once more the voice came from the bed. "Turn on the light. Let me look at you, boy."

Noah fumbled for the promised light, found it momentarily, and switched it on. The small wattage bulb illuminated the head of the bed and the old man's face. Atticus stared up at his son. His red-rimmed eyes were dark and piercing in the bone thin face that barely resembled the powerful man he'd once been. Noah felt for the chair behind him and sat down heavily.

Atticus cackled. "Do I look that bad?"

"No, it's just been a while."

"Miss me, did you?"

"Not really."

Atticus smiled, then chuckled, then fell into full out laughter. When he started turning red and then blue, the laughing turned into coughing. Noah slid to the edge of his chair and eyed the door. As he started to rise in preparation of going for help, Atticus waved a frail hand directing him to stay put. Noah remained on the seat's edge and watched as the coughing diminished and the pallor returned once more to his father's wrinkle skin.

"Should I get someone?" Noah asked when the room was quiet again.

"My nurse is gone for the night. And Tiffany is…well, you've probably met her. She'd just as soon see me dead than call for assistance."

Noah looked at the collection of pill bottles on the nightstand. "Can I give you something to help you sleep?"

"Sleep? Why does everyone want me to sleep? Hell, I'm damn near dead and everyone wants me to sleep." He wiped an arthritic hand across his dry lips. "Sit back and relax, son. I'm not dying yet. This is going to drag on another few months. My doctor has me on a new regimen of pills. Says they'll perk me right up."

Noah seriously doubted anything could perk his father up at this point. "Why'd you want to see me?"

"I have something to discuss with you."

Noah leaned back in the chair, but he was far from relaxed. He scanned the medical equipment surrounding the bed, while Atticus took a few more minutes to recover from his episode. Noah had no idea what most of the machines did, but he assumed the flashing lights and constantly changing numbers served a purpose other than to prolong the inevitable. Atticus Wainwright was not long for this world.

Atticus stared at his son, then closed his eyes for a long moment, causing Noah's panic to return.

Atticus opened his eyes again and said, "I'm not a man to mince words." Something Noah was all too aware of. "So, I'll get right to the point. Out of all my children and all my ex-wives, you're the only one who shows even a hint of promise." This was news to Noah, who always thought he was a disappointment. "Therefore, I'm leaving the destiny of my wealth…" Coughing once more overtook his frail body.

Noah sat by and waited as a multitude of endings to his father's sentence ran through his head. Atticus pointed at the glass of water sitting by the light. Noah picked it up and tried to hand it to him, but soon realized his father was unable to drink from it without help. He hesitated for a moment, almost afraid to touch his father. Other than an occasional handshake, physical contact between the two of them was non-existent. He put a hand behind the old man's head while holding the glass to his lips. Atticus took a small sip, allowing his eyes, for the briefest of seconds, to make contact with his son. He then quickly lowered them and turned away from the glass.

Noah sat back in his chair once more and returned the glass to the table. The coughing subsided and Atticus closed his eyes. When he feared the onset of sleep would leave his father's sentence hanging, unfinished, Noah said, "Dad?"

Atticus startled. "What?" he opened his eyes and looked at Noah. "What?"

"You were saying something about…"

"The money, ah yes. The money. A question no doubt on everybody's mind." He took a deep raspy breath. "You'll decide."

Noah stopped breathing. "What?" He involuntarily gasped as survival overtook emotion. "Excuse me. What'd you say?"

"I've stated in my new will that you'll decide who it goes to."

"What?"

"Are you deaf? Must you make me repeat everything I say? You're to make the choice. I'm too sick, and too tired, and frankly I don't think any of you deserve it. So, I leave it in your hands."

"Mine? No, wait."

"That lawyer woman…"

"Ms. Schmidt." The fact he was able to pull her name out of thin air, was interesting and quite amazing, since he never met her. He only heard about her over the years.

"Yes, she has the paperwork, all drawn up and legal. I've made a couple of directives I expect you to follow, but the rest is up to you." He coughed again. "You may go, now."

As he mentally reverted to his childhood of fear and loathing, Noah got instinctively to his feet before his mind started working again. He looked at the shell of the man who oversaw the ruin of countless fortunes. "You can't be serious."

Atticus glared up at his son. "Do I look like someone who has the energy to be amusing? I'm dying. Now leave me to my misery." He switched off the light.

Noah stood in the dark next to his father's bed, then slowly made his way across the room and let himself out into the hall. He continued to his room in a fog, as he went in and sat on the bed.

Marcus was laying on his bed talking on the phone, but upon seeing the state Noah was in, he ended the call and sat up.

"What's up? What happened? Where've you been?"

Noah sighed. "Which of those questions would you like me to answer?"

"All of them."

Noah sighed. "Atticus."

Marcus stood up. "Stay there. I'll be right back." He left the room and returned five minutes later to find Noah still sitting on the bed. He carried two drinks and handed one to Noah.

"Drink, then tell me everything."

Noah wasn't one to down a drink, but he dispatched that one in a couple of swallows, then set the glass on the table separating their two beds.

"I saw him. He *summoned* me."

"Shut the front door. Just now?"

Noah nodded his head. "It was weird, and horrible, and scary as hell."

Marcus handed Noah his own drink. "You need this more than I do."

Even though it was straight scotch, Noah drank it, then set the glass next to the other one. "Why would he do this to me? Does he hate me that much?"

"Noah, please tell me what he said. I'm trying to be patient, but I'm about to grab you up by the shoulders and shake you."

"He looked…like a dead man. But he's still as ornery as ever."

Marcus leaned forward. "Noah, what did he say to you?"

"It has to be a joke." He looked at his brother. "Right? Or he's lost it and he doesn't know what he's doing."

"Well, I could better answer if you told me what he said."

Noah stood up and walked around the room. "He wants me to decide who gets what."

Marcus was silent for a moment, but then asked, "What does that mean?"

"The will, he's changed it, again. He's leaving it up to me to disperse his money."

"He's making you executor?"

"I don't know. Is that what it's called?"

Marcus nodded. "I believe so."

Noah sat on the bed. "Why?"

Marcus moved over next to Noah. "He's not doing this to punish you. Quite the opposite, in fact. He's doing it because he trusts you to do the right thing."

"He didn't say that. He just said he didn't want to do it." He looked at Marcus. "Why not you? You're the oldest son."

"Well, you know ever since he found out I was gay, he's pretty much written me off."

Noah stood up again. "He's such a bastard."

"Well, you could really stick it to him and give it all to me. That'd have him rolling around in his grave."

"How do I get out of it?"

"Well, I'm sure you can go to court or something if you really want to."

"I really want to."

"Or."

"Or?"

"You can use that anti-Wainwright brain of yours, and execute the hell out of the Wainwright fortune."

Chapter Twelve

The two men talked about the possibilities for several hours, but by midnight, Marcus was fading and wanted to go to sleep. For Noah, that wasn't going to be an option. He stared at the ceiling and listened to Marcus snoring, but when that stopped, the room became unbearably quiet. At 1:45, Noah threw back the bedspread, slipped on some pants, and headed for the door. He went out into the hall and closed the door quietly behind him.

On bare feet, he descended the stairs, crossed the tile foyer and entered the library. He switched on a small light on the end of the bar and went behind it, then grabbed a bottle of scotch. This would be his third one for the night, which was unusual. He much preferred beer over hard liquor. But after the bomb dropped into his lap early in the evening, three scotches seemed acceptable. He poured a shot into a glass and drank it in one swallow, feeling it burn all the way down. *And that's why I drink beer.*

He sat on a stool and stared at himself in the mirror behind the bar. The face that looked at him resembled his father forty years ago. Even though he spent his entire adult life trying to be everything, his father wasn't, he couldn't escape the face that greeted him every morning in the mirror. Noah spun around on his stool and put his back to the glass.

When the door opened, splashing light from the foyer into the room, Noah looked up to see Simms' silhouette. The man was fully dressed, and Noah wondered if Simms slept in his clothes in order to be available twenty-four hours a day for any Wainwright that might need him.

"Everything all right, Sir?"

"Would you care to have a drink with me, Simms?"

He took a step into the room. "A drink, Sir?"

Noah got to his feet and went back behind the bar. He took a second glass off the shelf and poured a shot of scotch into it. He then refilled his own.

"Come on in and join me." He set the glass on the far side of the bar.

Simms walked to the bar, but remained on his feet. He looked at the offered drink then at Noah. "I really can't."

Noah took a sip out of his glass. "Simms…just what the hell is your first name, anyway?"

"William. Sir, are you all right?"

Noah swirled the scotch around the bottom of the glass. "Why have you worked for my father for all these years?"

"I've never had a reason to go elsewhere."

Noah looked into the dark eyes of the man who'd been more of a father figure to him than Atticus had ever been. "Have you been happy here?"

"Of course."

"But you've given up having a life of your own. You've given up having a family of your own."

"I've had three families. Each new wife, each new set of children. I've been there through them all. And now, the new Mrs. Wainwright."

"I wouldn't hold your breath on having anymore little ones around the place."

"One never knows, Sir."

Noah circled the end of the bar and sat on the stool again. "You're a curious man, Simms. A very curious man."

"May I help you to your room, Sir?"

"Who do you talk to, Simms?"

"Perhaps you should go up to your room now. The sun will be up in a couple hours."

Noah got to his feet and headed slowly for the door. Before going out, he glanced over his shoulder. "Good night, Simms."

"Good night, Master Noah."

*****

Noah got a few hours of sleep, but he was awake by seven and since he missed dinner, he was starving. He borrowed Marcus' bathrobe and slipped it on over his t-shirt and boxers, then headed to the kitchen. At this hour there wouldn't be anyone there, and he could throw together something to eat.

He walked into the kitchen to find Charlie at the stove. She looked at his attire and smiled. "So, is it casual Saturday? I didn't get the memo."

Noah looked down at his robe and pulled it closed, then tied the belt. "Sorry, I didn't expect to find anyone here yet."

"The Wainwrights aren't going to feed themselves."

"This one was planning to."

"Sit, I'll make you some eggs." She opened the refrigerator and pulled out a carton of eggs. "Did you ever get dinner last night?"

Noah shook his head as he sat on the stool in front of the counter.

"May I ask what Simms wanted?"

"Umm, I'm not sure."

"You're not sure what he wanted or whether or not I can ask?"

He frowned at her.

"Okay, not in a joking mood today. Are you okay?"

"Okay?" He thought about the question. "Am I okay?"

"That's what I asked."

"No." She poured him a cup of coffee. He picked up the cup and blew on it before he took a sip. "But, why would I be? I'm Noah Wainwright, son of Atticus Wainwright III."

Charlie put the pot on the stove and broke three eggs in the frying pan.

Noah sighed. "I'm sorry."

She turned and looked at him.

"I'm being a Wainwright."

"You know, you have the power to be whatever you want to be."

"You don't know my father very well, do you?" He stood up. "I'm sorry, I guess I'm not hungry after all. And even I don't want to be around me right now, so I'm going to go back upstairs and try to get some more sleep."

Despite his rumbling stomach, Noah fell asleep, but it seemed only minutes passed before someone started shaking him. Noah opened one eye and saw Marcus standing over him.

"Wake up. Breakfast is in an hour."

Noah closed his eye.

"Oh no, you don't."

Noah rolled onto his back and looked at Marcus. "We were supposed to leave last night. That means I don't need to go to breakfast this morning."

"No, it doesn't. We didn't leave, and now we can't leave, not after your visit with the old man. So get up." He headed for the bathroom. "I'm taking a five minute shower. You'll be up and ready to take one when I come out."

"Yes, Sir. King of the showers, or something equally stupid." He shook his head. "I didn't get enough sleep." He rolled onto his side and closed his eyes.

"Get up, get up, get up, get up—"

Noah opened his eyes and glared at Marcus. "Oh my God, shut up. Are you five?"

"Hey, whatever works." He went to the closet and selected clothes to wear.

Noah sighed. "Fine, I'm up. But if you come into the bathroom and say, get out, get out, get out. I'm going to take my bag, which is still packed, and leave you here with the Wainwright ex-wives club to fend for yourself."

Marcus put on a shirt and buttoned it. "I won't come in, but I'm knocking on the door in ten. And I left my razor in there for you."

"I have my own razor."

"Really, I thought you must've left it at home, seeing as your sexy two-day beard look has turned into a scruffy, 'is he growing a beard or does he just not care', look."

Noah rubbed his chin. "How does Roberto put up with you?"

"Go take your shower."

*****

Simms met the two men, freshly showered and shaved, in the foyer. He looked at Noah.

"How are we doing this morning, Sir?"

At the sound of raised voices coming from the dining room, Noah said, "Seriously considering walking out the front door."

"That would seem to be a more favorable choice."

Noah studied Simms' weathered face. If there were any men of integrity left in this world, this was certainly one of them.

He smiled and glanced at Marcus. "Kitchen?"

"Definitely."

Noah looked at Simms again, who gave him a slight nod. "Have a pleasant breakfast, Sirs."

They ducked into the kitchen and found Charlie at the stove, and she smiled when they came in. "Well, look how pretty you both are." She put a hand on Noah's smooth chin. "Who knew?"

He pulled away from her. "I don't suppose you could scramble us up some eggs?"

"Are you going to stay long enough to eat them this time?"

"Yes." He glanced at Marcus, who raised an eyebrow, but didn't say anything.

She poured two cups of coffee and set them on the counter. "Coming right up."

Marcus looked at his coffee cup. "I'm going to need some cream and sugar for this."

Noah took a sip of his black coffee and sat at the counter. "What's the point of drinking coffee if you're going to put sugar in it and dilute it with creamer? The whole coffee experience is the strong, bitter, taste of caffeine pumping through your veins."

"Says the man who drinks scotch and soda on the rocks."

Noah shook his head. "That's not the same thing."

"Of course it is." He looked at Charlie. "Right?"

She set plates with scrambled eggs and bacon in front of them. "Don't drag me into this."

When they were half way through their breakfast, Ruth came into the kitchen. "There you are. Hiding out?"

Marcus looked at her over his shoulder. "Good morning, Mother."

She kissed him on the cheek. "Good morning, darling."

"The family is expecting you in the dining room. Tiffany hasn't shown up yet, but we all decided to eat without her." She looked at Charlie. "You can start anytime."

Noah took a bite of bacon. "I seriously doubt whether they care one way or the other if Marcus and I are there."

"Well, I care. Please come join us."

Noah sighed and looked at Charlie. "Sorry, Mom says I can't play anymore."

"Well, at least you made it through half the meal this time."

The men followed their mother into the dining room. The arguing had stopped and everyone but Buddy sat at the table in anticipation of breakfast.

Dell held up a Bloody Mary. "Buddy, be a doll and fix Noah one of these. He looks like he could use one."

"No, coffee's fine." Noah poured himself a cup from a dispenser and sat down.

Charlie appeared, followed by Richard. They set fruit plates containing grapefruit, strawberries, and chunks of melon in front of each family member, then put a large platter of scrambled eggs, bacon and toasted English muffins in the center of the table, before heading for the door.

Except for silverware scraping china, the room remained quiet. Noah glanced around the table at his family. How soon before they all know what the old man had asked him to do? He needed to get out of it. It was an impossible task, a task his father had no right to saddle him with. Right after breakfast he'd go talk to him. He'd plead with him if he had to. This was one time Atticus Wainwright wouldn't get his way.

Noah pushed a strawberry around his plate as he stifled a yawn. Buddy grinned at him. "Have a late night, did we? Perhaps another late night game of pool."

Before Noah responded, Tiffany came into the dining room. Though she was perfectly dressed and groomed, she seemed frazzled. Dakota was the first to break the silence that returned to the room as everyone watched Tiffany approach the table.

"Everything all right, honey?"

Tiffany looked around, then growing pale, she grabbed for the nearest support, which happened to be the back of Noah's chair. He got to his feet and offered it to her, and she sank into it.

"I'm afraid I have some rather difficult news." Her voice barely rose above a whisper. Noah put a hand on her shoulder and she reached up and held onto it. "Atticus has passed on."

Now it was Noah's turn to feel faint, and of all the stuff rushing through his mind, the only clear thought was that he wished he hadn't given up his seat. His legs suddenly felt like they couldn't hold him as his mind reeled.

He was committed now to deciding the fate of the Wainwright fortune. There'd be no convincing the old man to change his mind, nor a chance of having him declared unsound and therefore not fit to lay that kind of responsibility on his son. If the will truly was changed, his fate was sealed. He looked around the silent room. Not even a gasp escaped into the air. Everyone stared off in different directions or into their plates, not wanting to make eye contact, afraid their true feeling, or lack thereof, would be revealed.

Marcus was the first to react. He set his spoon down and said, "Shut the front door." He looked at Noah and mouthed, *say something*.

His mind that seconds ago was awash with panic, suddenly became blank. *Say something?* "Ah, when? When did this happen?" Noah shrugged as Marcus frowned at him and shook his head.

"Early this morning. The doctor said, probably around 3:30 or 4:00." Tiffany squeezed Noah's hand and laid her head back, resting it on his arm.

Dell suddenly got to her feet. "Oh hell, let's not pretend any of us in this room are sorry to see him go." She held up her glass. "A toast. To the meanest son of a bitch that ever walked this earth."

Buddy reached up and took her arm, attempting to pull her back into her chair. "Sugarplum."

She pulled away from him and walked to the bar. "Bloody Mary, anyone?"

"I think you're drinking enough for all of us, Dell." Laura slid her chair away from the table. "Come, Libby." Libby stood up. "We'll be in our room." They headed for the door, but before going out, Laura turned and looked at Tiffany. "If you think for one minute you're fooling any of us with the bereaved widow routine, you're not as smart as I thought you were." She left with Libby on her heels.

Tiffany stood up. "What do I need to do to convince you all I didn't marry Atticus for his money?"

Dakota laughed. "Honey, we're not judging you. All of us ex-wives married Atticus for his money." She looked at Ruth. "Well, maybe not Ruth. You actually loved him for a minute, didn't you?"

Tiffany shook her head. "Shame on all of you." With a doleful look at Noah, she left the room.

Noah watched her leave, then looked around the table at the collection of relatives he often regretted belonging to. This was most definitely one of those times.

"She's right, you know." He took his seat. "Shame on all of us." He pushed his plate towards the center of the table.

Buddy eyed it. "Are you going to eat that?" Noah shook his head and Buddy reached across the table. "Then you won't mind if I do?" He took the plate and set it down in front of him. "The way I see it, as the only non-Wainwright in the group, you're all here for the same reason. So why don't we wait a few hours for the dust to settle. No pun intended, then get down to business."

Ruth finished eating the fruit on her plate and drained her coffee cup, then reached into the pocket of her tweed jacket and pulled out a pack of cigarettes and a lighter.

"I assume it's safe to smoke inside now." She took one out, then leaned across the table and offered one to Noah. He pulled one out and stuck it into the side of his mouth.

Marcus dabbed at the corners of his mouth with his napkin, and tossed it onto his plate.

"I don't know about everyone else, but I for one would appreciate it if you continued to smoke outside." The rest of the room mumbled in agreement.

Ruth got to her feet. "Fine, I'll be on the veranda." She headed for the door. "Noah, you going to join me?"

Noah took the cigarette out of his mouth and looked at it. He rolled it in his fingers a few times before he broke it in half and dropped it on the table. "No, I quit."

"Again," Marcus added.

Dakota watched Ruth leave then looked at Noah. "Good for you. I hope you stick with it this time." She stood up, tugged on her short denim skirt, and tucked in the black bra strap that slipped down her tanned arm. "If you all will excuse me, I'm going to go take a swim." She retrieved the cowboy hat hanging on the back of her chair and plopped it on her head.

Buddy said, "When I went by a while ago, the pool guy was out there sweeping it down."

Dakota smiled. "I know. He sweeps the pool down every morning, about this time." She tilted her hat down over one eye as she walked out the door. "See you all later."

Dell got to her feet. "When is she going to realize she's well into middle age?"

Buddy got up and put his arm around her shoulder. "Some things get better with age."

He steered her towards the door. "What do you say you and I go up to our room and…" They disappeared into the foyer, taking the rest of the sentence with them. The last thing Noah and Marcus heard was an uncharacteristic giggle from Dell.

Marcus looked at Noah. "Well, it looks like everyone has found something to do to pass the next couple of hours. How about you, what are you going to do?" When he got no response, Marcus looked closer at his brother. Even though they just received notice of their father's death, he seemed to be more upset than Marcus would've expected him to be. "You want to tell me what's wrong?"

"I was going to go talk to him this morning and tell him to take his will and shove it."

"Really." Marcus smiled. "I would've loved to see that happen."

"I hate this."

"I know you do, little brother. But, I have complete confidence in you."

Noah looked at him. "I'll pay you $10,000.00 to take over for me."

"Well, first off, until the executor," he pointed at Noah. "executes the will. You don't have $10,000.00. But even if you did. It'd be totally worth that much to watch you squirm through the meeting with the lawyer tomorrow."

"Is she still coming tomorrow?"

"I don't see why not. He's actually dead. It makes a lot more sense, now."

Chapter Thirteen

Buddy laid on the rumpled bed and watched his wife get dressed. It was moments like this that made putting up with her abrasive attitude all worth it. She loved him, in her own special way. She loved him a lot. There was no doubt about it.

She looked over her shoulder at him. "What?"

"Just enjoying the view, buttercup." He stuffed a second pillow behind his head. "So, how much do you think you're going to get?"

She turned around and faced him. "It's finally going to pay off or you, isn't it?"

"What's that, sweet pea?"

"Putting up with me all these years."

He reached out and took hold of her arm, then pulled her down beside him. "You know I adore you."

She kissed him lightly on the lips. "You're such a liar."

*****

From her perch on the window seat, Libby could see a large section of the grounds. She could see Dakota at the pool in an animated conversation with the man who cleaned it. He was a lot younger than her stepmother was, and Libby couldn't quite figure out what they could possibly be talking about, but they sure seemed to be having fun. Dakota always had fun, so unlike her mother.

Libby glanced at Laura who was engrossed in a paperback novel. The things going on outside the window were much more exciting.

Recently, she saw Dell and Buddy heading to their room. She suspected what they were about to do. Everyone was having fun except her. But then, should she even be thinking about that when a few hours ago her father died?" She tried to put a name to what she was feeling. Grief, no, sadness? Not really. The closest emotion she could name was relief. Now whenever anyone asked her about her father, she could say he was dead.

No one would question her further. They wouldn't ask about who he was, where he lived, or what he did for a living. She'd never need to lie about him again.

"Libby?"

She turned and put her back to the window. "Yes?"

"What outside the window is keeping you entertained for such a long time?"

"Can I please go out?"

Laura looked over the rim of her reading glasses. "And do what?"

"I don't know. Anything."

"Libby, we must at least put on the pretense of mourning your father."

Libby studied the blue nail polish on her fingers. "Did you ever love him, even a little?"

Laura set her book aside. "I loved Atticus for what he could do for me. Just like I loved the two husbands since him."

"So, bigger houses, fancier cars and upward movement on the social ladder. That's what love is to you?" Libby stood up and walked to the door. "So, when you tell me you love me…" She opened the door."

"That's different."

"I'm going out to the garden." Libby said as she stepped out into the hall and closed the door on her mother's protests.

*****

Marcus spread mayonnaise on a piece of bread then laid it on top of the sandwich he was building out of leftover scrambled eggs and bacon. He set it on the butcher block counter and poured himself a glass of milk. As he sat on a stool, Tiffany walked in.

He looked up at her, not sure what to say. She gave him a small smile and sat across from him. He picked up half of his sandwich and held it out to her, and she hesitated a moment before taking it from him.

"Thank you," she said quietly. "I missed breakfast." She took a tiny bite. "So, I guess the waiting game is over now."

"Waiting game?"

"You've all been waiting years for him to die."

"Well, some of us have. He disowned me years ago, therefore the money has never been an issue for me. And Noah couldn't care less. He doesn't want it.'

Tiffany got up and went to the refrigerator, then opened it and took out a pitcher of juice. She returned to the table.

"Do you really believe that?"

"Of course. He hates money and everything it represents."

She filled a glass with juice and took another bite from the sandwich, then looked at Marcus. "Well, we'll see how that holds up when the will is read."

"Right, the will. Should be an interesting afternoon tomorrow."

"I'm afraid there'll be some unhappy people."

"I believe you're right, Tiffany. Things aren't going to go as everyone hopes they will."

*****

Noah was out on the tennis courts giving the wall a thorough workout when Charlie found him. She watched him for a few minutes before he noticed her. She was out of her uniform and dressed in jeans and a cotton shirt. The French braid was gone, and her hair was loose and tucked behind her ears. With her hair down, she looked younger than her twenty-nine years.

He used the tail of his shirt to wipe his damp forehead, then walked over to her. She handed him a bottle of water.

"Thanks." He took it from her and drank half of it.

"I wanted to see how you were doing."

Noah wiped his mouth with the back of his hand. "As much as you may like it to be different, there isn't anyone in this house upset about my father's death. And that includes his newest wife." Of course, he thought, that's going to change when the will is read. Then there's going to be a whole house full of unhappy people.

They sat in two plastic chairs on the side of the court. There was a slight breeze blowing and Noah leaned back and let the air cool him down. He looked at Charlie. "Are you still staying through Monday?"

"Tiffany seems to think everyone will leave by tomorrow night, so I'll wait and see, I guess."

"And then what?"

"I have my catering business. So, I'll be fine, even if Tiffany decides not to keep me on part-time. I was just working weekends anyway."

Noah leaned forward in his chair. "I don't know what's going to happen after tomorrow, but Tiffany most likely won't have any say in whether or not you keep working here. So, I wouldn't count on it."

"You don't think she's going to get it all?"

"Let's just say, the new will isn't exactly what she's expecting."

"And how do you know that?"

Noah looked around to make sure they were alone. "When Simms called me out last night, it was to go talk with my dad."

She leaned forward. "What? Oh my gosh. What'd he want?"

"Well, let me preface this with, I haven't seen him in five years, but he looked like he aged twenty. He looked like death. And seven hours later he *was* dead."

She put a hand on his arm. "What'd he say to you?"

Noah sighed, and took a moment before he answered her. "He made me executor of his will. At least, that's what I think the paperwork Ms. Schmidt is bringing will say."

"Oh my God, that's crazy."

"I knew you'd get it."

"No, I didn't mean it like that. I mean it's a crazy responsibility, not crazy he entrusted you with it." She squeezed his arm. "You don't look too happy about it."

"It's ridiculous. I don't understand why he picked me to do it."

"Well, if not you, then who. Who else in the family would you want to be in charge of the Wainwright family fortune?"

Noah took a moment to assess her question. "None of them."

"There you have it. You, like it or not, are the best man for the job. So, you'll be my new boss."

Noah laughed. "Well, we'll see about that. In any case, tomorrow when Ms. Schmidt shows up, you might want to make yourself scarce."

"I'll hide in the kitchen."

He studied her for a moment. "I'm glad we crossed paths again."

"You are?"

"Yes. Can we stay in touch?"

"I'd like that." She gave him a small smile. "Did you just fire me?"

"I might have. For now, I'd say don't depend on this job for a while until the dust settles. I don't know what's going to happen to the house or who will live in it."

"Fair enough." She watched him as he finished the water in the bottle. "Give me your phone."

He took his phone out of his pocket, unlocked it, and handed it to her.

She looked at him. "So, if I go to your contacts is there going to be a long list of women?"

"The only woman in my contact list is my mother. And hopefully, you."

She smiled and went to the contact list. "Impressive, but also sad." She looked at him. "You have four names in here."

"I'm not a big phone guy, unlike my brother who lives on his."

"I wonder how long his contact list is?" She started to put in her number then stopped and erased it. "On second thought, I'll call you."

"Why?"

"To save myself the disappointment of you not calling."

"If you give me your number, I'll call you."

She handed him his phone and stood up. "This is better. Don't worry, I won't wait too long."

He stood up too, and she hugged him. Noah held her tighter and longer than he should have. When he felt her try to pull away, he released his grip and stepped back.

She smiled at him. "I thought I was going to need to tap out there for a moment."

"Sorry. You've just been…a light in a very dark tunnel. Which is pretty much what you were during the last time we were together in this house."

"If things go the way you think they're going to go tomorrow, just take some time to figure all of this out."

"That's the plan."

"And maybe keep the flinging down for a while. You know, to minimize the distraction."

"I'll do that."

"I still want to know how many lonely housewives you've flung."

Noah shook his head. "Never going to happen." He sat back down. "So, is this goodbye? I'll see you tonight at dinner, and for breakfast in the morning, right?"

"Yes, you will. But if things get crazy tomorrow afternoon, I might sneak out. So, this is the goodbye we might not get tomorrow."

"Okay, that works. And you'll call me."

"I'll call you." She took a couple steps back. "And now, I need to go get dinner ready."

"See you around, kid."

*****

Dinner was oddly quiet and Tiffany was a no show, which seemed to be a relief to everyone. Even though Noah had barely eaten since lunch yesterday, he wasn't hungry. The anticipation of Ms. Schmidt's visit was overshadowing everything he did.

There were a few squabbles, but mostly everyone ate and excused themselves. Noah found himself alone with his mother, pushing food around his half-empty plate.

"I don't think I've ever known you not to be hungry," Ruth said as she watched her youngest son. "Do you want to tell me what's going on?"

"I just want this weekend to be over. I wish I'd left yesterday before dinner. Marcus talked me into staying for the meal, then the sky fell on me."

Ruth studied him for a moment. "I wish you'd tell me what's really going on. You've been distracted ever since you left with Simms."

"I just didn't expect him to die while we were here, that's all."

Ruth shook her head. "No, that's not it. You know, I know when you aren't being truthful to me."

"Is that why I never got away with anything when I was a kid?"

She stood up. "Come out onto the terrace with me and have a cigarette. You look like you could use one."

Noah stood up and followed her out through the French doors. "My mother is encouraging me to smoke. That doesn't seem quite right."

She handed him a cigarette and took one herself, then Noah lit them both.

"Well, I've never been that good of a mother."

Noah kissed her on the cheek. "You were a fine mother."

"You and Marcus basically raised yourselves. I'm well aware I failed you two. But I always loved you, you know that, right?"

"Of course. There was never any doubt."

She smiled. "Somehow, despite the parents you were saddle with, you and your brother turned out pretty damn good."

"Well, Marcus did."

She put a hand on his cheek. "You're a better person than you think you are. As soon as you realize that, you'll do fine."

Chapter Fourteen

Ms. Schmidt had been employed by Atticus Wainwright for close to fifty years. As a young woman right out of school, she emigrated from Germany to the united States and got her first job as a secretary in one of the many businesses owned by Atticus. She enrolled in night school, perfected her English, and developed an interest in the law. By the time she reached her fifth anniversary as a Wainwright employee, she passed her bar exams. At ten years, she was one of his top lawyers. For the last twenty years, she had the final say over all legal matters in Atticus' private life. She was possibly the only human being he even came close to trusting.

She arrived in a small black town car and wore an olive green suit that resembled a military uniform. Her gray hair was pulled into a tight bun and her face bore no sign of make-up. She'd never been an attractive woman, not even when she was young, but she accepted her looks and never tried to achieve beauty artificially. She never married and as far as anyone in the family knew, she never had a lover. She was a spinster in the purest sense of the word.

The Wainwright family members were gathered in the library, all lost in their own little worlds of anticipation. Ruth had changed into a black wool suit for the occasion. She seemed unaffected, but Noah suspected she was feeling a bit nostalgic for the man she once loved.

Laura was also dressed in black to further her charade of mourning, and had a tight grip on Libby's hand, as though she thought the girl might run off if she let go.

Dakota, fresh from a swim, decked out in a white satin shirt and jeans, looked a tad buzzed, but hadn't reached the state of inebriation her daughter had. Dell also opted to forgo black and was wearing a purple cheetah print top with purple leggings.

Tiffany appeared to be a mess, though Noah doubted anyone believed it. She sat in a large armchair with her feet tucked under her. She was dressed and coifed, but she looked like she'd been up all night. Tiffany didn't marry Atticus for love, so it was all for show, right down to the simple black dress she was wearing.

Noah looked at them all and wished he could read their thoughts, but he knew he'd soon hear, in no uncertain terms, what was on everybody's mind. He was standing next to Marcus as the two of them tried to melt into the massive bookshelf behind them.

Ms. Schmidt stood behind a large mahogany desk and looked around the room at the expectant faces of her audience. When she cleared her throat in preparation to speak, everyone froze. She smiled curtly, but then instead of speaking, she clicked the latches on her black leather briefcase and slowly opened it. After pulling out a sealed manila envelope, she closed the case and once more looked around the room.

She cleared her throat again. "I have here the amended will and testament of Atticus Wainwright III. The will has been changed several times over the years, as circumstances warranted. The newest revision was right after his recent honeymoon."

All eyes in the room turned to Tiffany, who wiped at her eyes, and rearranged herself in the chair.

"But two weeks ago, Atticus asked me to make another, and it turns out final, revision to the will."

Tiffany stood up, and the grieving widow disappeared. "That can't be right."

Ms. Schmitt gave her a small smile. "I'm afraid it is." She waited for Tiffany to sit, which she did once she remembered she had a part to play. "If I may go on. The fact is, this latest version, is the final will and testament of Atticus Wainwright III. It will be followed to the letter including the supervision of the distribution of his estate."

Dakota got to her feet. "What the hell does that mean?" Dell reached for her and pulled her down to her seat.

"It was Atticus' wish to put his estate and the disbursement of it into the hands of an executor, who in his mind, would have an unbiased opinion of how the money should be allocated."

Laura raised her hand. "And is that person, you?"

Ms. Schmitt shook her head. "Oh goodness, no." She held up the envelope. "That person is Noah. It was Mr. Wainwright's request his son Noah, open and read this letter he wrote regarding the allocation of his estate."

In a room so quiet the hum of the air conditioner was an intrusion, all eyes moved from Ms. Schmitt to Noah. He seemed incapable of moving, and he glanced at Marcus who was motioning towards the front of the room with his head. When Noah still didn't move, Marcus put a hand on his back and gave him a gentle shove.

"You're up, Brother."

Noah took a step, then another. He felt like he was walking in wet cement as he continued to the desk and took the envelope from Ms. Schmitt.

With steady hands that belied the reality of his emotional state, he took a small penknife out of his pocket and sliced open the envelope. He then pulled out a single sheet of paper. He glanced over his shoulder at Ms. Schmitt.

"Read it," she said.

Noah looked at the letter written in his father's hand, unmistakable with its large letters and random mix of cursive and print, a sign of his limited education. He hated school and dropped out at fifteen to work for his father. Atticus the second, who never made it past fifth grade, believed education only slowed a man down, and pigeon holed him. He was a self-made man who rose out of poverty and illiteracy to build an empire on the ashes of weaker men. Atticus the third was just like him.

Noah looked once more around the room, before reading the letter.

"I, Atticus Wainwright III, being of sound mind—"

"For God's sake, Noah," Dakota interrupted. "Quit dallying with the legal stuff and get to the part we're all waiting to hear."

"The I bequeath part," Dell added.

Noah skimmed the first paragraph, then dropped to the second.

"In my seventy years, I've had the misfortune of being married to some of the..."

He paused again and looked at Tiffany, who raised her eyes from the floor and was watching him with a look he couldn't quite decipher. He went on.

"...greediest women the planet had to offer".

"Talk about the pot calling the kettle black," Dell said, as she pulled out a small compact, clicked it open and checked her lipstick.

Laura got to her feet. "This is an outrage. The man was obviously not of sound mind and body when he wrote that."

"Oh, come on, honey, Atticus may not have been many things, but he wasn't a fool," Dakota said as she stood up and walked to the bar. "He was just as aware of our motives as we were of his." She looked at Dell, who nodded at her unasked offer for a drink. "Anyone else want anything while I'm pouring?" Receiving only silence from the group, she poured two brandies. "Go ahead, Noah. Let's hear what else he has to say."

Noah continued.

"It was my ongoing hope that one of these women would at least serve the worthwhile purpose of giving me children to be proud of. At this too, they all failed miserably with the exception of two possible diamonds in the rough, I still hold a sliver of hope for."

When Dakota handed her a glass of brandy, Dell took a drink. "You'd at least think a man on his deathbed could come up with something decent to say to his children." She held up her glass. "Thanks for the memories, Dad."

Ms. Schmidt cleared her throat again. "Please go on with the letter."

Noah went on.

"Libby, you've yet to be corrupted by your mother. There may still be hope for you."

Noah looked at his little sister who was staring out the window, looking as though she'd rather be anywhere but there in the library with this strange assortment of relatives. Atticus was right, there was still hope for her.

He returned to the letter, but resisted reading the words that would change his life the moment he said them out loud. No matter what he ultimately did with his father's fortune, most of the people in the room with him would be unhappy about it. There'd be no pleasing everybody, of that, he was certain.

"Come on," Buddy said impatiently. "Just get on with it." He took the glass of brandy from his wife and drained it. She frowned at the empty glass when he handed it back to her, then got up and headed for the bar. "Better fill one of those up for me, buttercup," Buddy said, as he watched his wife walk away.

Noah took a breath and went on.

"The only other heir who shows any promise is my son, Noah. Even though he has spent his entire life trying to deny his parentage, he is his father's son, and I have every faith in his ability to make the right decision as to the fate of the Wainwright holdings".

If it was at all possible, the room got even quieter. Noah tried to swallow and dampen the desert that now lived in his mouth. He licked his dry lips and went on without looking out and meeting any of the eyes that were boring into him.

"Therefore, I leave it in his hands."

Dell slammed the bottle of brandy down on the bar. "What the hell does that mean?"

"Let him finish," Ms. Schmidt said, quietly.

"It's my final request that Noah Evanston Wainwright be the sole executor of my estate. All decisions made by him will be

binding and upheld by this directive. Signed by me, Atticus Wainwright III on this day…"

Noah trailed off, knowing his audience was no longer listening.

Buddy looked at Ms. Schmidt. "Can he do that?"

"Yes, he can."

Laura spoke up. "But that's ridiculous. Why did he change it? When did he change it?"

Marcus went to the front of the room and took the letter from Noah. "It's signed and witnessed. It looks like a legal document to me."

Dell laughed. "You're a waiter. What do you know?"

Laura started pacing the room. "He basically has left it all to Noah." She glared at him. "If he has the power to do whatever he wants with it, he can just keep it. Right?" She looked around the room. "Am I right?"

"That would be his option," Marcus said. "But there was a reason Atticus left it in Noah's hands. He knew, as I believe all of you do, Noah has no interest in keeping the money."

Buddy stood up and looked at Noah. "I love you man," he glance at Marcus. "But that's a hell of a lot of money to not have any interest in."

Ruth stood up. "I for one, trust Noah to do the right thing."

"Well, sure," Laura said. "He's your son, and you know he'll take care of you."

Ruth ignored her and looked at Noah. "Do you have anything to say about this?"

Noah sighed. "This is a burden I'd just as soon not carry, but I'll try my best to do the right thing and pass Dad's assets on to those who deserve it."

Laura sniffed. "And you're going to be the judge of that? You're going to decide who deserves it?"

Noah looked at her. "Yes, that's exactly what I'm going to do. Or at least die trying."

Tiffany, who remained quiet until then, stood up and started walking towards the door.

"Not quite what you expected?" Laura said to her back.

Tiffany turned around. "That letter was written two weeks ago. I don't believe Atticus was physically or mentally stable enough to make that kind of decision. I have a copy of the will revised two months ago. I'll do whatever I can to make sure it's his last will and testament."

Dakota said, "I suppose it leaves you the bulk of his estate."

Tiffany smiled before turning and going out through the door.

Buddy joined Dell at the bar and slipped his arm around her shoulder. "The way I see it, my sweet, is basically we're screwed, whichever way it goes."

Ms. Schmidt tapped her fingers on the top of her briefcase, then clicked the latches shut. "Mrs. Wainwright can dig up any old copy of the will she can find, but it won't change anything." She nodded towards the letter Noah was still holding. "That's the only one that counts."

Laura stopped her pacing, coming to an abrupt stop in front of Dakota. "Just who does she think she is? She's been married to Atticus for less than three months."

Dakota smiled up at her. "Yeah. You and I are veterans. Between the two of us, we suffered through more than ten years with the man." She looked at Noah. "That ought to be worth something, hazard pay or some such."

Dell spoke up from behind the bar. "So, how much do you think you should get paid for time serve? About a million a year?" She turned to the mirror behind her and ran her fingers through her hair, then checked her make-up.

Dakota looked at her daughter. "That'd be a good place to start.'

Dell glanced over her shoulder. "You were both paid generous divorce settlements. The money should go to his heirs."

"Seems to me," Dakota replied. "you were around to help me spend most of that settlement."

With his father's letter still in his hands, Noah sat down wearily and set the letter on his knees, before rubbing the back of his neck. *Here we go.*

Marcus came to him and patted him on the back. "I'll make it easy on you, brother. I just want enough to pay off my loft and my car, maybe a little nest egg in the bank." He headed for the door. "But whatever you decide, I'll support you. I need to go call Roberto and fill him in." Giving a little wave over his shoulder, he went out the door.

Dell waited a minute to assure Marcus was out of hearing distance. "Didn't Dad disinherit him when he moved in with Roberto?" She glanced around the room at the remaining family members.

Noah looked at her, not quite believing she brought it up. "Since I've been put in charge, it doesn't matter what Dad did or said about that subject. Marcus has my full blessing and support and if I want to give him the whole damn pie, I will." He picked the letter up again and looked at it, still hoping for some miracle to get him out of the situation. He wanted no part of this. The money, the fighting, the back stabbing…it was going to be a long and drawn out battle. One he'd just as soon sit out.

Buddy chuckled from behind the bar. "Come, come now, children. Let's not fight." He put an arm around Dell's waist and kissed her on the cheek. "We're all family here."

Laura glared at him. "Is that what we are?" She took Libby's arm and pulled her to her feet. "Let's go, Libby."

"Where're we going?"

"To our room."

"Libby looked pleadingly at Noah as Laura led her out of the room. He gave her a little smile as she disappeared through the door.

Ruth stood up and tucked her black silk blouse into her wool skirt. "My son, Marcus is a wonderful human being. A hell of a lot better than any of you. So, keep your prejudices to yourselves." She walked over to Noah. "I know this is the last thing you'd ever volunteer for, but you can do this."

"Thank you, Mom."

She patted him on the knee, then headed for the door.

Buddy poured two more brandies and handed one to his wife. "Come on lamb chop, let's go take a stroll around the grounds. Might be the last chance we get to do it." Dell sighed, then took buddy's arm and headed to the door with him. They both gave Noah a nod before exiting.

Ms. Schmidt came to him and took the letter out of his hands. "Perhaps you should leave this with me for safekeeping." She opened her briefcase again and tucked the letter inside, then pulled out another thicker envelope. "This is for you. Atticus wrote you a letter and made a couple of stipulations to the will. They need to be followed. The rest is a concise breakdown of his assets and business interests. Unless you have a business degree or are well versed in accounting, I suggest you get someone to help you with some of it. You have your job cut out for you." Her last words faded when she suddenly slumped into the chair and laid her head on the desk.

Noah moved quickly to her side. "Ms. Schmidt, are you all right?" He started to put a hand on her back, but then thought better of it. Ms. Schmidt didn't strike him as the kind of person who welcomed a comforting touch, especially from a man.

She moaned and shook her head. "I can't believe he's gone."

Noah went to the door and called out for Simms, who as always, appeared out of nowhere.

"Yes, Master Noah."

"Can you bring some water for Ms. Schmidt? I'm afraid she isn't feeling too well." Simms peered into the room. His right eyebrow rose slightly upon seeing Ms. Schmidt, but he gave no other sign things were amiss. He bowed slightly before turning and going off to fetch some water. Noah went back to Ms. Schmidt's side.

She lifted her head and looked at him with damp eyes. "You look so much like him. He was such a strong handsome man in his day." She dabbed at her flushed cheeks. "Don't look so worried, I'm just a silly old woman."

Noah sat on the couch. "You were in love with him." The thought of it was absurd, but there it was in her eyes, too obvious to deny. But this was perhaps, the one woman who loved him for reasons way beyond his fortune.

She smiled, something Noah didn't expect. "I'm afraid so. But only for the last forty years." Her smile faded as she leaned back in the chair and rested her gray head against the brown leather.

Noah leaned forward, resting his elbows on his knees. "I don't get it. How could you possibly have found anything about that man to love?"

She stared at the ceiling, lost in thought, then sighed. "There's a lot about your father you don't know." She closed her eyes. "He could be very kind and even generous if conditions warranted it."

"Just how often did those conditions arise?"

Simms returned with a glass of water and handed it directly to Ms. Schmidt, then bowed and left the room. Noah watched the woman drink while he mulled over the possibility of his father being more complex than he always thought. *Kind and generous?*

Ms. Schmidt regained her composure. She straightened up in her chair and ran a hand over her hair, tucking a few stray strands into her bun. "I don't know what came over me." She glanced at Noah. "I just felt a bit faint for a moment."

Noah took the glass from her. "Are you sure you're all right?"

She seemed to have regained control, and she said, "Yes, of course."

"Do you mind if I ask you a question?"

She shook her head for an answer.

"Did you and he…never mind." There were some images children didn't need or want to conjure up where their parents were concerned, even when they were well into adulthood.

"Have an affair?" She looked at her hands. "I'm afraid Atticus never knew how I felt. As you know, he had a penchant for young pretty women." She looked up at him, and it was clear she didn't expect him to argue the point she was about to make. This was a woman who knew what she was, and where her place in the world was. Certainly not on the arm of a man like Atticus Wainwright. "It really wouldn't have made much difference. In fact, I'm sure it would've made our working relationship almost impossible."

Noah leaned on the desk and studied the older woman who selflessly served his father for forty years. "What're you going to do now?"

"Retire, I suppose. Not much sense in me trying to find another job at my age."

"I assume my father paid you well."

"Oh, don't you worry about me. I'll be fine. I've got a small nest egg set aside." She stood up and smiled for the second time that day. "Maybe I'll take a trip."

She picked up her briefcase, then held out a hand to Noah. "If you have any questions, call me. I'll be available for you until this is resolved."

"Okay, I appreciate that."

She headed for the door, but paused in the doorway and looked back at Noah.

He gave her a nod, reassuring her that her secret would be safe with him.

Chapter Fifteen

Noah, alone in his father's study, still held the packet Ms. Schmidt gave him. He circled the desk and sat in the big leather chair behind it. His father's chair. It probably cost a small fortune. He sat down and concluded it was worth every penny.

Marcus returned and sat on the corner of the desk. "So, yeah. That went well, don't you think?"

Noah dropped the packet on the polished mahogany surface of the desk and looked at Marcus. "I still say he did this to punish me." Noah laid his head back and spun around a full circle on the chair. "I hate this."

They both looked towards the door when Charlie tapped on the doorframe. "Can I come in?" Marcus waved her in and she came up to the desk and studied Noah for a moment. "Dare I ask what happened?"

Noah shook his head. "Well it's official. You're looking at the executor of the Wainwright fortune."

"How'd everyone take it?"

"Pretty much as you'd expect the Wainwright ex-wives to take it."

She looked at the manila envelope on the desk in front of him. "What's in the envelope?"

"I haven't opened it."

She went to the bar in the corner of the room. After reading the labels, she selected an expensive bottle of scotch and two glasses. She put ice in one, and poured a healthy shot into each glass. After adding a dash of soda, she brought the drinks to the desk. She handed the neat scotch to Marcus and the other to Noah.

"Okay, so drink, and then open it up."

Marcus took a sip. "You're not joining us?"

"Not really a scotch girl. Or hard liquor in general."

Marcus tilted his head at her and smiled. "Seems to me I remember a Facebook post that showed you putting back shots of tequila."

She rolled her eyes. "Damn social media. That was my birthday. And yes, I've been known to drink tequila from time to time, but very infrequently. If you must know."

"Oh we must." Marcus tipped his glass to Noah, who hadn't yet taken a drink. "Drink up, so we can get on to the reading of the letter."

Noah sighed. He didn't want to read a personal letter from his father. It'd make it real. Right now it was a bizarre dream he hoped to wake up from. Once he opened the envelope, all hopes of waking up would vanish. He picked it up and looked at it. The envelope was blank. *He couldn't even bother to address it to me.*

He set it down and took another drink. When the alcohol was gone, he chewed on a piece of ice, all the while staring at the envelope that would change his life.

Marcus grabbed the glass out of his hand. "For God's sake. Open the damn letter."

Noah picked up the envelope and after a moment's hesitation, slid a finger under the flap and opened it. After waiting a few more moments, he pulled out the contents. There were five sheets of paper.

He held it out to Marcus. "I can't. Here, you read it."

Marcus took it from him with unexpected enthusiasm. "My pleasure." He slowly scanned the first page. "A private letter to you."

"Go ahead."

Marcus cleared his throat. "It's dated the same as the will." He glanced at Noah, before he read the letter.

"Noah, I'm sure this comes as a surprise to you. You've always assumed you were a disappointment to me. But I assure you it's quite the opposite. I admire the fact you went your own way and didn't fall prey to the Wainwright business trap that most of the

Wainwright men fell into."

Marcus looked up from the letter. "What about me? I didn't fall into the trap either."

Charlie patted his arm. "This isn't about you, Marcus. Go on."

"It's because of your independence and your lifelong goal to distance yourself from me and my money, that makes you the perfect person to decide who gets what.

I've made a couple stipulations, and bequeaths, and leave the rest to you. I have complete confidence in your ability to make fair and honest decisions as to the disbursement of my wealth.

Your father,
Atticus Wainwright III"

Marcus tucked the first page behind the others, but when Noah held his hand out, Marcus gave him the papers.

Noah read through the second paper, then looked at Marcus and Charlie. "Dammit. He's leaving the house to me."

"Congratulations," Marcus said, quietly.

"And. *The car collection shall go to Marcus."*

Marcus thought about it for a moment. "Okay, the bastard."

Charlie smiled. "Why is he a bastard for leaving you the cars?"

"Because he knows I'll never be able to sell them. They're classic, virtually irreplaceable vehicles worth a fortune, that I can look at from time to time, but never get a cent out of."

"Well, good thing your brother has a big garage for you to store them in."

Marcus got up and went to the bar. "What else does it say?" He filled his glass and the one he confiscated from Noah, and brought them both to the desk.

"There is a trust set up for Libby's education, and a separate sum of money set aside for her to be made available on her wedding day.

I also set aside a sum for Dell, which won't be released until she has been sober for one year. It will require close monitoring and documentation to attest to her sobriety.

The rest of the estate I leave in your hands to disperse as you see fit. You may or may not want to keep any for yourself, but I suggest you at least set aside enough to maintain the house and the grounds."

The rest of the pages were legal documents and a financial statement, which Noah scanned. The bottom line was more than he expected. The fifty million figure everyone had assumed was short by several million.

Noah stuffed the papers into the envelope. "And that's that. My life is over."

Charlie leaned forward in her chair. "Or maybe you're starting a new chapter."

"I was perfectly happy in the old chapter."

*****

Noah sat on the edge of the pool. After the reading of the letter, as Marcus called it, he needed some fresh air. He decided a swim would clear his head and help him think. But now that he was at the pool, he hadn't gotten beyond dangling his feet in the water.

He sighed and lowered himself into the pool. *A couple laps. It'll do you good.* He swam across to the other side, turned, and headed back to his starting point. When he got there, he found Tiffany waiting for him. She was standing a few feet from the pool's edge with a cigarette in one hand and a towel in the other.

He hoisted himself up out of the pool and took the towel from her to dry himself, before dropping it onto a chair and sitting under the umbrella sticking out of a glass-topped table. Tiffany sat too, and fiddled with the cigarette case sitting next to a lighter.

"What do you want, Tiffany?"

"I want to know what you're going to do."

He smiled. "I have no idea. It's going to take some time for me to wade through everything."

"You should save yourself a lot of time and trouble and reinstate the last will. He obviously wasn't thinking clearly when he dismissed it and got this ridiculous idea to put you in charge."

"Gee, thanks for the vote of confidence, Tiffany."

"Well, no offense, but he was on his death bed. Certainly it wouldn't hold up in court if one were to contest it."

Noah studied her for a moment. "Are you planning on contesting it?"

She leaned back in her chair and took a long slow drag from her cigarette. "My lawyer believes it'd be prudent to do so."

Noah got up and grabbed his t-shirt from a nearby chaise. He'd always been comfortable with his body, but she made him feel uncomfortable. She looked at him like he was something she wanted to devour. He suddenly became aware of how women must feel when they're viewed strictly as an object of desire.

He pulled the shirt on over his head, before he returned to his seat at the table. "Ms. Schmidt seemed pretty confident the new will would hold up in court. You'll have a hard time proving he wasn't of sound mind, when his lawyer of forty years is saying he was."

Tiffany thought about that for several moments. "What about the house? I get the house, right?"

Noah shook his head. "The house is mine now."

She stood up. "You little bastard. I knew you couldn't be trusted. You're going to take it all, aren't you?"

"I didn't take the house. He left it to me."

He could see the wheels turning in her head and he waited to see what her next move would be.

She sat and reached for his arm again. "I love this house. And...well, I'd do most anything to remain here."

Noah pulled his arm out of her grasp once more and leaned back in his chair. "I'll give you until the end of the week to get your things moved out."

She stood up. If this was a cartoon, steam would be billowing from her ears. "You're not going to toss me out of here. I was his wife. This is my house."

"Tiffany, you moved in here two months ago. I, on the other hand, was born here. So, dibs."

She huffed and turned away from him before she stalked off and left her cigarette case and lighter behind. Noah looked at them and shrugged, then opened the case and pulled a cigarette out. He lit it with her lighter and got comfortable in his chair.

That was easier than he thought it would be. Maybe he was the right man for the job. He laid his head back and closed his eyes. *Don't go patting yourself on the back just yet.*

When he heard someone approaching, he thought it was Tiffany returning for her case and lighter. He opened his eyes and was happy to see it wasn't his step-mother, but Charlie. He smiled at her and nodded toward the other chair.

She sat down. "Tiffany nearly ran me over when I came out the door. Did that have anything to do with you?"

He took a puff from his cigarette and blew the smoke away from Charlie. "I told her to move out by next weekend."

"Wow. You're taking this master of the house seriously."

"I would've given her more time, especially since I have no interest in living here myself. But when she told me she'd do most anything to stay, I had to send her packing."

"Oh my. That's positively scandalous. So, do you think everyone will leave tonight or in the morning?"

"I don't know, but I'm staying until they're gone."

"Then I'll stay as long as there are Wainwright's to feed. Or until tomorrow night. I have a catering job on Tuesday."

He watched her for a moment as she tucked some hair behind her ear. In the sunlight, her light blue eyes were almost gray. "So, that first day in the kitchen…"

"When you didn't remember who I was."

"Yes, jerk that I am. But you said you were working here along with your catering business because you needed some extra money."

She nodded.

"So, you want to tell me why?"

She stared at the table for a moment. "It's my dad. He's been sick. And even with his insurance, the co-pays are outrageous."

He leaned forward in his chair. "What's wrong with him?"

"Lung cancer."

Noah looked at the cigarette in his hand. He needed a final push to force him to quit. If this wasn't it, nothing would ever convince him. He dropped it into a puddle of water on the pool decking, then took her hand. "I'm sorry. If there's anything I can do…"

"Now that your rich?" She pulled her hand away. "Thank you, but we'll manage."

"Okay, well, just ask. And I inherited a big damn house, but it doesn't put any money in my pocket. I'm still just a tennis pro."

"Who drives a BMW."

"I have really good credit."

*****

Noah skipped dinner, as did most of the others according to Marcus who came up to the room at eight. Apparently there was a lot of drinking, and a fair amount of passive aggressive 'pass the salts', but nobody punched anyone, so it was a win as far as Marcus was concerned.

Noah didn't want to spend another night at the house, but now that it was his, or at least his responsibility, he decided to wait until the others left. But Marcus was leaving tonight, and was waiting to say goodbye.

Marcus sat on the bed. "You sure you don't want me to stay tonight? I hate leaving you here with four angry women."

"I'll be fine. I'm planning on avoiding them as much as possible. Go home to Roberto. But you better call and give him a heads up so he can clear out the Chippendale dancers before you get there."

"Funny." He stood up and went to the closet. "He actually dated a Chippendale dancer several years ago."

"That doesn't surprise me."

Marcus grabbed a handful of hanging shirts and laid them on the bed. "Apparently, what you see on stage, isn't exactly what you get, if you know what I mean."

"I do, and I really didn't need to know that."

"They have these—"

Noah put his hands over his ears. "Stop."

Marcus removed his shirts from the hangers, folded them, then placed them gently into his suitcase. Noah watched him for a few minutes, ever amazed by his brother's eccentricities. Marcus had always been particular about his clothing. Even as a child, he folded his underwear and rolled his socks up in perfect little spheres, while Noah's drawers were apocalyptic in comparison. Their mother ironed every item of Marcus' clothing, even his jeans. Noah always teased that he was the favorite son, because she could drop a basket full of clean clothes onto the bedroom floor, and be done with Noah's laundry for the week.

Marcus looked at him. "What?"

"Why'd you bring ten shirts for a four-day weekend?"

"I like to be prepared. You never know what might come up."

"Yeah, well all the shirts in the world couldn't have prepared you for this weekend." He watched Marcus empty the dresser drawer and tuck the items into the suitcase.

Marcus closed his suitcase and looked at Noah. "You seem slightly less freaked out."

"I'm not, but I decided to give it a few days and see how I feel mid-week."

"Okay, well, if you need any help figuring out who gets what, let me know. Roberto's business degree might be of some help."

"Thanks."

"Are you going to give up your condo and move in here? It'd probably impress the hell out of your…clients."

Noah looked around the room. "This is what they're trying to escape from. The fantasy is a clandestine affair with someone below their station."

"Like the heiress and the stableboy."

"Umm sure, something like that."

"Oh my gosh, I need to add that to my list of plotlines. Dashing young heir falls for the equally dashing stableboy. Delicious."

"With a bit of spicy sex thrown in."

"Well obviously."

Chapter Sixteen

Ruth leaned on the polished white surface of her Mercedes and blew out a puff of cigarette smoke. Laura stood downwind, watching her with disdain. The sun had gone down and the sky was full of stars. A slight breeze filtered the air between the two women and added to the chill already present between them, replacing the warmth and humidity of the afternoon.

Laura studied Ruth for a moment before asking, "So, what're we going to do about this?" She rubbed at the goose bumps on her bare arms. "I know you feel you need to be loyal to him and all, but Noah doesn't know the first thing about financial matters. He's never even held down a real job. To leave this all in his hands is ridiculous."

Ruth dropped the stub of her cigarette on the ground and rubbed it into the brick drive with the toe of her shoe. It joined a half dozen other spent cigarettes piling up next to the car.

"There's more to executing the will than business savvy. He can hire people to help him with the accounting. Atticus chose him because he won't be swayed by all the bitterness running rampant in this family." When she spotted Noah coming out the front door, she added. "Well, here he is now. Why don't you voice your concerns to him?"

Noah dawdled towards the women, and Ruth could tell he wasn't expecting to run in to anyone. Her youngest son was overwhelmed, but she knew he had what it would take to get the job done fairly.

She lit another cigarette. "Laura's having a bit of a problem accepting Atticus' will." She offered a cigarette to Noah.

He started to take it, then shook his head and stepped back as she exhaled. She looked at Laura. "What was it you were saying about Noah before he came out?"

Laura glared at Ruth and gave Noah a slight smile. "I have concerns about your qualifications as executor of such a large estate. Your experience in the business world is pretty much nonexistent. Before you arrived, I was about to suggest to Ruth that we call in an outside party to supervise the dispersal of funds."

Ruth blew smoke in her direction. "And who would you suggest?"

Laura waved her hand in front of her face and forced a cough. "Well, I know someone who might be willing to help." Noah and Ruth looked at her, waiting for her to go on. She paused a moment, then said, "Mike Westcott."

Noah laughed as Ruth shook her head in disbelief. "Your latest ex-husband?"

"I'm sure he'd be totally impartial," Noah added.

"We parted on amicable terms."

"My point exactly." Noah turned and headed for the house. "I may not be the best man for the job, but like it or not, you're all stuck with me."

Laura looked at Ruth, then at Noah's departing back. "Do you really think I had ulterior motives when I suggested Mike?"

*****

As Noah crossed the foyer, Simms appeared and bowed slightly. "Can I get you anything before I retire for the evening, Sir?"

"I'm fine Simms, thank you."

"Good night, Sir." He bowed again, before he headed off towards his room.

Noah called out after him. "Simms?"

The old man stopped and turned back.

"What're you going to do now? Do you have someplace to go?"

"I've been contemplating a visit to my sister in California."

"Well, it's going to take a while before I figure out what to do with this house. I hope you'll stay and do your thing until it's all sorted out. I could use your help with the employees. Who does what and when they do it. Stuff like that."

"Of course Sir, anything you need." He turned once more and started to leave, then stopped. "May I ask about Mrs. Wainwright? Will she be staying in the house?"

"Tiffany? No, she'll be gone by the end of the week. Regardless of how I divide up the inheritance, the house won't be part of the deal for her."

"Very good, Sir." He turned once more and headed for his room.

Noah started up the stairs, then changed direction and headed for the veranda. He needed to do some contemplating over a beer or two. He grabbed a beer out of the refrigerator behind the bar, before going out through the French doors. He took a seat on the wicker couch, leaned back to put his feet up on the glass table, then cracked open his beer.

His father's wishes had come as a complete surprise. Even now, eight hours after reading the will, the implications behind the responsibility hadn't quite sunk in. Laura was right about one thing, he was ill equipped for the job. Two years in college hadn't prepared him for taking control of a fortune. He didn't even know where the money was. Atticus had his fingers in so many pies, it'd probably take years to sort it all out. The house alone was worth several million. He sighed and put the cold bottle to his forehead. The simple little life he'd been leading for the last several years was at an end.

When he felt two hands on his shoulders, he looked back then sat up abruptly.

Tiffany smiled at him. "You're looking a little stressed out." She started massaging his shoulders. "Let me fix that for you."

Noah slithered out from under her grasp and stood up. "I'm fine, but thanks." He took a sip of his beer. "So, you're not mad at me anymore?"

"Of course not, how can I stay mad at you?"

He didn't respond as he noticed Tiffany had changed out of her black dress and was now wearing a long floral print skirt with a slit on the side reaching well up her thigh. The complementary pink blouse left little to the imagination. He averted his eyes away from her chest and looked her in the eye.

"Short mourning period."

She looked at her clothing. "Atticus wouldn't want me moping around in black. He loved this outfit."

"I'm sure he did." Noah moved to a chair and sat down. It would be refreshing to find that everyone was wrong about the newest Mrs. Wainwright, but obviously they weren't. He was all too familiar with the look of a woman in search of a rich man to carry her comfortably through life. He worked with them daily. This one was younger and prettier, but he had no doubt thirty years down the road, she'd be flirting with some young tennis pro, or trainer in search of a brief respite from the wealthy husband who'd lost interest in her.

"No luck finding that will, huh?"

"What do you mean?"

"If you had the old will, you wouldn't need to bother with me. You'd have what you set out to get. A dead husband and a healthy inheritance."

Tiffany walked around the couch and sat down. She crossed her legs and studied her nails. "Maybe I'm not just after the money. Maybe I've set my sights on something else." She looked at him.

As much as he hated to admit it to himself, Noah was uncomfortable, and he shifted in his chair. He took another drink, hoping Tiffany wouldn't notice she was causing him to squirm. Because of his job, he got hit on more than most men, but this woman was different. This one scared him and made him feel like he wasn't in control.

He instinctively knew she wasn't one to take no for an answer. In a lot of ways, she was a perfect match for his father. Not sure how to respond to what she said, he held her stare and waited for her to back down. She didn't.

Instead, she slid to the end of the couch and put her knees a few inches from his. "The moment you walked into the dining room Thursday, I knew I had to get to know you better."

"And the fact I was your dying husband's son didn't bother you?"

"Not in the lease." She reached over and put a hand on his knee. "But that's not even an issue anymore."

Noah once more stood up. "Yes, wasn't it convenient for your husband to die."

Tiffany sighed and leaned back on the couch as she folder her arms across her chest and looked up at him. "You're not making this easy." She crossed her legs again, causing the skirt to fall away.

"You want it easy? Well, let me help you out. I'm not interested, Tiffany. And if you think all this…stuff you're throwing at me is going to get you what you want, you've got the wrong man. I'm immune."

He walked away, not sure whether or not she was convinced. In actuality, he wasn't so sure if he convinced himself.

"Noah."

He stopped and looked back at her.

"If you weren't so intent on not looking at my legs, I'd almost believe you."

"Friday. I want you out of here by Friday."

*****

"So, you ladies have any thoughts on this? Is Noah going to give it all away to some obscure charity, or what?" Buddy rattled the ice in the bottom of his glass as he looked across the room at his wife and her mother. "It wouldn't come as a shock to me if he did."

Dell stood up from the edge of the bed and crossed the room to the window. She looked down on the pool. The light was on, illuminating the decking around the water's edge. She pulled the red silk robe she wore, tighter across her chest and watched as the pool boy stepped into the light, naked as a newborn baby, and dove into the crystal blue water.

"As much as Noah would like us all to believe he isn't interested in the money, I don't buy it." Dell turned and put her back to the window.

Dakota looked at her daughter from the comfort of the small love seat in the corner of the room. "Noah isn't like the rest of us, Dell. He'll mull this over, and look at it from every angle, and when we're all about ready to go stark raving mad, he'll decide." She looked at Buddy. "And when he does decide what to do with it, it'll be the right decision."

Buddy stood up and stretched, then walked over to Dell. "I don't suppose that decision will involve leaving any of it to us." He kissed his wife on the cheek then looked out the window at the swimmer in the pool. "He's at it again, huh?"

Dakota came to attention. "Is my little Latin darlin' down there again?" She got up and joined them at the window, smiling as she looked at the pool. "Isn't he the prettiest thing?"

"Mother, please." Dell walked away and returned to the bed.

Dakota glanced over her shoulder for a moment, then returned her eyes to the pool. "Now you can't tell me you don't find him the least bit attractive."

Dell looked at Buddy. "Why would I be looking at some young stud bare naked in the pool, when I have Milton Albright, aka Buddy, all to myself?"

"My little sweet pea." Buddy tried to kiss her, but she put a hand up to stop him, and he sat down heavily on the bed.

Dakota turned around and stared at him. "Your name is Milton?"

Buddy fell back onto the bed and put his arm up over his eyes and let out a groan.

Dell grabbed his arm. "Why do you think he goes by Buddy?" She pulled her husband up to a sitting position, then to his feet. "Come on stud, let's go raid Dad's bar."

Dakota glanced at them over her shoulder as they headed for the door. "You two sleep tight, now."

Buddy gave her a wave. "We're just a couple of nightcaps away. A few shots from oblivion." They closed the door behind them as Dakota returned to her view out the window.

Chapter Seventeen

Noah was dozing off to sleep when he heard something that brought him instantly awake. He sat up and listened. He heard it again and turned his head towards the wall separating his room from his father's. The sound was coming from that direction. Noah glance at the clock. It was way too late for someone to be rummaging around his father's room. He tossed back his covers and stood up, then grabbed his jeans from the floor and slipped them on as he headed for the door. He eased the door open and peered out into the dimly lit hall. A light shone from underneath the door to Atticus' room. Noah walked over to it, and after a slight hesitation, turned the knob and slowly opened it.

The short wiry man, intent on rummaging through the medicines on the bedside table, didn't hear the door open or Noah approaching his back.

"What the hell are you doing?" Noah asked.

At the sound of Noah's voice, the color drained from the man's face and he jumped and spilled the contents from the pill bottle he was holding.

The man sat on the edge of the bed and took a deep breath. "By God, you scared me." His voice was as thin as his frame, and he ended his sentence more like a question than a statement. He removed his black-framed glasses, pulled a white handkerchief from the chest pocket of his plaid sport coat, and polished the lenses.

"Who are you and what are you doing in here?" Noah asked.

The man replaced his glasses and carefully folded the handkerchief before tucking it into his pocket. He stood up and held a hand out to Noah. "I'm Dr. Beals," he said, once more accentuating the final syllable of the sentence. He picked up the spilled red pills, checking the floor for any strays, then returned them to the bottle. "I've been Mr. Wainwright's physician for the last six months." He glanced briefly at the label on the bottle, before dropping it into the pocket of his brown slacks.

Noah studied the balding man in front of him. He couldn't have been more than 5'6" or 5'7", and wouldn't make much of a dent past the hundred pound mark on a scale. He obviously wasn't a threat. But there was something about him Noah didn't like. Dr. Beals returned Noah's stare. "And who might you be? One of the sons, I presume."

"You presume right. I'm Noah."

"Ah, yes. Of course."

The sound of the doctor's voice and the way he oddly accented his words was annoying Noah. "You still haven't told me what you're doing here in the middle of the night." He folded his arms across his bare chest, suddenly aware of being half-naked, and found it odd a thing like that could make him feel so vulnerable in this situation.

The little man didn't seem to notice or care. He resumed picking up pill bottles, reading the labels and setting them back on the table.

"What are you looking for?"

Dr. Beals looked at Noah over the rim of his glasses. "Your father was on some potent medicines. I wouldn't want them to fall into the wrong hands." He walked to the bookcase and ran a finger along the spines of the books, taking in the titles. He pulled two of them off the shelf and carried them to a soft leather bag. He tucked them inside on top of a neatly folded stack of clothing.

Noah took a step towards the bag and peered inside. "Are those my father's things?"

Dr. Beals zipped the bag and picked it up. He gave Noah a strange little smile as he said, "I spent a fair amount of time caring for Mr. Wainwright. I'm afraid I left a few things here. Just tidying up, that's all. Tidying up." He took a few steps toward the door, then stopped and turned to face Noah. "I'll be sending some people around in the morning to pick up these medical supplies."

Noah looked at the equipment that was humming and beeping the last time he saw his father. It was all silent now, turned off, unplugged and ready to be transported to some other man's deathbed. Suddenly, he realized he had no idea where his father's body was.

"Where's my father? His body, that is."

"He was delivered to Heaven's Gate Mortuary. I'm sure they'll be contacting you about the arrangements." He put his hand on the doorknob.

"How do I contact you, if I need to?"

"Mrs. Wainwright has my contact information."

He opened the door and stepped out into the hall, then closed it behind him. Noah sat on the bed and stared at the silent equipment, trying to justify Dr. Beals' middle of the night visit. When the door opened again, he was surprised to see Simms, once more fully dressed, step into the room.

"Is everything okay, Sir?"

Noah stood up. "Who the hell is Dr. Beals?"

"Dr. Beals was your father's latest doctor."

"He was just here."

"At this hour, Sir?"

"Yes. How'd he get in here? The guy is creepy as hell."

"He has the access code to the gate, since he was often needed during the night. What was he doing, Sir?"

"Tidying up."

"That seems odd."

"Will you make sure he's gone and check the doors? I don't want any more mysterious visitors."

"Right away, Sir."

"And change the gate code."

*****

The new day brought another visitor to the Wainwright estate. Mr. Weatherby from heaven's Gate Mortuary showed up at nine, and Simms took him to the library. Simms served him coffee and fresh pastry, then asked him to wait for the family to get themselves together. Simms left with a bow and a promise to send the entire family in soon. But fulfilling that promise proved to be no easy task.

Simms proceeded to the dining room, where most of the family was gathered. Dell and Buddy were somewhat color coordinated with his orange shirt complementing her giraffe patterned jumpsuit. They were halfway through tall Bloody Mary's, choosing to forgo the Spanish omelets, bacon and fried potatoes spread out buffet style on one of the long tables. Laura, still in black, but with a splash of color in her blouse, sat across from them drinking black coffee and drumming her fingers on the table, silent and lost in her own thoughts. Libby, the only one with an appetite, was heartily enjoying her omelet except for the onions, which she meticulously picked out and swept to the edge of her plate.

Ruth in her usual attire of blouse, blue today, and black slacks, was sitting apart from the others at the end of the table. She tossed the piece of toast she was gnawing, onto the small plate in front of her and took a sip of hot tea. "Where the hell is everybody?" she said, aiming her question at no one in particular.

Simms, standing in the doorway, said, "Excuse me," giving a nod of his head to Ruth and the others. "Mr. Weatherby from the mortuary is here about the arrangements."

Laura, with her back to the door, glanced over her shoulder at Simms. "Let Noah handle it. He's the one in charge these days."

"Master Noah hasn't yet come downstairs, and Mr. Weatherby requested the whole family's attention."

Dell drained the last of her enhanced tomato juice. "Dad has probably requested some elaborate burial scenario."

Laura smiled a sour little smile. "He once told me he wanted to have a sendoff like the Vikings."

Dell looked at Buddy and patted him on his head. "I wonder who we could get to play the dog at his feet?"

Buddy pulled away from her as he stood up. "My little drop of dew, are you suggesting I accompany your father to the hereafter?"

Dakota stepped around Simms as she walked into the room, picking up on the end of the conversation. "Milton, you're much too sweet to be dragged down to the depths of Hell with Atticus." She grabbed a plate from the buffet. "Dell's mind has been too clouded for the last five years to notice. You pay her no mind." She was without her customary cowboy hat, but had her short red hair in two braids tied with leather lacing.

"Thanks Dakota, and good morning to you, too." Dell said, quietly.

Simms adjusted his tie and cleared his throat. "Shall I tell Mr. Weatherby you'll be along shortly?"

"Who is this Mr. Weatherby?" Dakota asked as she filled her plate.

Buddy came up beside her and took a plate of his own. "He's from the mortuary." After snagging the last crispy piece of bacon, he leaned in close to her and said, "I'll stop calling you mother if you forget you ever heard my given name."

"Deal," Dakota replied, and suddenly laughed. "Viking! Now I get it. Did you know Atticus once told me he wanted to be put to sea on a burning ship when he died, just like the Vikings?"

Buddy shook his head and grinned. "Yeah, I heard that somewhere."

Ruth was the only one to notice Simms was still waiting for an answer. "You tell Mr. Weatherby, we'll all be along in a few minutes."

With relief showing in his eyes, Simms bowed slightly and left the room.

*****

Simms next headed for the stairs, taking each step slowly. He took several minutes to reach the top, stopping on the landing for a few moments to catch his breath, before he headed for

Noah's room. He paused for a moment, then knocked softly. When he received no response, he knocked again, using a little more force.

A muffled, "Who is it?" came through the door.

"Simms, Sir."

Noah opened the door mid-yawn and stretched.

"Sorry to bother you, Sir, but Mr. Weatherby from the mortuary is in the library. He wishes to talk to the whole family."

"I'll be down in a few minutes."

"Very good, Sir." He bowed, turned and continued down the hall, but stopped when Noah called out after him.

"Better make it a half hour."

Simms nodded his response, then continued his trek towards Tiffany's room. This time, when he arrived at the door, he paused a bit longer. Mrs. Wainwright wasn't too fond of being aroused before ten. He took a breath before he knocked on the door. When he got no response, he knocked again.

"What the hell do you want?" came through the door.

"It's Simms, Ma'am. I'm sorry to bother you."

"Then don't. Go away."

"Mr. Weatherby, from the mortuary is here. He wishes to see the whole family, Ma'am."

The door opened a crack. "Can't this wait until a decent hour of the day?"

"I'm afraid not, Ma'am."

"Fine, I'll be down soon." She closed the door, and Simms headed back down the stairs.

When he returned to the library, Mr. Weatherby had finished his pastry and poured himself another cup of coffee. He perched on the edge of an overstuffed chair in anticipation of the family's arrival.

"The family will be in shortly," Simms said with his customary bow.

"Very good, very good," Weatherby said, getting to his feet.

*****

As if on cue, the group from the dining room appeared at the door and entered the library. Ruth made the introductions and everyone uttered polite greetings before taking up residence in the various places around the room. Dakota, Dell and Buddy took the couch while the rest of them occupied various chairs. Mr. Weatherby resumed perching on his chair while sipping coffee from his cup.

As the silence was closing in on unbearable, Noah showed up.

Mr. Weatherby stood up once more. "Would this be everyone, then?"

Noah looked around the room. "Mrs. Wainwright isn't here." He looked at Laura, Dakota, and Ruth. "The fourth, that is."

Mr. Weatherby pulled a large gold watch from his pocket and flipped it open. "I need to be getting back. I have a viewing at noon."

"Oh, honey, you go right ahead with whatever it is you came here to say. We'll see to it Mrs. Wainwright…" she glanced at Noah. "the fourth, is filled in."

Mr. Weatherby checked the time once more than dropped the watch into his pocket. "Well, I suppose I should." He ran his hand through his mousy brown hair, straightened his wire-framed glasses, then moved to the desk and opened his black leather briefcase. After rifling through a stack of papers, he pulled one out and briefly read it. He returned the paper to the case, before he closed it and turned back to the family.

"Mr. Wainwright had specific directions as to his burial. He wants to be cremated. Then, one week from the day of his death, he wants the family to gather here in the library, where Dr. Beals will present the ashes with instructions detailing Mr. Wainwright's wishes."

As everyone exchanged blank stares, Dakota spoke up and asked, "Who the hell is Dr. Beals?"

"He's Mr. Wainwright's physician," Mr. Weatherby said.

"Why will he be presenting Atticus' ashes?" Ruth asked. "And just how does he present ashes?"

"It's a formality, Ma'am." Mr. Weatherby looked around the room and smiled a sterile little smile. "By Mr. Wainwright's request, Dr. Beals is in charge of the body." Mr. Weatherby took a sip of coffee. "That is, until he hands them over to you." He set his cup down. "Dr. Beals took possession of Mr. Wainwright's remains shortly after his death. He'll deliver them to us on Tuesday for cremation, then bring the ashes here on Saturday."

Dell got up and went to the bar. "Isn't this just a little strange?"

Dakota laughed. "Consider who it is we're burying here, dear." She joined Dell at the bar and look at Mr. Weatherby. "Where is this Dr. Beals keeping Atticus' body until Tuesday?"

"That," Mr. Weatherby said quietly, "is not my concern." He picked up his briefcase to

prepare to leave. "Now, I really must go. I have a viewing to get to."

Noah got to his feet. "I'm sorry, but Dr. Beals said the body was at the mortuary."

"You've spoken to him?"

"Yes."

"Well, surely you're mistaken. Now I need to run." He headed for the door. "Don't forget, Saturday, everyone must attend."

After Mr. Weatherby disappeared through the door, Laura got up and straightened out her black jacket. "I can't stay until Saturday. I have a business to run. I have clients waiting, meetings to attend, subordinates to order around. It's impossible for me to stay."

Dakota dropped two cubes of ice into a glass. "Look at it as a long overdue vacation." She poured a shot of gin over the ice and splashed in some soda water. "Besides, aren't you a little curious about where he wants the ashes to go?"

Laura and Libby headed for the door. "You can send me an e-mail."

Noah was still standing in the middle of the room, trying to sort out the conflicting stories of Mr. Weatherby and Dr. Beals. Buddy stood up and walked over to him. "So, when did you meet this doctor Beals?"

"Last night. I caught him poking around Dad's room."

"Poking around?"

"Yeah." He looked at the family. "I think Laura's idea of not staying here for another week is a good one. There's really no point. The funeral is on Saturday, too, so why don't we all go home and come back on Saturday." The thought of spending another five days with the family was alarming. He wanted to go home, and he wanted them all to leave him alone for a while. He needed time to digest everything that happened since Thursday. To help them on their way, he added, "Charlotte, the cook, is leaving today. So you'd need to fend for yourselves."

As everyone grumbled, mostly in agreement, Tiffany walked in the room, interrupting the conversation. The soft yellow sundress she wore, complimented her figure in such a way as to make Buddy's jaw drop and Noah forget what he was saying. She smiled a bright smile.

"So, what's this about a family meeting?"

"Over and done with," Dakota said. "Nice of you to get here on time." She headed for the door. "I think I'll take a swim before I pack."

Dell went to Buddy, took his arm and led him a safe distance away from Tiffany. "So," she said, transferring her glare from her husband to the newest Mrs. Wainwright. "Do you have any idea what Dad's plans were for his ashes?"

"Plans?" Tiffany thought about if for a moment. "I assumed after the ship burned, the ashes would go straight to the bottom of the ocean."

Chapter Eighteen

Noah got everyone to agree to leave and return on Saturday, then went to the kitchen to let Charlie know she was free to leave anytime. He found her arguing with Richard.

She stopped when she saw Noah and gave him a strained smile, while Richard grabbed his things and scurried out the back door.

Noah returned her smile. "What was that all about?"

"I swear that man has never worked in a kitchen before. He was less than useless this weekend."

"Maybe he hasn't."

"Tiffany said she got him from a temp agency. I assumed she asked for someone with experience."

"You know what happens when you assume?"

She sat at the counter. "Yeah, yeah." She looked up at him. "So, you look like you came to say goodbye."

Noah nodded. "I've convinced them all to go home until next Saturday."

"What's next Saturday?"

"Tentatively the funeral, and definitely the presenting of the ashes."

"Oh, sounds…formal. Why tentatively on the funeral?"

"There seems to be some discrepancy around where my father's body is."

Charlie pointed to the other stool. "Please explain that."

Noah grabbed a beer from the refrigerator. "You want one?" he asked over his shoulder. She nodded, and he brought two beers to the counter and sat on the stool.

"Dr. Beals, the extremely creepy doctor, said it was at the mortuary. But Mr. Weatherby, the equally creepy mortuary guy, said the doctor had it." He took a sip of beer. "Maybe I'm reading too much into it. I'm not thinking as clearly as I could be."

"It's definitely something worth looking into. That seems a little weird to me."

"The doctor was creeping around Dad's room at two in the morning, collecting some meds and his things. Tidying up, he said." He held up a finger. "Or the way he said it, tidying up?" Noah tried to imitate Beal's odd speech pattern.

"Yeah, that's weird."

"I'll check him out tomorrow after I've gotten some good sleep in my own bed."

*****

Noah got everyone out of the house by one, then took a last swim before heading up to his room to change and grab his bag. At the top of the stairs, he saw Simms coming out of Atticus' room. He bowed when he saw Noah.

"Will you be leaving soon, Sir?" He was wearing a bib apron over his shirt and his sleeves were rolled up to his elbows. He was carrying a small bucket with cleaning supplies.

"In a few minutes." He nodded towards his father's room. "Did everything look okay in there? I'm still a little freaked out by Dr. Beal's middle of the night visit."

"I saw nothing missing, Sir, but I can't be sure if the medications are all there. But I left them on the nightstand."

"Just curious. I think I need to check into Dr. Beals."

"I believe that'd be a wise move, Sir."

"As far as Tiffany goes. If she gives you any trouble, please let me know. She's supposed move out by Friday."

"Very good, Sir."

Noah held out his hand and after a slight hesitation, Simms switched the bucket from his right hand to his left and took it. "Thank you, Simms, for all you've done for this family. We didn't deserve you."

"It was my pleasure, Sir."

The two men shook, then Simms left Noah and headed slowly down the stairs.

Instead of going into his room, Noah continued down the hall to his father's. He went in and sat on the freshly made bed, then remembered who the last occupant was and stood up as he looked around.

He was only in his father's room a handful of times over the years. It was off-limits, but he vaguely remembered sitting on the bed with his mother as a young child. And he hid in the closet once while playing hide and seek with Marcus. His brother never found him, because he refused to enter the room. The last time was when he came in to see Libby right after she was born. Laura, still young, pretty, and amicable, invited him in to see his baby sister. At twelve, he wasn't impressed.

Which brought him to Friday night, seven hours before his father died. He looked at the prescription bottles on the night stand. The equipment had been removed, but the medication remained. He picked up a couple bottles and read the labels. He couldn't pronounce most of them, and didn't know what any of them did. Which reminded him of the bottle Dr. Beals stuck in his pocket. Why'd he take the one bottle and leave the rest? As he remembered the Doctor dropped the container and spilled its contents, Noah knelt and looked under the table. *Maybe you didn't get all of them, you creepy little man.*

Noah's hunch was right, and he found two red pills hiding under the far side of the table. He pulled it away from the wall and retrieved the pills, studying them for a moment in his outstretched hand. He put them into an empty bottle, then went to the closet.

He was suddenly hit by déjà vu. The closet, full of black, brown, and gray suits smelled of his father's aftershave. It was the smell, Noah always associated with Atticus, though he couldn't tell you what it was. Something expensive, no doubt.

He shook that off and looked at the dozen neatly stacked shoe boxes on the floor. Noah removed a pair of black wingtips and took the box to the nightstand, then took all the medication and stashed the bottles. He needed to find out what the old man was taking, especially the mysterious red pills.

He looked around the room for a moment. It was an intimidating room, and he suddenly felt uncomfortable in it. He left and closed the door behind him. He wouldn't be going back in there for a while. With the box in hand, he headed for his room, but before he got to it, Tiffany intercepted him. She seemed pleased to see he was wearing only swim shorts and a wet t-shirt. She put a hand on his chest, but he backed away from her.

She pouted. "Are you leaving too?"

"Yes, as soon as I get dressed."

"What am I going to do here all by myself with only grumpy old Simms to keep me company?"

"You can start packing."

She sighed. "You're as grumpy as he is. You were much more fun the first day we met."

"Well, a lot has happened since then."

She stepped towards him again. "Are you still going to insist I leave by Friday?"

"Yes, Tiffany. And I don't want you taking anything you didn't arrive with."

"What about Atticus' gifts?"

"Simms knows what belongs to you and what my father gifted to you. Everything else stays."

"Fine."

"I mean it."

She saluted. "Yes Sir, Mr. Wainwright."

She flounced off and Noah went into his room and closed the door. It wouldn't be that simple. She was going to fight it, and he pitied Simms. She wouldn't make it easy on him.

He got dressed, then sat on the bed and called Marcus. He needed some advice.

Marcus answered with a, "Hey are you home yet?"

Noah thought about the question. Yes and no would both be proper responses. But he went with, "Just heading out."

"So, you sound down. What's going on?"

"Not down, just curious. Do you know anyone who can identify medications? What they're used for specifically?"

"Why?"

"Dad was on a lot of meds. I'd like to know what they did, or didn't do, I suppose. And I have two of the mystery medication Beals took in the middle of the night."

"Yeah, that wasn't suspicious at all." Noah heard him humming while he pondered the question. "Rosita."

"Roberto's cousin?"

"Yes, she's a pharmacy tech."

"She is?"

"Yes. If you'd talked with her instead of jumping into bed, you might've found that out."

"I didn't jump into bed with her. I told you, she was very…insistent."

"How long?"

"How long, what?"

"Before she got you into bed?"

Noah paused for a moment. "Ahh, probably…two hours or so."

Marcus laughed. "Which means, in actuality, under an hour."

"Whatever. Do you think she'd help me?"

"I don't know, Noah. You slept with her and then never saw her again."

"Isn't she married now?" Noah asked.

"Yes, but still."

"Will you ask her please?"

There was a hesitation, before Marcus said, "I'll ask her."

"Thank you."

*****

Noah sat on the couch in his living room that seemed even smaller now that he'd spent time at the Wainwright family home. He looked around. "You may be small, but you're cozy and you haven't been tainted by three generations of Wainwrights." He thought a few minutes about leaving the condo he lived in for four years and moving into his father's house. As long as he referred to it as his father's house, he didn't see how he could be comfortable there. But he couldn't see selling it either. And no one else in the family deserved it.

He leaned back and stared at the ceiling. "Thanks Dad."

*****

He slept soundly for the first time since he left on Thursday morning. And he was still lounging, attempting to hold on to the comfort, when his phone rang. He assumed it was Marcus, but it was a number he didn't recognize.

"Hello?" he said, hoping it was Charlie calling already.

"Noah?" The voice and the accent came back to him, and he remembered why he'd never called her after their one night together. Her heavily accented nasal whine, was agonizing and he assumed he must've let her seduce him so quickly because anything was better than listening to her talk.

"Rosita?"

"So, you remember me."

"Of course. How could I forget?"

"Oh, don't be teasing me now, I'm a married woman."

She obviously wasn't aware of the fact it wasn't necessarily a deal breaker for him.

"Did Marcus tell you my dilemma?"

"Yes, he did, and I'd be glad to help you out. In fact, I can do you one better. My husband is a Pharmacist."

"Oh, perfect."

"So, when can you come over? We're both off today if you want to come by the house."

"Today, sure. That'd be…great. Thank you."

"Oh, no problem. But just so you know, I'm not doing it for you. I'm still mad you didn't call me again. I'm doing it for Roberto."

"Okay, well, thanks. And I'm sorry. It wasn't personal. It was just…"

"Oh, don't you worry about it. I'm teasing you. If I hooked up with you, I wouldn't have met my Leo."

"You and I weren't meant to be, I guess."

Noah hung up after getting her address and setting the time to meet at one. He looked at his watch. He could lie in bed for at least another hour if he wanted to.

He lasted thirty minutes, then out of boredom got up to shower and dress. He made a breakfast sandwich with an asiago bagel, fried egg, a slice of ham, and a slice of cheese, then went out onto his patio. He hoped Diana was off shopping or at the gym, because he really didn't want to deal with her. He had his fill of women over the weekend. And soon he would meet up with another. His only consolation was her husband would be there and he'd more than likely be safe.

Chapter Nineteen

Noah pulled up to the address Rosita gave him. It was a multi-story complex of condos in an expensive part of town. Rosita's Pharmacist made good money dispensing drugs. He parked in the underground lot and took the elevator up to the eleventh floor. As he cradled the shoebox in his arms, he followed the hallway down past ten identical doors, before coming to 1188, a corner unit that would have views of the city on two sides.

He knocked and a moment later, Rosita flung open the door and greeted him with a kiss on the cheek. Then she stepped back and looked at him.

She leaned in close and whispered. "I forgot how good looking you were." Before she opened the door wide and yelled out to her husband. "He's here, my love."

Noah stepped into the room and was overwhelmed by the assault of colors and patterns from every surface. Rosita's house was as extroverted as she was.

She noticed his reaction and said, "I decorated myself."

"Wow," was all he got out.

Leo the Pharmacist entered the room and shook hands with Noah. "Welcome to our home. Come sit and show me what you have." Leo wasn't at all what Noah expected. He was mid-forties, with a full head of slightly greying hair, and a handsome face. He stood a couple inches shorter than Noah and was in good shape. When he passed his wife, he gave her a little pat on the rear.

Noah followed him to the dining room table, with a wood inlay pattern that resembled a turtle shell. He sat and removed the lid from his box, took out the bottle with the red pills, then pushed the shoebox across the table to Leo.

Rosita sat next to her husband, and she and Noah watched as Leo took each bottle, read the label, then opened it and checked the contents. As he set each bottle down and moved on to the next, he arranged them in small groups.

This continued for almost ten minutes. When he got to the last bottle, he pushed the box aside and smiled at Noah.

"I see nothing unusual here. How old was your father when he passed?"

"Seventy."

"The prescriptions here are for conditions you'd expect someone his age to have, meds for high blood pressure and high cholesterol, blood thinners, etcetera. Like I said, nothing unusual, or life-threatening." He nodded towards the bottle Noah still had. "And what's that one?"

Noah held it up. "This is what Dr. Beals came into the house in the middle of the night to remove." He handed the bottle to Leo. "I put them into an empty bottle. He took the original bottle with him, these were left behind."

Leo poured the pills out into his hand and studied them. "These aren't FDA approved medications."

"What does that mean?"

"They weren't ordered from any pharmacy. They were handmade."

"Is that legal?"

"Not really. Depends on what's in them." He held one up and showed it to Noah. "See this crease around the pill? That's from a press. You make your concoction and compress it into a neat little package for delivery."

"How do we find out what's in it?"

Leo set the pill on the table and smiled at Noah. "Well, you're in luck, my friend. I am a bit of a chemistry nerd." He looked at Rosita. "Will you fetch me my kit, dear? And bring Noah here something to drink. Coffee, iced tea, beer?"

"Coffee would be great, thanks."

When Rosita left the room, Leo studied Noah for a moment before he smile and leaned forward in his chair. "You can relax."

"Relax?"

"I know my wife had a…carefree youth. Whatever happened between you two, is in the past, forgotten."

"Um, okay. But really, it was—"

Leo put up a hand. "In the past, I don't need details or excuses."

Rosita returned to Noah's relief and set a cup of coffee in front of him. He looked at it and wished now he'd asked for a beer instead. He blew across the cup, before he took a sip.

Rosita sat a wooden case in front of her husband, who opened it up to reveal a collection of vials. He looked up at Noah. "Since we have two pills, can we grind one up? It's the only way I'll be able to discern what it contains."

Noah nodded. "Of course, whatever you need to do."

Leo kept on out, then dropped the second one into the bottle and handed it to Noah. Leo crushed the pill into a fine powder in a small contraption that made a neat and tidy job of it. He divided it into several piles, then put drops of liquid from various vials into the powder. After five minutes, he sat back in his chair and scratched his head.

Noah watched him for a moment. "You seem perplexed."

"I am. There's nothing illegal or unidentifiable here. It's all common, inert compounds mostly added for color, flavor, and preservation."

"So, are they placebos? Was Beals flaunting some miracle drug that was in actuality nothing?"

"Well, I didn't say they were nothing. There's also selenium and vitamin E, along with another odd ingredient I wouldn't expect to find in pill form."

"And what's that?"

"Charcoal."

Rosita spoke up. "Like for a BBQ?"

Leo patted her hand. "No, my dear. Activated charcoal. Something you'd prescribe to treat a drug overdose or a poisoning." When she and Noah both looked confused, he continued. "When you give a patient activated charcoal, the drugs or toxins in their body bind to it, and it helps the body eliminate the substances."

Noah thought about it for a moment. "So, my father overdosed on something?"

"Or," added Rosita, "someone poisoned him."

Noah stood up. "Or someone poisoned him." He looked at Leo. "Is that possible?"

Leo still seemed confused. "I suppose so, but this is an odd way to treat it. Selenium and vitamin E help with the symptoms of arsenic poisoning. But giving charcoal in pill form is odd."

"How do we find out? There must be a way to find out if he was poisoned, right?"

"Depends on the poison. But your best option would be through an autopsy. If there's something to find, that's how they'll find it."

Noah dug his phone out of his pocket. "Tuesday. They're going to cremate him today." He stared at his phone as he realized he didn't know the number for the mortuary.

Rosita opened a laptop on a nearby counter. "What's the name of the mortuary, hon, I'll get the number for you."

His mind was suddenly blank. "Mr. Weatherby from…" He put a hand on his forehead. "Heaven's Gate." He looked at Rosita. "Heaven's Gate Mortuary." He sighed and sat down.

She found the website and rattled off the number to him. He dialed, got to his feet again, and walked into the living room.

"Heaven's Gate Mortuary. Were here to help you celebrate the life of your loved one."

"Mr. Weatherby?"

"No, may I ask who is calling please?"

"Noah Wainwright."

Noah thought he heard a gasp on the other end of the line, then a mumbled, hold on please. In a few moments, Mr. Weatherby came on the line.

"Mr. Wainwright. I'm so very sorry. This is highly unusual, and I assure you we're doing everything in our power to resolve the issue."

"Issue? What issue?"

"Why the issue with your father's body. Isn't that why you're calling? I spoke to Mrs. Wainwright this morning."

Noah sighed. "No, I haven't heard from her. What's wrong with his body?"

"Well, it's missing, Sir."

"Missing?"

"Yes. Dr. Beals insists he sent it to us on Sunday, but we haven't received it."

"You don't know where his body is?"

"No, Sir."

"So, he hasn't been cremated yet?"

"No, not by us, anyway. I've put in calls to all the local mortuaries. He hasn't turned up at any of them, either.'

Noah sat on the couch. "Mr. Weatherby."

"Yes, Mr. Wainwright."

"If my father's body shows up, I want you to call me right away. Me, not Mrs. Wainwright. And whatever you do, don't cremate him."

"Of course. I'll contact you straight away when we find him."

"Thank you."

Noah ended the call, then leaned back on the couch and closed his eyes. When he heard Leo clear his throat, Noah sat up.

Leo asked, "Everything okay?"

"The mortuary seems to have misplaced my father's body." He stood up. "I've got to go." He went to the table and picked up the single bottle with the red pill in it and dropped it in his pocket. "Can you keep the other medications for me? I'll come back and get them soon."

"Of course. Where're you going?"

Rosita put a hand on Noah's arm. "Your father's missing?"

"I'm pretty sure I know exactly where my father is." He headed for the door, but stopped before going out? "Thank you so much for all your help."

"Let us know if you find him," Rosita said quietly.

Noah smiled. "I will."

*****

He rode the elevator down and accidentally got off on the first floor. Frustrated, he took the stairs the rest of the way to the garage and jogged to his car. Once in behind the wheel, he pulled his phone out again and dialed Marcus.

"What are you doing right now?"

"Why thank you, Noah, I'm fine, how are you?"

"Yeah, yeah, blah, blah, just answer the question."

"It's not blah, blah. It's a matter of manners. Which you seem to lack."

Noah sighed. "Good afternoon, Marcus. How are you?"

"Much better."

"So, what are you doing right now?"

"Roberto and I are enjoying each other's company until I have to go to work."

"Oh good. He can come too."

"Come where? What's up with you?"

"Dad's body is missing.'

"Good Lord. Missing?"

"Yes, but not really. I know where it is."

"Have you been drinking?"

Noah started his car. "No. I need you and Roberto to come with me to Dr. Beals' office."

"Are you driving and talking on the phone?"

"No, I'm sitting in a parking lot and talking on the phone. I'm on my way. Be ready to leave the house when I get there."

"Where are you coming from?"

"I'm ten minutes away."

"Jesus, Noah we—"

Noah ended the call and backed out of his parking space. "Dr. Beals, you sneaky bastard, you won't get away with this."

Chapter Twenty

Once Noah arrived, it took another fifteen minutes to get Marcus and Roberto out of the house. Followed by twenty minutes of listening to Marcus complain while they drove across town to Dr. Beals' office. Roberto was manning the GPS and trying to calm his husband, while Noah drove.

When they arrived at the medical building where Beals had an office, Marcus refused to get out of the car until Noah told him exactly what was going on.

Noah gave him an abridged version of what transpired at Rosita's house, and ended with the three of them confronting Beals, who Noah was sure was hiding their father's body.

Roberto seemed excited by the prospect. "Get out of the car, *el carino*. This is going to be fun."

Marcus peer at him through the window. "Going into the office of the man, Noah described as creepy, doesn't sound like fun to me."

"Think of it as an adventure."

Marcus got slowly out of the car and Noah went to him. "This guy is very unassuming. I don't think he's any threat to us."

"Then why didn't you just come by yourself?"

"I thought a show of force would make him give up his plan."

Roberto put an arm around Marcus' shoulder. "When that little man sees us three walk in the room, he'll spill his guts."

Marcus rolled his eye. "Fine, whatever." He caught the reflection of the three of them in the window glass. Roberto's dark hair and skin was a pleasing contrast to the two blond Wainwright brothers. "We are pretty damn impressive. But if you make me late for work…"

Noah checked his watch. "This won't take long."

They crossed the parking lot and entered the building. The directory mounted on the wall inside put the doctor's office on the second floor. There was no elevator, so they took the stairs up. Beals' office was two doors down. They stopped outside and took a moment.

Marcus sighed for the hundredth time, "What's the plan?"

"We're just going to go in and talk to him."

They entered the office which was a couple steps above the average waiting room, and the clients were older and well-dressed. Noah went to the reception desk and gave the young blonde behind the desk a smile.

"I need to see Dr. Beals."

"Do you have an appointment?"

"No, this isn't a medical issue. If you tell him Noah and Marcus Wainwright are here, I'm sure he'll want to see us." He leaned an elbow on the counter and smiled again, causing her to blush as she picked up the phone.

Noah glanced at Marcus and winked at him.

Marcus shook his head. "So stereotypical."

Roberto whispered in his ear. "Whatever works, *querido*."

Five minutes later, Dr. Beals appeared, looking nervous as he fidgeted with the stethoscope hanging from his neck.

"Gentlemen, what can I do for you?"

"Seems there's a problem with my father's body," Noah said loud enough for the people in the waiting room to hear.

Dr. Beals motioned for them to follow him. They did so, following him past the examination rooms and into his private office. He closed the door behind them, then looked at Noah.

"I did nothing wrong. I was following your father's wishes."

Noah took the pill bottle out of his pocket and rattled it. "You want to tell me what the little red pills are for?"

"They're nothing. Mostly inert ingredients."

"What about the charcoal?"

Dr. Beals grew pale and sat behind his desk. He looked up at the three men standing in front of him.

"I was only following your father's wishes. I was trying to…save him."

Noah was suddenly confused. "Wait, what?"

"I was trying to save him."

Marcus took over for his brother, who had lost his direction. "Trying to save him from what?"

"The poison."

Noah found his voice and took a step towards the desk. "You weren't trying to poison him?"

"No, I was trying to save him."

Noah held his hand up and took a moment to sort out his jumbled thoughts.

In the meantime, Marcus asked the question. "Who was trying to poison him?"

Noah glanced at his brother. "Yes, who? And what do you mean you were following his wishes?"

Dr. Beals leaned back in his chair in resignation. "Six months ago, your father was a healthy, robust seventy-year-old man. Then he met and married…that young woman, and everything changed."

Roberto sat in the only other chair in the room. "Are you saying Tiffany poisoned Atticus?"

"Yes, isn't that what I just said."

"No," Marcus and Noah said simultaneously.

Beals sighed. "It took me a while to figure out why he was failing so quickly. It was hard to pin down, but I finally figured it out. She was slowly poisoning him with arsenic. A little at a time. It builds up in the system and eventually kills you. I was trying different things, hoping to at least delay the inevitable until he came to his senses."

Noah nodded. "So, you were trying to slow the process."

"Yes, but I'm afraid I failed."

"The Pharmacist I took the pills to said it'd be a very inefficient way to cure him."

"It was the only thing I could do. He didn't want me to intervene. So, I didn't tell him what I was doing. The charcoal was a hail Mary."

Roberto stood up. "So he knew she was trying to kill him?"

Beals nodded. "He thought she wouldn't be able to go through with it. He thought she'd find some compassion and admit what she was doing. Until she did, he didn't want me to say or do anything."

Noah took another step towards the desk and leaned on it, putting his face a foot away from the doctor's. "You could've saved him. You could've stopped it."

Beal's rolled back in his chair, but hit the bookcase behind him. "He made me promise. Doctor patient privilege, and all."

Marcus shook his head. "But surely saving his life and stopping a criminal act, supersedes the Hippocratic oath."

"Exactly," Noah added. "What happened to protect and serve?"

Marcus cleared his throat. "Noah, that's the cop's oath."

He glanced over his shoulder. "What?"

"Cops protect and serve. Hippocratic oath is do no harm."

"Oh, right. That makes more sense." He looked at Beals again. "What happened to do no harm?"

He removed his hands from the desk and stood back upright. "Our father's death is on your hands. You're as guilty as she is."

Beals rested his elbows on the desk and put his face in his hands. "I know."

Roberto came up beside Marcus and put a hand on his back. "So, Dr. Beals, where's the body?"

"And why are you hiding it?" Noah added.

"I didn't want anyone to find out. I wanted to make sure no one performed an autopsy. I was going to take him to the mortuary tonight and cremate him myself."

Noah turned and sat on the edge of the desk. "You were going to cover up a murder?"

"Your father put me in a very compromising position. When he died... well, I didn't know what else to do."

"How about come clean and not let Tiffany get away with murder?"

"That would've been the smarter thing to do, I suppose."

Noah looked at Marcus and Roberto, then back to Beals. "You need to talk to the authorities and tell them what you know."

"Are you sure it was Tiffany?" Marcus asked.

"I'm not positive. I just know he started going downhill after they got back from the honeymoon. After he rewrote his will."

Noah sighed and rubbed his face. "Damn Tiffany. Of course it was her. And she's still trying to get a cut, even after he changed the will, again."

Marcus checked his watch. "I'd love to see how this all turns out, but I need to be at work in an hour."

Noah nodded at him. "Okay, go ahead. I got it from here."

"We all drove in the same car."

"Well, I can't drive you home. I need to call the cops and see that Beals here does the right things. Take an Uber."

Marcus folded his arms across his chest. "You know I don't Uber."

Roberto put his arm around Marcus' shoulder. "It'll be fine, just this once."

Noah studied his brother. Neither he nor Roberto were going to convince Marcus to take a ride share home. He sighed and dug his car keys out of his pocket. "Leave the keys under that ugly ass cat statue you have next to your door."

Marcus took the keys from him. "That cat statue was quite expensive."

"That doesn't make it any less ugly."

Marcus and Roberto headed for the door. "Are you sure you'll be all right here, alone with him?"

"Do I have a choice?"

"No, I just thought it'd be the proper thing to ask," Marcus said quietly.

"Go home and get ready for work. And Roberto, you drive, please."

Roberto smiled. "I always do."

*****

It was a long excruciatingly quiet thirty minutes until two police officers showed up. They introduced themselves as officers Parker and Bryant, then listened patiently as Noah gave them a fairly detailed accounting of what had transpired over the last few hours.

When Noah finished, Officer Parker addressed Beals.

"We need you to come to the station and make a full report."

Beals looked up at him from his desk chair. "Now?"

"Yes, that'd be best."

Beals studied the desk for a moment. "Am I in trouble?"

"That'll be up to the District Attorney, Sir."

Officer Bryant approached the side of the desk. "We're asking you to cooperate, but if you choose not to, we'd insist you do." He rested his hand on his gun and Beals' eyes grew a size.

"Of course I'll cooperate." He put his hands on the desk and stood up. He removed his stethoscope and pushed a button on the intercom. "Ms. Holmes. I'll be out the rest of the day. Please cancel the rest of my appointments."

A surprised, "Yes, Sir," came back over the speaker as Beals cleared his throat and nodded to the officer. "May I request we leave by the back entrance?"

Officer Bryant nodded. "Of course."

Officer Parker looked at Noah. "We don't need you for this, but stay available. A detective will be assigned to the case and will want to talk to you."

"Of course, no problem."

Bryant looked at him. "And leave any further investigative work up to us."

Noah smiled. "Yes, of course. I leave it in your hands."

Chapter Twenty-One

The rest of Tuesday was a blur and Noah spent another long night not sleeping. On Wednesday morning he called the club and told them he still wasn't ready to return to work. They of course understood and repeated their condolence for his loss, but in actuality, his father's death was an excuse. He had no desire to be there. The thought of catering to rich clients who'd never become even adequate tennis players, was disheartening.

After spending an hour sitting on his couch, he forced himself to get up. Dredging up some motivation, he cleaned his house and did his long overdue laundry, then went out on his deck and found Diana watering her hydrangeas.

He assumed she was watering with the hope of him venturing outside, as she was wearing yoga pants and a tight tank top. When she 'accidently' sprayed some water on her shirt, she squealed and looked at him as she insufficiently covered up the fact she wasn't wearing anything underneath.

She said, "Whoops," as she turned off the hose and went to the brick retaining wall separating their compact backyards, conveniently forgetting he could see everything mother nature endowed her with, or more likely, her plastic surgeon.

"So you've been gone awhile. How was your family thing?"

Noah took a sip of the beer serving as his breakfast. "My father died."

She was quiet for a moment as she seemed to consider a proper response. She finally came up with the standard, "Oh, I'm so sorry for your loss."

"He was murdered."

She put a manicured hand to her chest. "Oh, my."

He stood up, no longer interested in shocking her, and headed for the door as she called out after him.

"Do you want me to spray your lawn?"

He looked at the ten foot square plot of grass turning brown from lack of care and gave her a small smile. "Sure. That'd be great, thanks."

"Anytime. You know I'm here for you."

When he went inside, his phone was ringing. He picked it up from the counter where he left it. "Good morning, Marcus."

"I've been calling for an hour. Where were you?"

"On the deck."

"You know, the whole idea behind a cell phone is that it isn't connected to the wall, making it convenient to carry with you."

"What do you want, Marcus?"

"I've been getting hounded by the Wainwright women because they don't have your number. You need to call them at some point."

Noah leaned on the kitchen counter. "Why do they have your number?"

"Because I don't live in the stone age like you do. I communicate, keep in touch, and bring my cell phone with me so others may contact me and not consider calling 911 when they don't hear from me for days on end."

"I saw you yesterday." He stood up and went to the refrigerator.

"Please call them. I can give you all of their numbers."

"I have them. Ms. Schmidt sent me a detailed email with everyone's info."

"Ohh, I want to see that."

Noah took out a beer, then headed for the living room and sat on the couch. "No word from the cops, yet."

"These things take time," Marcus said, sounding like he actually knew what he was talking about.

Noah picked at the label on the bottle with his thumb nail. "Maybe, but while they're taking their time, Tiffany is living it up."

"You need to go back to work and stop mulling."

"I really don't want to go back to work."

"Whatever will the women do without their token gigolo?"

"I'm not a gigolo. I don't get paid for my services." He twisted off the cap and took a drink.

"Well then, you're selling yourself short."

Noah leaned back on the couch and put his feet up on the matching ottoman. The room was small, and the couch was the main piece of furniture. "Have you heard from Charlie by any chance?"

He could hear the smile in Marcus' voice. "No, why?"

"Just curious. It was nice to see her again, that's all. And she said she'd call and check up on me."

"Sounds like some of those twelve-year-old sparks have been fanned. Watch out you don't get burned. Unless of course you want to get burned."

"I don't think she's too interested in a gigolo who works for free."

"Maybe it's time to turn in your little white shorts and put on some responsible man pants."

"I don't wear white shorts, but I'll consider it," Noah said before taking a drink of beer.

"After all, you're a land owner now."

Noah swung his legs up onto the couch, then laid down and closed his eyes. After rubbing the bottom of the cold bottle across his forehead, he asked, "Would it be totally wrong of me to sell the Wainwright family home?"

"Yes."

"It's not like it was a happy family home."

"I really don't think that matters. We're the third generation."

Noah sat up and took another drink. "And there's some law that says you can't sell it after three generations have lived there?"

"If there's not, there should be."

He smiled. "Marcus."

"What?"

"I'm so glad you're my brother."

"Really? I think I might cry."

"So when can you and Roberto come over and wade through all this legal stuff with me?"

"We'll be there at six. And we'll bring sushi."

"I prefer my fish cooked."

"Oh my God, you're such a neanderthal."

"I'd venture to guess neanderthal men probably ate raw fish when they didn't have a fire handy."

"I'm hanging up now. We'll be there at six."

*****

Marcus and Roberto showed up promptly at six. Roberto carried two six packs of imported beer, which he took to the kitchen and stashed in the refrigerator after pulling out three bottles. Marcus set a tray containing a variety of sushi on the table and handed a brown paper bag to Noah, who was pleased to find it contained a burger and fries. He sat down and unwrapped the burger as Marcus slipped a plate under it.

"Now I just need to wash that," Noah said before taking a bite of the burger.

Roberto set down the three beers and three mismatched glasses. Noah grabbed a beer and drank directly from the bottle, drawing a look from both men.

"I hate washing dishes."

Marcus and Roberto sat down, opened the sushi, and poured their beers. The two men had been in a relationship for four years and lived together for three. Roberto was slightly less fastidious than Marcus, but still considered Noah to be a heathen when it came to eating, or dressing properly, or just about anything else.

After they ate, they spent several hours going over financial statements, lists of assets, money owed, and money coming in. The final picture showed Atticus to be a savvy business man who took the moderately prospering business he inherited from his father and made it into an impressively successful enterprise. Over the last two years, he'd sold off most of the original business for ten times what it was worth when he took it over.

Roberto took a sip of his beer. They were down to the last three. "So, unless you want to become a business mogul, you need to liquidate the rest of these commercial holdings."

Marcus straightened a pile of paperwork. "Which would end the Wainwright dynasty."

"Yes. Then you divvy it all up, however you see fit."

Noah leaned back in his chair and drained his beer. "What would you do, if this was your decision to make?"

Roberto answered without hesitation. "I'd keep it going."

His answer surprised both Noah and Marcus.

Noah shook his head. "This is all beyond me. And frankly, I have no interest in running my father's business."

"You don't need to run it. That's what CEOs are for. You just need to show up at the board meetings and act important."

"Yeah, see, no. I don't even want to do that."

Marcus thought for a moment. "Well, you could hire someone to represent your interests with the board." He glanced at Roberto. "Someone you trust, and who knows his way around a pile of legal documents."

Roberto patted Marcus' hand. "Now *querido*, don't be putting ideas in your brother's head." He smiled at Noah. "Of course, if you were so inclined to keep things going, I'd be more than willing to be your representative."

Marcus slapped the table. "Laura."

Noah shook his head. "What about her?"

"Well, she's a pain in the ass, but she's one hell of a business woman. She's fought her way up to the top. She'd probably jump at the chance to be CEO of what's left of the Wainwright Corporation."

Noah put his forearms on the table and laid his head on them. "I hate all of this so much."

Marcus patted his brother's blond head. "I know you do. But we're here to help you through it. And whatever you decide, we support you one hundred percent. Sell it all off, or keep it going, whatever you want."

"Can we go back in time and stop this from happening?"

"Anything but that."

*****

After Marcus and Roberto left, Noah was too hyped up to go to bed. His brain was on overdrive and he needed a distraction, something to take his mind off the Wainwright family business. He retrieved his laptop and opened the file with contact information for all of his clients. His phone may not have many contacts, but this file had over a hundred. They weren't all current. He started the file five years ago. Most of them weren't women he spent time with off the tennis courts. But that number was bigger than he wished it was. *I'm a horrible person.*

As that thought ran through his mind, he was dialing Missy Steinberger's number. As usual, Mr. Steinberger was out of town, and she jumped at the chance to come by and give Noah her condolences.

It took her about thirty minutes to coax him into bed, and once there he tried his best to enjoy himself. But his heart wasn't in it, and he found himself just going through the motions. However, Missy didn't seem to notice, and as she lay dozing next to him, he stared at the ceiling and hated himself for caving in and calling her.

What had always been an enjoyable, but admittedly shallow pastime, had turned into something he didn't want to do anymore. He felt it slowly happening over the last year or so, but now tonight, he was done. *What changed?*

"Charlie."

"What sweetie?"

"Shh, go to sleep, Missy."

She curled into a ball and molded herself into his side, and he resisted the urge to turn his back to her. He'd let her have this last night.

She tried to engage him in some early morning sex, but he begged off with the excuse of a beer hangover. She headed for the shower and he breathed a sigh of relief.

Then his phone rang.

He didn't know the number, but knew, instinctively, it was Charlie. Charlie who could've called any other time, but called when he had a woman in his shower. He debated for two rings on whether or not to answer it. He swiped answer.

"Hello."

"Master Wainwright," Charlie said, doing a poor imitation of Simms.

He could hear Missy singing in the shower and he got up and cradle the phone in the crook of his neck, while he slipped on his boxers and headed for the kitchen.

"Charlie, you called."

"I told you I would."

"So, how've you been?" he asked as he opened the sliding glass door and stepped out onto the deck.

"I'm good. Have you made any decisions?"

He glanced over his shoulder at the door and thought about who was behind it. "Not any good ones." He then noticed Diana, once again watering her hydrangeas, and realized he was only wearing his boxers. He gave her a little nod and turned his back to her.

"You sound distracted. Did I catch you at a bad time?"

"Um, no. It's all good." When the sliding glass door open next to him, he turned to see Missy in the doorway. He put a finger to his lips.

"Oh, okay," she whispered as she stepped back inside and closed the door.

"Noah?"

"Yes?"

"Oh my gosh, you're not alone, are you?" When he didn't respond, she continued. "It's okay. You can call me back when you're not occupied."

"No, no, it's not like that. Well, it is, I guess, but...dammit. I'm sorry."

"You don't need to be sorry, Noah. You're a grown man who doesn't need to answer to me."

"You think I'm a bastard. I think I'm a bastard. When can I call you?"

"Not today. Lunch with my dad, and a catering job tonight. Tomorrow's fine."

"Okay. I'll call you tomorrow."

"Okay. And for the record. I don't think you're a bastard."

She hung up and Noah nodded to Diana, before going inside. He found Missy still in her towel, sitting on the counter and eating a piece of leftover sushi.

She smiled at him and held up the fish. "I hope you don't mind."

"No, help yourself. I don't eat it."

She finished her bite, then licked her fingers, before giving him a suggestive smile. "So, have you ever made love in the kitchen?"

"Can't say that I have, no."

"They do it in the movies. Looks like fun." She released the towel tucked in above her bosom and let it drop to the counter. "What do you say?"

"I say, I'd never be able to eat in here again. So, probably not going to let that happen."

She pouted as he wrapped the towel around her. "Didn't you just shower in preparation of going home?"

She slid off the counter and headed for the bedroom. "I did. But no need to rush off."

Noah followed her. Not that he wanted to fall into her trap again, he just wanted to make sure she got dressed. When he came into the room, he sat on the edge of the bed.

She picked up her underwear. "Are you sure you want me to leave?"

"Yes. And once you're dressed, we need to talk about something."

"Uh oh, sounds serious."

"Just get dressed."

She disappeared into the bathroom, then reappeared five minutes later. She sat next to him on the bed and took his hand.

"So, what do you want to talk about?"

"This thing we do. It can't happen again."

She moved a few inches away from him and looked at him for a long moment. "The phone call. It was a woman, wasn't it?" She put a hand on his cheek. "You have a girlfriend."

"No, she's not a girlfriend."

"Yet." She stood up. "Well, I'm happy for you."

"You are?"

"Yes, of course. You deserve to have someone special. And not just special in the moment, special all the moments."

"Um, I'm not sure what you said, but thank you, I think."

She smiled and gave him a kiss on the cheek. You're a hell of a man, Noah. And one of the best lovers I've had. But I'd never stand in the way of your happiness."

"Well, thank you. Wait, *one* of the best lovers?"

"Easily in the top ten."

"Top…ten?"

She laughed. "I'm teasing you. Top three."

"Out of…?"

"Now you really don't want to know the answer to that." She gathered up her purse and sweater. "You take care Noah Wainwright. And I'll see you on the tennis court." She headed for the door.

Noah called out to her. "Missy?"

"Yes, handsome."

"I'm going to miss you."

She smiled. "I know."

He watched her leave, surprised by her reaction. He wasn't sure what he expected, but complete acceptance wasn't it. He'd been seeing Missy recreationally, once or twice a month for almost six months. Which was more than any other woman from the club. Usually it was once or sometimes twice period. Something about Missy made him break his one and done rule.

Chapter Twenty-Two

Noah arranged to have lunch with Dakota early Friday afternoon. The sooner he talked to everyone and got a sense of where they were at and how much money they hoped to get, the sooner it'd all be over with.

He was sitting at a table near the bar and was halfway through his beer when she waltzed in twenty minutes late. She was wearing a white leather skirt that hit her mid-calf, paired with a pink silk shirt. Her boots and hat were the same shade of pink as her blouse.

Noah was instantly uncomfortable when she headed his way. He never had to deal with her choice of clothing in a public setting. He only spent time with her at the Wainwright home.

He took a healthy swallow of his beer and indicated to the server to bring him another. Dakota yoo-hooed at him and then crossed the room to the table, causing a ripple effect of patrons turning heads as she whisked by. She seemed impervious to the staring and whispers, or maybe she misinterpreted them as favorable. Either way, she had making an entrance down to an art.

Upon her arrival at the table, she air kissed his cheek, then plopped down into the chair across the table from him. She removed her hat, patted the static out of her hair, and set the hat on the spare chair.

"Well, darlin', how's my favorite stepson?"

"You know, Marcus thinks he's your favorite stepson."

"If he were here instead of you, of course he'd be. I love you both equally."

Noah had to admit that despite the fact she ended his mother's marriage, she'd always been nice to him and Marcus.

The waiter delivered the second beer and asked Dakota what she wanted. She ordered a martini with three olives.

"So, you looked positively panic-stricken when Ms. Schmidt named you executor, but you look better now. Has it sunk in?"

"Well, had it been my option, I never would've volunteered, but since it was dumped in my lap, I'll do what I need to do."

"I have faith in your ability to do the right thing."

"And what, in your opinion, is the right thing?"

"Oh you little stinker, puttin' me on the spot like that." The waiter set her martini on the table and she smiled at him, then watched him walk away. He was easily twenty years younger than her, but he was a good looking twenty-something man, and she didn't hide her admiration.

She looked back at Noah. "Well, I definitely think the children should be taken care of, Libby, you, Marcus, and I suppose my daughter." She noted his surprise and went on. "Of course I love my daughter, but she'll drink away any money you give her. And God knows that pathetic excuse for a husband doesn't deserve anything."

Noah considered telling her about the stipulation Atticus put in his will regarding the money he set aside for Dell, but decided against it. Dell was an adult and deserved to be informed privately. It'd be up to her to tell her mother or not.

He picked up his menu. "Let's order and then talk about this some more."

They ordered and didn't talk much business during the meal, but Noah learned more than he wanted to about Dakota's year or two of mild success in Nashville. He remembered hearing her sing when he was a child, not on stage, but at the house. She sang to Dell, who was four years younger than Noah. In a private setting like that, her voice was sweet and quite good, but he imagined when she turned on the theatrics in front of an audience, the quality went down considerably.

She pushed her empty plate away and smiled at Noah. "So darlin' what's this meeting all about?"

He pushed his plate aside, as well. "I like you Dakota, I always have. You were good to Marcus and me when we came to visit. Why don't you tell me what you'd do with a chunk of Atticus' money."

She smiled and answered without hesitation. "I'd open a theater for up-and-coming performers. A place to give them the chance to shine without trying to compete with those who have made it."

"That's an interesting idea. Do you know how to run a business like that?"

"Of course not. I'd hire someone to run it. I'd be the face of the place, the MC, and of course perform myself, from time to time."

Time to time meaning every night, most likely. "Okay, that's not bad. Where would this club be?"

She seemed insulted by the question. "Well, in Nashville, of course."

"Of course. I should've known." He leaned back in his chair. "I'll tell you what, you come up with a business proposal, and I'll give it some serious thought."

"Really? You're not just shinin' me on, are you?"

"Of course not. I think the money should go to something specific. And that's pretty damn specific."

She stood up and gave him a hug. "You're an angel, you know that Noah Wainwright. How the hell did you spring from the loins of Atticus the scrooge?"

They both had another drink and talked more about Dakota's idea. She seemed enthusiastic, but he wasn't sure if she'd actually follow through with the work of figuring out the mechanics of such an endeavor.

They parted ways in the parking lot after another hug. Noah watched her drive out of the lot in her Jag, then got into his car. He pulled out his phone and called Charlie.

She answered after two rings with, "You actually called back."

"Of course I did. I said I would."

"I won't doubt you again."

"I'm going to remember you said that. So, where're you right now? What're you doing?"

"I'm at the Hilton setting up for my gig."

"The Hilton on East?"

"Yes. Why?"

"Can I come by and say hi. I'm not far. A few miles away."

She was quiet a moment, then said. "Sure, but I'll need to keep working."

"That's fine. Maybe I can help."

"Come in the back door. Room C. The entrance is off the parking lot on the south side of the building."

"I'll be there in ten."

He got there in less than ten minutes and drove around to the parking lot she indicated. He parked beside a bright blue van with Rosemont Catering painted on the side. As he got out, Charlie came out of the building. She greeted him with a smile as she unlocked the side door of the vehicle. She was wearing a tailored chef's tunic made from a light mauve fabric with her business name embroidered on the left shoulder. Her dark hair was up in a loose bun and she was wearing more makeup than she wore over the weekend.

"You look fancy," he said, returning her smile.

"As do you." She studied his outfit. "Were you on a date?"

Noah nodded. "Yes, Dakota and I have decided to run off to Nashville together."

She pulled a box out of the van and handed it to him. "You may have a lot of experience with older women, but I don't think even you, could handle Dakota."

Noah sighed. "Nor would I want to."

She patted the top of the box. "Take that to the bar, please." She picked up a box for herself, and they went into the convention room.

Noah could tell from the abundance of white decorations, the party was a wedding reception. He set the box on the bar and looked around. "Do you do a lot of these?"

"Quite a few. I stay busy. I have a pool of waitstaff to pull from, a pastry chef to help with the fancy stuff, and two cooks who help with the entrées."

"Wow, I'm impressed. And here I thought you were just a cook and dishwasher."

"So, you had lunch with Dakota?"

"Yes."

"That explains the smell."

"I smell?"

"Like a bed of lilacs."

Noah smelled the arm of his leather coat and shook his head.

Charlie came up close and sniffed at his collar. "It's more in there." She stepped back. "Did she hug you?"

"Twice." He took his jacket off and hung it over a chair. "I guess that'll be going to the dry cleaners."

"So, did she beg you for money?"

"No, she was rather well behaved, actually. When you separate them, they're much easier to deal with." He opened the box and handed the bottles of champagne to Charlie. "She wants to open a venue for struggling musicians in Nashville."

"Hmm, interesting. Does she know anything about running a venue?"

"No. I told her to come up with a business plan and I'd consider it."

"Okay, that's a smart move." She set the bottles on the shelf behind the bar. "So, is your father's funeral tomorrow?"

"Yes, tentatively turned into actually."

"Would it be alright if I came?"

"Why would you want to?"

"I've known your father most of my life, but I wouldn't be coming for him. I'd be coming for you and Marcus."

"Well, I wouldn't mind a familiar face. One that wasn't related to me."

"Okay then, I'll be there."

He handed her two more bottles. Even though he was told to keep it to himself, Noah was dying to tell Charlie about the poison and who might've administered it.

"So, would you like to hear the latest scoop about my father's death?"

She turned to face him. "There's a scoop? Of course, tell me."

"I checked out the creepy Dr. Beals and his mysterious little red pills."

"And?"

"Turns out he was trying to counteract the poison..." He paused for effect. "That someone, most likely his new wife, was dosing him with over the last couple of months."

"Well, to borrow Marcus' line, shut the front door!"

"I know, right? Crazy stuff."

"How'd you find out?"

"Roberto's cousin is married to a pharmacist. He gave me the breakdown of the meds, then Marcus, Roberto, and I, confronted Dr. Beals in his office."

"Oh my gosh, you guys must've scared the crap out of him. Three strapping young men."

"I must admit, the three of us together is pretty impressive."

She grabbed another bottle of champagne. "So, is Tiffany arrested then?"

"Not yet. The cops are investigating. I haven't heard from them yet. But Tiffany is still busy not moving out of the house, so nothing formal has happened, yet."

"That is so bizarre and..." She looked at him. "Are you okay?"

"Sure, why?"

"You just learned your father didn't die of old age, but was murdered. Probably by his wife. It's okay to be just a little freaked out about that."

"With everything that's happened in this last, extremely long week, it's just another brick falling from the sky. I'm just trying to stay vigilant and not let one hit me on the head."

He was quiet for a moment as he watched her. But then said, "So, about yesterday morning."

"Noah, you don't need to explain your actions to me."

"But I want to."

She took the empty box and set it behind the bar. "Why?"

He dropped onto a bar stool. "Because." He glanced at her. "Okay, fine. Whatever. You're right. You don't care, and I don't need to justify myself to you."

She took a step closer to him. "Noah. I'm going to go out on a limb here and say you think this friendship we rekindled over last weekend, could turn into something more."

He looked at her for a moment. "Am I just totally off base, then?"

She put a hand on his arm. "You're incredibly cute, and funny, and when we were seventeen, I had a major crush, but…we live different lives. You've made choices in your life that work for you. And I'm in no way judging you for them. But they're not necessarily things I could overlook in someone I wanted to pursue a relationship with."

"You think I'm a bastard."

She stepped back and smiled. "No, I don't. And I'd love to carry on a friendship with you."

"Ouch. The, we're just friends line."

"Can you handle being just friends?"

He thought about it for a moment. "Sure."

She looked at him. "Don't say that unless you mean it."

"I mean it."

She held out her arms. "Then hand me that other box."

He picked up the box and handed it to her. "So, you think I'm incredibly cute, huh?"

"You know as soon as it came out of my mouth I knew it was a mistake."

"So, is it the hair, the two-day growth of beard? Maybe it's the blue eyes."

She started pulling more champagne bottles out of the box. "I think I changed my mind. Maybe I don't want to be friends with you after all."

Chapter Twenty-three

Noah decided to numb the pain of Charlie's rejection by some really expensive food he didn't need to pay for. So, he headed across town for Callahan's where Marcus ran a tight ship, and would always comp his brother a meal.

He didn't want to put his lilac laced jacket back on, but he needed to give the pretense of at least trying to dress appropriately. It was an hour before the official dinner hour, but a line was already forming. Callahan's was the place to go on Friday night. Noah left his car a few blocks away in a parking structure and walked down the street, contemplating whether he should bother Marcus on such a busy night.

With a shrug, he went to the front of the line and got a handshake from the man at the door who knew he was Marcus' brother.

"It's super busy tonight. But we'll find a place for you."

"Has my brother reached Zen mode yet?"

The doorman smiled. "The busier it is, the calmer he gets." He opened the door and let Noah in, leaving a line of people wondering who he was, celebrity or sports star?

He approached Marcus, who was giving a last-minute pep talk to his dinner staff. When he spotted Noah, he came to him and studied him for a moment. "Lunch with Dakota must've gone bad."

"No, actually, it was all right. Just wanted to see my brother."

Marcus cocked his head. "On a Friday night?" He waved at a waiter. "Show my brother to the waitstaff table. That's the best I can do tonight. And when I get a chance, you can tell me why you're really here."

"I know you're busy. I'm fine."

Ryan, the waiter, took Noah to a large table set up behind a panel a few feet from the entrance to the kitchen.

"It's not fancy, but you should have it to yourself for a while." The table sat right under a speaker and Ryan glanced up at it. "And sorry about the music. It's loud back here, but we're all used to it."

Noah sat. "It's perfect, thanks. Can I get a Heineken when you have a chance?"

"Sure thing," Ryan said as he rushed off.

Noah checked out the reading material left on the table. There was today's *New York Times*, two gossip magazines, a month old *Sport's Illustrated*, and a *National Geographic* from last year. He had no interest in the *Times* or the gossip magazines, and he'd read the *Sport's Illustrated*, which left him with *The National Geographic*.

He opened it up to the cover story, which was an in-depth article on killer whales, and settled back in his chair. Ryan returned in a few minutes with his beer, water, napkin, silverware, and a basket of bread.

"Thanks. What's the special tonight?"

"Calamari."

"Ah, no. How about Callahan's famous prime rib, medium well with a baked potato, and clam chowder."

"I'll get that started for you." The waitstaff all knew who Noah was, and that he tipped well on his comped meal. So, they took care of him as best they could, while serving their paying customers.

When he was two pages in on the whale article, and halfway through his clam chowder, a perky blonde came up to the table.

She smiled and said, "Hi, I'm new, but they tell me you're Marcus' brother."

He checked her name tag and held out a hand. "Nice to meet you, Khloe."

She nodded towards the magazine. "So, are you into marine life?"

"Never have been, but I now know everything there is to know about killer whales."

She laughed. "If you need anything when I'm flying by, just holler."

"I'll do that, thanks."

Marcus came up as she was leaving. "Don't distract my waitresses."

"I didn't, she came up to me."

"Well, try to look less sexy then. That jacket is great." He came closer and ran a hand down the sleeve to feel the leather, then wrinkled his nose and stepped back. "Oh, it smells like Dakota."

"That was pointed out to me. I think my olfactories have become immune."

"Self-preservation is a wonderful thing." He glanced around the partition. "I've got to run, but I'll be back to get the poor me story."

"So, you don't think it's even a possibility I came here just to see you?"

"Not a chance." He ran off then, almost bumping into Ryan who was carrying Noah's prime rib.

When Noah was halfway through his dinner, Marcus returned and sat down. "Okay, I have three minutes. Give it to me."

"After you left Wednesday night, I had a weak moment and called...a friend. And well, she was still there the next morning when Charlie finally called."

"And she found out you weren't alone. Why'd you answer the phone?"

"I don't know."

"Yes, you do."

Noah shook his head. Then realization hit. "I wanted to get caught."

"Exactly."

"So, I'd be forced to make a choice."

"Bingo. What do psychiatrist make per hour? You owe me .05 percent of that."

"I tried to explain, but she said it wasn't her business, basically, and I was free to do whatever I wanted."

"Friend zone."

"Friend zone." He took a sip of beer. "I went to see her right before I came here, and she basically told me some of the choices I've made aren't things she could accept in a relationship."

"Well, she has a point." Marcus stood up and squeezed Noah's shoulder. "Hang in there, kid. She may be saying friends, but the way she looked at you a couple times last weekend, when she thought no one was looking, doesn't back that up."

"You think she'll come around?"

"How could she not? Look how sexy you are in that jacket." He rushed off again with a promise to return when he could.

Noah smiled. *She did say you were incredibly cute.* As he took a bite of prime rib, his phone vibrated in his pocket. He pulled it out and was pleased to see it was Charlie calling.

He answered the call. "See, I knew you'd miss me."

"Are you in an elevator?"

"Um, no." He took a moment. "Oh, the music. I'm at Callahan's."

"Didn't you eat lunch a couple hours ago?"

Noah checked his watch. "Four hours ago."

"Callahan's seems too fancy for you."

"Marcus is the head honcho, I come get a free meal every once in a while."

"Oh, okay."

"So, why are you calling?"

She was quiet for a moment. "I feel like I was a little harsh earlier."

"You were a lot harsh."

"I'd like to make it up to you."

"I like the sound of that," he said with a smile.

"Can I cook you dinner on Sunday?"

"Definitely." He leaned back in his chair. "What time?"

"Four?"

"Four it is. Can I bring anything, wine, beer…tequila?"

"Beer will be great."

"I'll see you Sunday. Well, actually, I guess I'll see you tomorrow at the funeral. You sure you want to come? You don't need to, and I understand if you don't want to."

"Noah, I want to come. I'll see you tomorrow at the church."

He hung up and stashed the phone in his pocket, then finished his meal. He was glad she was coming to the funeral. He could use another ally. He expected he wouldn't know many of the guests Tiffany invited. But he wouldn't think about that right now. *She wants to cook me dinner on Sunday.*

Marcus returned as Noah was finishing his second beer. His intention seemed to be a quick wave as he rushed by, but he stopped and studied Noah.

"So, what changed?"

"I just got a phone call. She wants to cook me dinner on Sunday."

"Hmm. Don't get too excited. She's not going to flip flop that quickly. She'll stick to her morals for a while."

Noah smiled. "That's okay. I can wait."

*****

When Noah pulled up to his house, there was a black SUV and a police cruiser waiting for him. After he parked in his drive and stepped out of the car, he saw a stocky, mustached man in a black suit coming up the walkway.

"Good evening. Mr. Wainwright?"

"Yes."

The man held out his hand. "I'm Detective Reece. Can we talk for a minute?" He gave Noah a firm handshake.

Noah glanced at the officer coming up behind the detective.

"Sure. You want to come inside?" When Reece nodded, Noah headed for the front door, and the detective followed him after instructing the officer to remain outside by the door.

The two men went inside and Noah dropped his keys on a chest by the door and hung his jacket on a hook attached to the wall.

He nodded towards the lone chair in the room. "Is this a sitting conversation or a standing conversation?"

The detective smiled and sat down in the chair. Noah went to the couch and sat as well.

Reece cleared his throat. "I'll be handling your father's case and I wanted to update you on where we're at so far."

"Okay, I appreciate that."

"Dr. Beals turned your father's body over to the mortuary and they sent it out for the autopsy yesterday morning."

"Right, I was told."

"You won't get an official report on the results, but I can tell you, it seems Dr. Beals' conclusions were correct. There was a high level of arsenic in your father's bloodstream and organs, and it was determined to be the cause of death."

"So, why is Tiffany still running around planning a funeral?"

"She's our top suspect, but we only have Dr. Beals' suspicions. We don't have proof she poisoned your father."

Noah stood up. "Well, that's discouraging. It has to be her. Who else would poison an older wealthy man, other than his new bride, forty-five years his junior?"

"I understand your frustration. Nevertheless, we need proof. Is there anyone else in the family who had an issue with your father?"

Noah smiled. "All of them. My father was not a well-liked man. But as far as I know, none of them have seen him in over a year. I haven't seen him in five years, and he turned his back on Marcus ten years ago."

"Yet, you all showed up when he asked you to."

"He was Atticus Wainwright III. You don't say no to him."

"Well, we'll interview everyone, but in the meantime, I ask that you keep this all to yourself. I don't want Tiffany thinking we're on to her and taking off. Does she have access to money?"

Noah shook his head and sat down. "She has no money of her own. And as long as she thinks she's gotten away with it, she's not going anywhere. She's still hoping to get her hands on some of the family fortune."

"Is she going to?"

"No. My father rewrote the will right after the honeymoon, so she thought she was going to get most of it. But a few weeks ago, he changed it again."

"And left her out of it?"

"He actually put me in charge of it. I get to decide who gets what. And I pretty much decided she wasn't going to get anything, or maybe a token amount. But, now, she's not getting a cent."

"Even if she's not guilty?"

"She's guilty. I'm sure of it."

Reece jotted something in his notepad, then asked, "What about your brother-in-law?"

"Buddy?" Noah laughed. "Not possible."

"Why is that?"

"He's…a buffoon. And an idiot." He thought about what he just said. "And I know, that's redundant."

"That doesn't make him incapable of murder."

"When you question him, you'll see what I mean. He's weirdly dedicated to his wife, Dell."

Reece leaned forward in the chair. "Would Dell ask her husband to kill her father?"

Noah stood up again and shrugged. "I don't know." He headed for the kitchen. "Do you mind if I grab a water?"

"No, go ahead."

He returned with a bottle of water, but didn't sit down. "Dell's a lot of things, but planning to take out the old man? No, I don't think so."

Reece studied him for a moment.

"Are you and Dell close?"

"Close? No, not at all. The Wainwright family doesn't do close. My brother and I, definitely. My mother, of course, but the rest of them, I barely see. As dysfunctional as my family is, I don't see any of them taking that step. And like I said, they haven't spent time with him recently. If he was slowly poisoned over time, it wasn't any of them."

Reece stood up. "Okay, I agree with your assessment. Like I said, Tiffany is our prime suspect." He went to the door. "We'll be in touch. And don't talk to anyone about this until we've made an arrest." He opened the door, then turned to Noah. "No more investigating. Leave it up to the professionals."

"Right, gotcha."

When Reece closed the door, Noah sat down and leaned back on the couch. As conniving as Tiffany had shown herself to be, he was still having trouble believing she was that devious and a murderer. Yet, the facts all pointed to that conclusion. He checked his watch. It was too early to call Marcus. He looked at his laptop. "No, not going there."

He went to his room and changed into shorts and a t-shirt, then grabbed his bike, which was hanging from the ceiling near the door. He headed out into the cool night air.

He took an hour bike ride, then returned home. After grabbing a water, he checked the time. Marcus would be home now.

Marcus sounded less than enthusiastic by Noah's late-night phone call.

"I had a horrendous night at work. If this isn't earth shattering news, call me in the morning."

"So, did the place catch on fire after I left? Because it seemed things were running pretty smoothly up to that point."

"I'm hanging up now."

"No, wait. Guess who was waiting for me when I got home?" There was only silence on the other end. Marcus hated guessing games. So Noah went on. "A detective."

"Well, it's about time. We gave them Beals three days ago. What'd he say? Are they going to arrest Tiffany?"

"He says, she's their main suspect, but they don't have the proof they need to arrest her, yet."

"Well, what do they want, a damned signed confession? Of course she did it."

"Until they get that, or something else, he wants us to keep it on the downlow."

"Of course. Who are we going to tell? Does he think I'm going to announce it on Facebook? Hey guess what? My newest step-mother just took out my old man with arsenic."

"Just don't say anything to the family."

"Well, I was going to go hang out with them tomorrow, but I won't say anything."

"Why are you in such a mood? Is it seriously just work?" He was quiet for a moment. "No."

"What is it?"

"Roberto brought up the, you know what, subject again."

"I'm sorry. But at the risk of you hanging up on me. I kind of agree with him."

"Don't go taking his side."

"I'm not taking sides. I just think any kid would be lucky to have you guys as parents."

"You're sweet."

"I know."

"Sometimes. But until you're faced with the prospect of being a father, then you don't get to judge my misgivings."

"So, I have to find a girlfriend first, get married. All that."

"Preferably a girlfriend still of childbearing age."

"You had to go there."

"Good night, Noah."

"Night, Marcus."

Chapter Twenty-Four

Noah stared at his reflection in the bathroom mirror. The dark gray suit he was wearing belonged to Marcus, but the maroon tie was a gift a few years ago from a client. She wasn't one of his special clients; she was just very thankful for his attention during their lessons and showed her appreciation with a Christmas present. The gray shirt was his too. Somehow the combination came together nicely. He got a haircut first thing in the morning and had shaved. He was as presentable as he was going to get for his father's funeral.

It'd been a week since Atticus summoned him to the bedroom and dropped the responsibility of the estate in Noah's lap. A week since the old man died because he let his wife slowly poison him. *Why would he do that? Wouldn't he at some point figure out she wasn't going to stop?* Atticus was just as responsible for his death as Tiffany and Dr. Beals.

Tiffany insisted on taking on the funeral arrangements, and Noah was happy and relieved to let her do it. But he told her to run any expenses by Simms first. He didn't want to give her carte blanche with the checkbook. He hadn't seen the receipts, but he knew it was going to be an overblown affair celebrating the life of a man few people actually liked.

Noah left the house without eating breakfast, he wasn't hungry. He did however allow himself a scotch and tonic before leaving.

When he arrived at the church, he parked under a large oak tree two blocks from the building since the lot was full. He sat in his car and wondered if the birds he heard singing in the branches above, would leave a mess on his car. As he watched a multitude of people, mostly dressed in black, head into the church, he considered if anyone would miss him if he drove away.

When he saw Marcus approaching through his rearview mirror, he sighed. There'd be no escaping. Noah lowered his window and looked up at his brother.

Marcus squatted next to the door and put his hands on the edge of the open window. "So, whacha doing?"

"Remember how much I didn't want to go to the house last week? Well, I want to go to this, even less."

"We're his family. Dysfunctional at best, but still family."

Noah watched a group of people walk by the car. "Who are all these people?"

Marcus stood up, smoothed his pant legs, and straightened his tie. "Well, like it or not, our father was a big deal. So, come on. Get out of the car."

Noah closed the window then got out and stood next to Marcus, who looked him up and down. "You look very handsome. Charcoal is definitely your color."

"Last week you said blue was my color."

"Same color pallet. Come on, let's go." Marcus studied him again. "I think it looks better on you than it does on me."

"Can I keep it?"

Marcus laughed. "No. But you can borrow it again."

They headed for the church and Noah spotted Charlie standing with Roberto. She smiled when they came up and she gave Noah a hug, then ran a hand down the front of his suit jacket.

"Gray is your color."

Noah glanced at Marcus. "So I've been told."

Charlie took his arm, and they headed for the church. She was wearing a simple black dress and her hair was down. She looked good. Noah mostly saw her dressed for work. This was a change, and he liked it.

She walked slowly to match his reluctant pace. "So, how you doing with all this?"

"I'll be glad when it's over."

They entered the church and since the family was seated in the first two rows, Charlie stayed behind and took a seat near the back while the men continued to the front of the church. The pews were full with people from Atticus' life. Noah didn't know any of them. Nor did he wish too. His father's life was not

Noah's life. He wondered how many of them were there because it would've been bad form not to be, a checkmark on the steps to financial success; attended the funeral of Atticus Wainwright III.

On his way down the aisle, Noah recognized three women from the club, along with their husbands. He gave them all tennis lessons over the last couple of years. But one of them he slept with. It was one time, two years ago, but awkward, none the less. He hoped she wouldn't see him, but it'd be hard to be invisible at the funeral of the family patriarch.

He, Marcus, and Roberto sat on the second pew next to Ruth. On the other side of her were some distant cousins he only met a time or two. He couldn't even remember their names or how they were related.

Tiffany sat in the front pew, dressed in a black lace dress. She wore a small hat with a veil covering her eyes, which she dabbed at occasionally with a handkerchief. He could only see the backs of most everyone else, but from what he could see, they seemed to be dressed appropriately. Even Dakota was sans cowboy hat.

The black coffin was covered with a blanket made of white roses. Several more vases surrounded the coffin and also contained the same white roses. An easel next to the coffin held a picture of Atticus, taken several years ago. He looked like Noah remembered him, middle-aged, serious, and healthy. A far cry from the man who summoned him a week ago.

Noah leaned in to Marcus' ear and whispered. "This is so weird. How does someone like our father fill a church like this?"

"Ass kissers," Marcus whispered back.

"It's a little late for that, isn't it?"

When Ruth shushed them, Noah straightened up in his seat and tried to stay awake while the minister droned on, followed by an endless line of friends and business associates who wanted to pay tribute. When Tiffany stepped up to the lectern, Marcus's elbow to Noah's ribs roused him out of the stupor he'd fallen into.

"This should be good," Marcus whispered.

Noah put his hand over his mouth to cover a yawn and glanced at his mother, who was frowning her disapproval. He shrugged and turned his attention to Tiffany.

She gave a teary-eyed dedication to the man she knew less than six months, but everyone in the audience seemed to believe her grief was genuine.

Marcus whispered in Noah's ear again. "Did you bring a shovel? It's piling up." This time the reprimanding frown came from Roberto, but it didn't deter Marcus.

Tiffany finished and walked back to the pew, collapsing dramatically into the wooden seat. As the minister stood once more and moved to the lectern. "If there's no one else wishing to speak—"

"Hold on." Marcus stood up and the entire front row turned to look at him, along with Roberto, Ruth, and Noah. "I'd like to say something."

Ruth whispered to Noah. "What's he up to?"

Noah, who truly had no idea, shrugged.

Marcus adjusted his tie and tugged on the hem of his jacket before he side-stepped out of the pew and went to the front of the church. He cleared his throat. "Some of you may not know me. I'm the son Atticus turned his back on ten years ago."

Noah mumbled to himself. "Oh boy."

"Marcus Wainwright, the oldest son of Atticus Wainwright III. I guess I'm lucky I wasn't named Atticus the fourth." He looked at Ruth. "Thank you Mom. I'm sure you had something to do with that."

Ruth grabbed Noah's arm. "Get up there and stop him."

"So, while you're all going on about his accomplishments, I want you to know the man you saw in the office, was not who he really was."

Noah stood up and squeezed by Roberto's knees, then approached his brother.

Marcus smiled at him. "And here's my brother. Also a great disappointment to the old man, when he led his own life and didn't follow the Wainwright family tradition of being a business mogul and an asshole."

Noah put a hand on Marcus' shoulder and muttered to him. "Come on, let's sit down."

Marcus looked at him for a moment, then nodded and headed down the aisle, passing the row he was sitting in and headed for the door in the back of the church.

Noah gave the crowd a small smile. "I'm not going to reprimand my brother or apologize for him. Those are the first negative words Marcus has ever spoken publicly about our father, despite the fact Dad ignored him for ten years." He glanced at his mother, but couldn't read what she was thinking.

"I'm proud of him for not bowing down to the will of our father. You all may consider Atticus' unyielding persona as a strength, and it may well be in the business world. But as a father and a husband, he sucked, plain and simple. I can say this to you at his funeral, because most of you already know that."

He looked at the ground for a moment. "Anyway, I wasn't planning on saying anything, and I probably shouldn't have, but I didn't want you all assuming Marcus is lacking in some way and deserved our father's disdain. He didn't. All he wanted to do was love who he wanted to love. That's it. We should all be able to do that without judgement." He smiled. "And there ends the longest public speaking I've ever done."

He left the front of the church to go join Marcus. The crowd was quiet and seemed determine to avoid looking at Noah as he passed by. Noah assumed they all knew his and Marcus' assessment of the man in the coffin was accurate and well-deserved.

The minister once more stepped up to the podium to announce there'd be a wake at the home of Senator Skarsgard. Tiffany didn't even asked if she could hold the event at the Wainwright home. Perhaps she knew Noah would've said no.

As the church emptied and headed towards Noah and Marcus, Noah turned abruptly, putting his back to most of the guest.

Marcus looked at him. "What's up? Who are you hiding from?"

Noah glanced over his shoulder. "Three women from the club, with their husbands."

Marcus looked at the crowd. "Which ones?"

Noah grabbed his arm and turned him around. "Just chill for a minute."

"Are these ladies special clients?"

"Only one of them."

Marcus turned and looked again. "Which one?"

"I'm not telling you."

Ruth was talking with the other ex-wives, who dawdled at the front of the church while it emptied. As most of the crowd dispersed, she came up to her sons and took Marcus' arm, then kissed him on the cheek. "Feel better?"

"Yes, much, thank you. Been holding that in for ten years."

She took Noah's hand. "Never a dull moment with you two."

Noah looked at her. "We've done our due diligence. Can we go home now?"

"You may certainly not. You need to make an appearance at the wake."

"A brief appearance?"

"Give me an hour, then you can disappear."

Noah nodded.

Outside the church, Noah tried to find Charlie in the crowd. But he was quickly approached by strangers, who seemed to forget, moments ago, he disparaged his dead father. They shook his hand and offer their condolences, and by the time he managed to untangle himself from them, he figured Charlie had left. Marcus somehow managed to sidestep the crowd and he and Roberto were waiting for him by the car.

Noah shook his head when he saw them. "How'd you get past the mob?"

"Well, sometimes it helps to be the black sheep of the family."

Roberto added, "We went out the side door of the church."

Noah followed Marcus and Roberto to the Senator's house and they found two spots to park fairly close together. The home was outside of the city like the Wainwright house, so cars were parked on both sides of the road for several blocks in either direction.

It was a five minute walk from the cars to the house, and when they got there, Noah found Charlie sitting on the front porch.

She stood up as Noah approached. "I tried to find you at the church. What're you doing out here by yourself?"

She shrugged. "I don't know any of those people."

"Neither do we. And the few we do know, we don't want to hang out with. But I promised my mom an hour." He looked at his watch. "I'll give her exactly that and not a minute more."

The group from the club came walking up the sidewalk and Noah turned his back and said, "Dammit."

Marcus smiled and answered Charlie's question before she asked it. "Some of Noah's clients from the club."

Noah gave Marcus a small shove. "Dude. What happened to the bro code?"

Marcus put an arm around Charlie's shoulder. "She's one of us. An honorary bro."

Noah shook his head. "No offense, but I don't see you that way."

She smiled. "That's fine." She looked at the group who stopped on the lawn to mingle with a few other couples. "So, which ones, and are they, *special* clients?"

Marcus laughed and Roberto took his arm. "Come on, let's go get you a drink and leave your poor brother alone."

Noah watched them go into the house, then looked at Charlie. "We're not going to talk about this."

"Okay. I think you need a drink, too." She took his arm, but he resisted her pull towards the door. "What's wrong?"

"I need a minute. Can we take a walk?"

Of course. She steered him away from the house, avoiding the couples from the club, and they headed down the street lined with pretentious homes set behind manicured lawns and security gates.

She gave him a few minutes before she asked, "Are you okay?"

He stopped and looked at her, but when he felt his eyes start to water, he turned away. "God damn it."

She put a hand on his back. "Noah."

He rubbed his eyes and glanced back at her. "What the hell is wrong with me?"

"You just lost your father."

"But he wasn't a father you miss." He cleared his throat and wiped at his eyes again. "Certainly not one to cry over."

Charlie put her arms around his neck and hugged him. "Even so, he was your father. And now he's gone."

He stepped away from her and sighed. "And he left me to clean up his mess." Back in control, he leaned on the hood of a black Mercedes.

She stood a few feet in front of him. "Pretty impressive speech."

Noah shook his head. "Probably not the best time or audience to express my feelings about my father."

"Well, I thought it was great. If it hadn't been a funeral, I would've started chanting, Noah! Noah!"

"I'm sure that would've gone over real well."

She moved next to him and leaned on the car as well, then started digging through the small purse she carried, finally pulling out two small glass bottles of tequila. She handed one to him.

"Maybe this will help you get through the next hour."

He took the bottle, then looked at his watch. "Forty-five minutes."

They both unscrewed their lids, then Charlie held up her bottle in a toast. "To Atticus Wainwright III. May he rest in peace."

"To Atticus." He took a sip and watched Charlie take hers. She grimaced as it went down, but she ended with a smile. "So, funerals and birthdays?"

She questioned him with a raise of her eyebrows.

"When you drink tequila."

"Oh, right. Funerals and birthdays." She took another drink, then glanced at him. "You look really handsome today, by the way." She touched his hair. "Haircut, shave, expensive suit."

He tilted his head away from her. "Had to play the part of the Wainwright heir." He stood up. "The suit is Marcus'. I don't own one. Never had the need."

"Well, you wear it well."

"We should get back."

"Wait, I have a request."

"Okay," Noah said, warily.

"Give me one moment in your life with Atticus that wasn't bad."

"I wish I could."

"Come on. There has to be one."

Noah thought for a moment. "I was twenty-one, and just dropped out of school."

"What was your major?"

"Business." At the look on her face, he smiled. "I know. Me in business school doesn't quite fit. That's why I dropped out."

"So, he must've found out."

"I was required to set up an appointment to see him. I creeped into the office and he was on the phone, with another line waiting. He glanced up at me and nodded towards a chair. I sat. He finished his call and told the second one he'd call back. Then looked at me."

"Scary?"

"You have no idea. I stuttered around a bit, then told him I dropped out. He already knew, but he made me confess, because, you know, it was the manly thing to do. But, for about a second." Noah held up his thumb and forefinger and held them a hair a part. "The briefest of moments, I thought I saw something resembling pride. But it was gone so fast, I've never been sure I saw it."

"Pride that you went your own way?"

"Yeah, I think so. But then he spent forty-five minutes yelling at me about being irresponsible and unmotivated, and letting me know in no uncertain terms I'd never amount to anything."

"I'm sorry you had to grow up with that. But now, I think you can believe it was pride you saw. He asked you to execute his will."

"I still don't know how I'm supposed to do that."

"I have complete faith in you. You're stronger than you think you are."

"I'm not that strong."

She touched his bicep. "I don't know, you seem pretty strong to me."

She stood up, and they both finished their tequila, then stashed the empty bottles in her purse. She took his arm, and they headed for the house.

"So, if I guess which one of those ladies you flung, will you tell me?"

"Nope." They walked in silence for a few minutes, then Noah asked, "Do you always carry tiny bottles of tequila in your purse?"

She laughed. "Only to funerals and birthdays."

Chapter Twenty-Five

Noah stayed exactly one hour, then kissed his mother on the cheek. "I'll see you at five for the ashes thing."

"Okay, dear."

Marcus and Roberto, who were leaving too, both kissed Ruth, then Marcus smiled. "So, can I be the one to light the ship on fire?"

Roberto took his arm. "You know what happens when you play with matches, *el carino*. Thank God we have an electric stove."

The three men, along with Charlie, walked the few blocks to their cars and Marcus glanced at Noah. "So…"

"No."

"Just let me guess."

"Fine, guess all you want, but I'm not telling you which one was the one."

Marcus smiled and rubbed his hands together. "The one in the dark purple dress. Ash blonde, overweight husband."

Charlie shook her head. "No way, the one in the black slacks and silk shirt. She's much more his type."

Noah looked at her. "You don't know what my type is."

Roberto shrugged. "You're both wrong, it was the other one. Blue sweater."

Marcus looked at him. "You really think so?"

He shook his head. "I have no idea. I was just stirring the pot a bit."

They reached Roberto and Marcus' Prius and Noah stopped. "Say goodbye to your husband. You're coming with me to the house."

"When did I agree to that?" Marcus asked.

"You didn't. But I know if you go home, you won't want to go back out and I'll be there alone with the Wainwright women."

Roberto gave Marcus a quick peck on the cheek. "He's right. I'll see you later."

The three of them continued on to Noah's BMW and as Marcus grudgingly got into the passenger seat, Noah said goodbye to Charlie.

"So, I'll see you tomorrow at four."

"Looking forward to it. Good luck with the ashes thing."

"Thanks."

*****

Noah and Marcus had a couple hours to kill, so they ate a late lunch, then made the thirty minute drive to the house. When they pulled up to the security gate, they were buzzed in before Noah even announced himself.

"Simms is on it, today."

They pulled around the drive, and the only other car was Dakota's Jag.

"Okay," Marcus said as he climbed out of the car. "Not a big turnout."

Noah checked his watch. Dr. Beals would be there in twenty minutes. Still time for late arrivals, but he suspected everyone that was coming was already there.

Simms met them at the door with a look that could only be described as relief.

"Good afternoon, Sirs." He bowed slightly and ushered them into the foyer.

Noah smiled at him. "You okay there, Simms?"

"Very glad to see another male in the house, Sir."

Marcus patted Simms' shoulder. "You could always hang out with the pool boy."

"I'd rather not, Sir." He stepped out of their way. "The ladies are in the library."

"Thank you, Simms. Go take a breather."

When they entered the library, Dakota rushed up to Noah and hugged him. "Thank God you're here. I thought I was going to be stuck with just Tiffany."

She kissed Marcus on the cheek then wiped off the lipstick she left behind. "Let me get you a drink. You'll probably need one."

She poured two scotches on ice and handed them to the men. Marcus nodded a thank you, then studied the ice in his glass. He glanced at Noah, who shook his head.

"Just go with it."

Marcus looked at the ice again. "Sorry, can't do it." He grabbed Noah's glass and poured his scotch into it, then filled a fresh glass with straight scotch, no ice. "Much better."

They took a seat on the couch and nodded at Tiffany, who was on her phone texting. She gave them a small smile, then resumed typing.

Marcus leaned towards Noah and whispered. "So, she totally thinks she got away with it."

Noah shrugged. "Apparently. Certainly doesn't look or act guilty."

A few minutes later, Simms showed up at the door and announced the arrival of Dr. Beals. The little man came in and glanced nervously at Noah and Marcus, then nodded at the women. He was carrying a small wooden box in his arms.

Tiffany put her phone aside and assumed her grieving widow persona. "So, let's get on with this please. It's been such a long, devastating day."

"Of course." He glanced at Noah again. "Mr. Wainwright was very specific with his request for the care of his ashes." He cleared his throat as he opened the wooden case and revealed twelve small glass vials filled with ash. Beals held one up. "He requested one vial be set in each main room of the house, at your discretion of course, so he may always oversee the goings on of the family home."

The room was silent for a moment, then Dakota snickered, tried to stop herself, but finally gave up and laughed out loud.

"The arrogant bastard. He has to have control, even in death."

Noah glanced at Marcus, who was trying hard to control his own laughter, then stood up. "Thank you, Dr. Beals. We'll seriously consider his request and give the ashes the respect they deserve."

Dr. Beals nodded. "May I talk to you alone, please?"

"Sure."

Beals headed for the door and Noah followed him, closing the double glass doors behind him. Beals continued across the foyer and stopped by the front door.

"I was shocked to see Mrs. Wainwright. Why is she still here?"

"They've assigned a detective to the case, they need solid evidence before they can charge her with anything."

"But I know she did it."

"We need to be patient. What about you? How much trouble are you in?"

"I've been told under no uncertain terms to not leave the city. I expect they'll charge me with something." He studied the floor for a moment. "Which, of course, I deserve." He looked up at Noah. "I was trying to do the right thing. Your father was such a…force."

"I know. But still."

"Of course."

Dr. Beals left, and Noah returned to the library and went to the desk. He looked at the box of vials, then pulled one out and studied its contents. "Anybody have any suggestions?"

Dakota raised her hand. "Can I have one? I'd love to run over it with my car."

"No, you can't do that."

Tiffany stood up. "I'd like one for my room, please."

Noah looked at her. "Tiffany, you don't have a room. You were supposed to be out of here yesterday."

"Can I take one with me when I go?"

"No. The ashes stay here."

Tiffany huffed, then flounced out of the room as Dakota got to her feet. "Well, if we're not going to have some fun with them, I'm out of here, too. I can't believe I drove here for this. I turned down a dinner invitation from the Senator's speech writer. Stunning young man."

She headed for the bar to pour one for the road, but Marcus stood up and intercepted her. "You wouldn't want to crunch that pretty Jag of yours, would you?"

She sighed. "No, I suppose not." She looked at Noah. "Don't forget about our little lunch conversation. I was completely serious."

"I'll give it some serious thought, then. Take care, Dakota."

She left, and Noah and Marcus looked at each other.

"You're not going to stash those around the house, are you?" Marcus asked as he poured himself another scotch.

Noah closed the box and opened the bottom drawer of the desk. "Like I told Dr. Beals, I'll give the old man's ashes the respect they deserve." He set the box in the drawer and closed it. He stood up and removed his jacket and loosened his tie. "Pour me another one of those."

They both had a couple more, and by the time Simms came in to check on them, they were giggling over the list they wrote entitled, 'Things to do with Dad's ashes'. When Marcus, who was at the desk and in charge of the pen, saw Simms, he flipped the list over on the desk and smiled at him.

"What's up, Simms?"

"I came to check on you two. Is everything okay?"

"Everything is perfect," Noah said as he gave Simms a thumbs up. He was reclining on the couch with his head propped up on a cashmere pillow that had probably never been touched, let alone laid on.

"Should I go prepare your rooms?"

Marcus nodded. "I believe that'd be a wise thing to do, Simms, thank you."

"Very good. I'll leave you to it, then."

Noah looked at Marcus. "You better call your husband and tell him your brother is too drunk to drive you home."

Marcus pointed a finger at him. "Good idea. Though I suspect he already knew I wouldn't make it home tonight." He pulled out his phone and sent a text.

Noah sat up slowly. "Okay, one last thing to add to the list."

Marcus flipped the paper over and grabbed the pen.

"We make a tiny little boat, put one of the vials on it, set it on fire, and send it off across the koi pond."

"Oh, I like that." He added it to the list.

"No, no, we can't do that. We don't want to poison the fish."

Marcus crossed it off the list. "And Mr. Kwan Jr. would probably kill us."

"I'd have to go mow the front lawn with the push mower."

Marcus sat forward in the big leather chair. "How about we put a vial on the mower and push it out into the middle of the lawn and set it on fire?"

"Yes, let's do that." Noah laid back down. "Tomorrow. We'll do it tomorrow."

Chapter Twenty-Six

Noah plugged Charlie's address into his GPS and traveled the twenty minutes to her house. It was a small older home in a neighborhood probably built in the seventies. But the homes and yards were well maintained, and it was located at the edge of the foothills where the Wainwright home was. The neighborhood was the gatekeeper to the expensive homes in the hills.

He pulled into the driveway behind Charlie's Honda and sat for a moment. *Just be cool. You're friends, you can do it.*

After Noah knocked on the door, Charlie opened it and greeted him with a smile, then stepped aside and let him into her living room.

He looked around while trying not to be too obvious. It was about what he expected, nice, neat, and conservative. The furnishings appeared to be moderately priced, so either she didn't make much money, or she was frugal. Or, she was like him, and made plenty of money and didn't care what people thought about her home, choosing comfort over making impressions.

"Does it pass inspection?"

He smiled. "I wasn't…yes, yes it does. It's no Wainwright mansion, but it's nice." He sniffed the air. "And smells wonderful." He handed her the six pack he brought after taking a bottle out. She grabbed one too, and put the rest into the refrigerator. He followed her into the kitchen and went to the stove. There were several pots simmering and when he reached to lift a lid, she slapped his hand.

"No peeking."

He sat at the breakfast bar while she put a salad together.

She glanced over her shoulder at him. "So, do you cook, or are you a takeout guy?"

"I have about three things I cook well, and I make a pretty good sandwich. Other than that, I grab takeout after work from a couple favorite places."

"What three things?"

"Bacon and eggs, chili, and spaghetti."

"Well, you'll need to make me spaghetti someday."

"I can do that." He twisted the cap off his beer and took a sip. She may not be frivolous with her furniture, but her kitchen was decked out. He watched her expertly chop onions, carrots, and celery, and toss them in a mix of lettuce leaves.

"So, any word from the cops?"

"A Detective Reece was waiting for me Friday night when I got home."

She finished with the salad, stuck it in the refrigerator and came to the counter in front of him. "What'd he say? Tiffany was at the funeral, so obviously they haven't arrested her yet."

"No proof."

She shook her head. "What do they want, a signed confession?"

"That's exactly what Marcus asked."

Her unopened beer was sitting behind her on the counter by the stove. She picked up Noah's and took a sip. When she saw the surprised look he gave her, she set the bottle down and put a hand to her mouth.

"Oh my gosh, I'm sorry. That was rude."

Noah shook his head. "No, it's fine. Help yourself."

She went to get her bottle and returned to the breakfast bar. "Honestly, what kind of proof could there be?"

Noah shrugged. "How do you even go about slowly poisoning someone?"

She took a sip of beer. "Well, the last time I did it, I put it in their food."

Noah sat up straighter in his chair. "That's how she did it. You're right."

"You think?"

Noah nodded.

Charlie thought about it for a moment before she said, "The problem with that, unless she turns into Susi homemaker during the week, I've never seen her make a sandwich, let alone a meal for her sick husband."

"How do they eat during the week when you're gone?"

"I make meals for the week and freeze them."

Noah picked up his beer, took a sip then pointed the bottle at Charlie.

"It was you. You killed my father."

She raised her hands. "I confess, you got me."

"Well, I won't hold it against you."

"This is all so weird." She gave him a half-smile. "More weird for you, I guess. Has it sunk in yet? That he's gone?"

Noah shrugged. "It's not like he was a big part of my life. But now that he's gone. It's a little weird."

"So, when are you going to move into the big house?"

Noah shook his head, then took a sip of his beer. "I can't see living there."

"Why? The bad memories you have, aren't of the house, it's the people who lived there. Don't you think the house deserves to have someone make it a happy home?"

"After eighty years? My grandfather built the house in the forties. He owned all the surrounding land. Maybe even where this house is. In the sixties and seventies he sold it to a developer and just kept the five acres around the house."

"So was grandpa like his son?"

"I never met him. He died before I was born. But I've heard some stories from my mom. Apparently, he was a decent businessman, a womanizer, and an alcoholic. He put the moves on my mom before she married my dad."

"Oh goodness. That's so wrong. Like father, like son." She looked at him.

"Don't look at me like that. That's not what I do."

"I know. It's pretty much the opposite of what you do."

"Did. I'm changing my stripes."

She pointed her bottle at him and took a sip, then said, "I've heard a tiger can't change its stripes."

"Well, you heard wrong. A tiger can change if he wants to."

She went to the stove and stirred a couple of pots, tasting them each before turning off the heat under them. "I believe this is done."

Noah stood up. "Where do you want me?"

"Go sit at the table, and I'll bring it to you."

"Wow, fancy."

Charlie set a plate with a grilled halibut filet and a side of asparagus, sweet peas, and yellow bell pepper slices. She then delivered the salad and a basket of sliced French bread, along with a fresh beer.

She sat across from him and smiled. "You eat fish, right?"

"As long as it's cooked, yes. This is great. Thank you, but you didn't need to go to so much trouble. I would've been happy with…well, most anything."

"It's my pleasure. This is what I do."

"Well, you do it well." She was waiting for him to take a bite, so he did, and the food tasted as good as it looked. He finished chewing, then said, "Wow. Impressive."

She started eating then, and for several minutes they were quiet as they ate. She was the first to talk again.

"So, about the house, wouldn't it be nice to have the tennis court and the pool, and your pick of bedrooms? Not to mention, the wine cellar, and an incredible kitchen. I'd die for that kitchen."

"The koi pond, the piano room, and a dumb waiter. That's all pretty tempting," Noah added.

"What's with the piano room, anyway?"

"I believe my father felt every rich guy should own a piano. Even though not one of us plays."

She smiled at him. "Well, there you go. You could learn. It's your piano now."

"So, you like my kitchen, huh?"

"I do. Aside from it being a great kitchen, I have fond memories of it from when dad was the on-call chef for your father. He worked there for about ten years and I hung out once in a while."

"But that summer we spent together, he and you were there fulltime."

"Yes, I believe your father was experimenting with having a chef on staff."

"I guess that didn't work out."

She shrugged. "I'm not sure if it was your dad or mine, but the experiment didn't stick and Dad went back to being on call for another two years before he finally had enough of Atticus Wainwright."

Noah finished his fish and took another serving of the salad and a slice of bread. "I'm fine with you using the kitchen. It's not like I'm ever going to do anything in there."

Charlie put her fork down and studied him for a moment. "Are you serious?"

"Of course. Do whatever you want. I'll get you a key." He smiled at her. "No ulterior motive here, just an offer from one friend to another. Although, I wouldn't mind a meal like this every once in a while."

"Well, that's the least I can do. Thank you so much."

They finished dinner and Noah offered to help her with the dishes.

She handed him their plates. "Okay, you clear and I'll go fill the sink."

Noah followed her to the sink. "You don't have a dishwasher?"

She looked at him. "You volunteered because you thought I had a dishwasher?"

"No, I thought everyone had a dishwasher."

"I have one, I just don't like to use it."

"Okay." He left to continue clearing the table. When he came with the rest of the dishes, she nodded towards a towel.

"You can dry and put them away."

He looked around the kitchen. "Am I going to get some sort of directions, or are you going to leave me searching for the right cupboard?"

She nodded to a set of cupboards. "Everything will go in those two."

They finished the dishes, then went out to the patio. Charlie lit the gas fire pit, and they sat in two rustic wooden chairs. They each had a fresh beer and were comfortably full from dinner. Her back yard was small, but nicely landscaped with flowerbeds along the perimeter of the cedar fence. There were two large trees in the center of the yard and a hot tub at the end of the patio. The space was lit up with twinkle lights along the roof over the patio and wrapped around the trunks of the trees. It made for a very cozy space.

Noah took a sip of beer and glanced at Charlie.

She turned her head and looked at him. "What?"

"Nothing."

"Hmm."

"So, let's pretend for a moment Tiffany didn't do it. Which Wainwright would you suspect of poisoning my father?"

"Wow, um. Let me think." She took a sip of beer.

"If you had to pick one Wainwright, who would have no problem taking the old man out, who would it be?"

She took a few moments to think about it. "Laura."

"Really?"

"She seems to be the angriest of the bunch. Your mom and Dakota, don't seem to care too much one way or the other. But Laura seems like she feels she deserves to be compensated for putting up with him all these years."

"Interesting. For a minute there, I thought you were going to say me."

She turned in her seat and looked at him. "Why would I think that?"

"You're already of the opinion I'm a heartless bastard who preys on women. Murder probably isn't that big of a leap."

"Okay, once and for all, I don't think you're a bastard. Nor do I think you prey on women. I think you offer them…respite from their unhappy marriages."

"But you don't approve of my…benevolence?"

"Do you really want to know what I think?"

"Yes, please."

"I think it's sad."

Noah set his beer next to the chair and got up to stand by the firepit. "Sad?"

"Yes. I think you're lonely, and a bit lost, and you've fallen into this lifestyle to compensate for those feelings. I think, you wish, you made different choices along the way."

He stared into the flames for a long moment. "You could be right. Or maybe, I just want to have no strings attached sex."

Charlie sighed and shook her head. "If I believed that, I never would've invited you over here tonight."

He picked up his beer and took a drink. "Why did you invite me over here tonight?" He wasn't sure why he was being defensive. Her assessment was probably right, and certainly easier to accept than his. But for some reason, he didn't want to admit his vulnerability to her.

She stood up. "Well, maybe it was a mistake."

Noah sighed and rubbed the back of his neck. "I'm being that thing you say I'm not. I'm sorry."

She gave him a little smile. "Maybe we should call it a night."

Noah nodded. He didn't want to go, especially with her mad at him. "Can we do this again, only with a different ending?"

"Maybe. I'll call you in a few days."

"Okay, please do."

He left and berated himself all the way home for being an idiot. When he pulled into his driveway, he sat for a few minutes. "You won't call her tomorrow. You'll wait and let her call you." He got out of the car. "No matter how long it takes."

Chapter Twenty-Seven

The phone ringing woke Noah up. It was across the room on his dresser, so he let it ring and tried to ignore it. He started drifting off when it started ringing again. The only thing that got him out of bed to answer it was the chance it could be Charlie.

It wasn't. It was a number he didn't recognize.

"Hello?"

"Jesus, Noah, why didn't you answer it the first time?"

He sat on the end of the bed. "Who is this?"

"Tiffany!"

"What do you want?"

"What's wrong with you? Why are you being so mean?"

"I'm not being mean, I didn't sleep much last night." He looked at the clock.

"It's ten, no one sleeps in until ten."

Noah knew she was rarely up before ten, but decided not to state the obvious fact to her. Instead, he flopped back on the bed. "I won't ask again. I'll just hang up. What do you want?"

"I need to talk to you."

"I can meet you later today. Right after you finish moving out of the house." He heard from Simms she was still there despite him giving her until Friday, now three days past.

"Can you meet me at the house?"

Noah squeezed the bridge of his nose. "Sure. I can be there at one."

"Thank you."

He hung up, tossed the phone aside, then crawled up the bed to his pillow. Within a few minutes, he was asleep.

He woke at 11:30, still groggy, but feeling better than he did when Tiffany woke him up. He checked his phone and found two text messages from Dell. She wanted to meet him for an early dinner at a restaurant with a bar.

He texted her back. *Five at The Roadhouse Bar and Grill.* He sighed, a day full of ornery women ahead. He showered, drank a bottled smoothie, then contemplated calling Marcus so he'd have someone to commiserate with. He decided against it though, because his brother would want to know all about his dinner with Charlie. He was actually surprised he hadn't heard from him. But it was Marcus' day off, so he and Roberto were probably off shopping or getting brunch, or doing whatever happily married couples do.

*****

Noah arrived at 12:45 and after searching the house, he found Tiffany in the pool. She was floating on a lounge in a tiny white bikini, no doubt worn for his sake.

He stood on the edge of the pool. "Tiffany?"

She lifted her head and blocked the sun with her hand. "Is it one already?"

Noah checked his watch and nodded, then sat at the table.

Tiffany slid off the raft and made her way to the built in steps at the end of the pool. She climbed out and stopped to ring the water from her hair.

"Can you bring me that towel, please?"

Noah picked up the folded towel on the table and tossed it to her. She caught it with a frown, then dabbed at her arms and chest, before she wrapped the towel around her waist and sat across the table from him.

Noah took his sun glasses off and laid them on the table. "So, what's the emergency?"

"You want me out of here, but I've got nowhere to go."

"I find that hard to believe."

"Well, it's true. When I met Atticus, I was a dancer."

"So, go back to that."

"I don't want to. I thought I was starting a new life. Now, I've got nothing." She pouted and gave the best puppy eyes she could manage.

"There're plenty of jobs out there that don't require you taking off your clothes. I'm sure you'll find something to better fit your new life."

"You're so mean to me."

"I'm not being mean, Tiffany. You waltzed in here two months ago and expect me to give you a huge inheritance. That's not going to happen."

She leaned back in her chair. "What am I supposed to do?"

He studied her for a moment. He didn't want to give her anything, but he also didn't want her taking off to a distant relative in Kansas or something that would make arresting her more difficult. "Get your stuff and move out of here. The estate will pay for one week in a hotel to give you a chance to get on your feet. If you find a job and a nice apartment to move into, I'll pay your deposit and first month's rent. Then you're on your own. At least until I figure out what to do with all of Atticus' money."

"Can I stay at the Plaza?"

"Let's go with something under $200.00 a night. And an apartment rent you can afford on minimum wage and tips." If all went well, he'd only pay for the hotel. Her accommodations after that would be paid for by the state.

"Fine." She leaned forward and twisted a lock of wet hair around her finger. "But, what about the baby?"

"Excuse me?"

She put a hand on her flat stomach. "I'm two months pregnant. Must've happened on the honeymoon. I'm sure Atticus would want to take care of his child."

Noah stood up and walked to the edge of the pool, but the sparkling water didn't offer the response he was seeking. He turned and looked at her. "You're pregnant?"

She nodded.

"And I'm supposed to, first off believe you, and secondly trust you it's Atticus'?"

"Of course, who else would be the father? I don't sleep around. I'm a married woman." She sighed. "Or at least I was."

Noah went back to his chair and sat down. She'd propositioned him twice. There was no telling how many men she'd flirted her way into bed with while her husband was on his death bed.

"I'm going to need proof."

"You don't believe me?"

He shook his head. "Not really, no."

"Would you like to see the pregnancy test? It's probably still in the trash."

"No, a doctor's confirmation, please."

"And how do I prove to you it's Atticus'?"

"That, I'll need to figure out."

"It's so sad that it'll never know its father."

"He's better off, trust me." Noah stood up again. "This doesn't change the fact I want you out of here today. By five." He walked around the table and stopped next to her. "If you're lying about this, that'll be it for you. You understand?" She nodded. "Leave your keys with Simms. And don't give him a bad time. He's suffered enough from you."

He walked away and headed for the house. This was something he didn't see coming. But he wasn't convinced by her story. She'd say and do anything to get her hands on some of Atticus' money.

When he came into the house, a plump older woman was waiting for him. She'd apparently been watching them through the window, but turned away and started madly dusting the bookshelf when he came in.

Noah looked at her. "Who are you?"

"I'm Martha, the housekeeper. I come three days a week."

"Oh, right."

"Will Mrs. Wainwright be leaving today?"

"Yes. If she's not gone by five, call me."

"Yes, Sir."

"And can you get the bedroom at the end of the hall ready for me? I'll be back tomorrow and will stay for a few days."

"Yes, of course, Sir."

He smiled. "And please, you don't need to call me Sir."

"Okay, Mr. Wainwright."

"Noah. Just call me Noah."

She nodded, not sure how to respond.

He headed for the door. "Call me if she gives you any trouble."

"Yes, Mr. Noah."

He stopped and looked back at her. "Where's Simms?"

"I believe he's in the library reprimanding the young man who services the pool."

Noah changed directions and headed for the library. As he approached the double doors, a deeply tan young man dressed in shorts and a t-shirt came through and almost ran into him.

"Sorry Sir, Excuse me," he mumbled as he continued on his way.

Noah went into the library and found Simms standing next to the desk.

"Everything okay?"

"Seems Aaron has been enjoying the pool at night." He cleared his throat and fiddled with his bow tie. "Without the benefit of a swimsuit."

Noah chuckled. "I guess you put a stop to that."

"Of course."

"Thank you."

Simms bowed and headed for the door but stopped when Noah called out after him.

"Who fixes the meals during the week? I can't really see Tiffany doing anything in the kitchen, even just warming up the prepared meals."

"That would be me, Sir. Or, Martha, the housekeeper, when she's here until the dinner hour."

"Huh. Okay. Did Tiffany ever come in and oversee what you were doing?"

"Perhaps occasionally. She did like to bring a tray up to Mr. Wainwright once he was bedridden."

"Of course she did. Thank you, Simms."

He left the library and went out the front door to stand on the flagstone porch. He always hated the place, because it meant spending time with his father and possibly the family. But what Charlie said was true. It wasn't the house he hated, it was the people who lived here. He looked out at the acre of grass he mowed with the push mower almost twenty years ago. He'd spend a few days here and see how he felt.

Chapter Twenty-Eight

Even though it was close, Noah ran into traffic, and Dell and Buddy were waiting for him when he walked into the restaurant. When he sat down, Dell was halfway through her drink and Noah wasn't sure if it was her first or second.

He smiled. "Sorry, I'm late."

Buddy reached across the table and shook his hand. "No worries, it gave my little ray of sunshine here a chance to have a drink."

Dell frowned at her husband, then smirked at Noah. "So, don't keep me in suspense, I can't sit here and have a polite meal with you without knowing what's going on."

Buddy waved the waiter over. "Can you get another one for my sweet wife here, and I'll take a beer." He looked at Noah. "What'll you have?"

Noah looked at the waiter. "Beer's fine." When the waiter left, Noah looked at Dell. "Okay, Dell, I'll give it to you straight. It seems our father at least wanted to make sure his kids were taken care of, so he set some money aside for you and Libby."

"How much? When do I get it?" She finished her drink and set the glass aside. "And what'd you and Marcus get?"

"This isn't about me and Marcus, it's about you."

"Fine, don't tell me. What'd he leave me?"

"First off, this is apart from whatever else you may get once I figure out what to do with the estate. This was put into a trust fund for you." He glanced at Buddy. "And you alone."

"How much?"

The waiter returned and set the drinks down, then rushed off, apparently picking up on the rising tension at the table.

"He set aside $500,000.00 for you."

Dell glared at him. "A half a million dollars out of fifty?" She drank half of her drink. "That's...insulting. And woefully inadequate."

"Well, there's a stipulation."

Buddy glanced at Dell, as she leaned forward and asked. "What stipulation?"

Noah watched Dell down the rest of her drink. "You won't have access to it until you've gone through AA and have been sober for a year."

Dell stared at him, and Buddy leaned back into his chair. It appeared as though he wished to melt into it and disappear.

Dell finally said, "You can't be serious."

"He set it up, not me. A year sober with documentation from a reliable source."

She looked at Buddy. "Get that waiter over here."

"Sweetie, maybe you shouldn't."

"Now."

Buddy sat up in his seat and waved at the waiter who was hiding near the kitchen, but reluctantly came to the table with a small smile.

"Can you bring the little missus another one, please?"

The waiter hurried off and Buddy retreated into his chair once more.

Dell squinted her eyes at Noah. "What if I refuse?"

"That's totally your option."

"Are you going to keep the rest of my inheritance away from me too? Put some ridiculous restrictions on it?"

"I don't know what I'm going to do, Dell."

The waiter returned and set Dell's drink in front of her. She immediately picked it up and drank half of it.

"I want Ms. Schmidt's contact information. I'm going to fight this."

"You'll need to get a lawyer, go to court. But I'm pretty sure it'll stick."

Dell finished her drink, then stood up. "Well, we'll see about that." She glared at Buddy, who got to his feet, then she returned her wrath to Noah. "And you, you little shit. If you try to screw me on what's owed me, I'll take your ass to court, too."

She stalked out of the restaurant with Buddy on her tail. He glanced over his shoulder at Noah before they both disappeared out the door.

Noah leaned back in his chair and took a sip of his beer. When the waiter approached, he gave the man a smile.

"Sorry about that, she's pissed at me, not you."

"She's…scary."

"She definitely is scary." He took another sip of beer. "Will you bring me the biggest burger you have on the menu, with everything on it and a side of fries."

The waiter smiled. "You got it, Sir."

Noah pulled out his phone and dialed Marcus. He was about to end the call when Marcus finally answered on the fifth ring.

"This better be damned important, Noah."

"Sorry, is this a bad time? You weren't doing something I don't want to know about, were you?"

"No, but I was in the middle of whipping up a bowl full of egg whites."

"Egg whites?"

"Yes, and now they're ruined, I need to start all over."

Noah heard him calling his cat. "That's probably not very good for Desmond."

"Oh, a little taste won't hurt Sir Desmond, now will it. That's a good kitty."

Noah took another sip of beer and waited for Marcus to finish spoiling his cat.

"Okay, so why'd you call me and interrupt my whisking?"

"I met up with Dell and Buddy."

"Well, my God, why didn't you lead with that? What happened? She exploded, right? Did she throw something? Did she punch Buddy? Come on, tell me, tell me."

"Are you done?"

Noah heard him take a breath before he said, "Yes, go ahead."

"Yes, she exploded. No, she didn't throw anything, though I'm pretty sure the waiter thought she was going to. And Buddy walked out of here unharmed. But who knows what happened to him once they got outside."

"So, what now?"

The waiter returned with Noah's burger and set it on the table along with some mustard, ketchup, and a fresh beer.

"The beer's on me," he whispered.

Noah gave him a smile, then returned his attention to Marcus. "Now, I'm going to eat this beautiful burger sitting in front of me and not think about Dell anymore. The ball's in her court. She'll either comply to the old man's wishes or she won't."

"Never going to happen."

Noah took a bite of his burger, chewed, and swallowed. "I believe you're right, brother. Which makes my job easier. If Dad didn't want to enable her, then I won't either. I'll scratch her right off the list."

"She'll take you to court."

"Oh, I look forward to it." He took another bite.

"Well, I guess that was worth interrupting my whisking for."

"You haven't heard the best part yet."

"What part? What are you talking about?" He took a moment. "Did you and Charlie—"

"No. Charlie's a whole other story. This is about Tiffany."

"I don't know if I can take all this intrigue. Hold on. I need to go sit on the couch." He was quiet while apparently navigating from the kitchen to the living room. "Oh, Roberto's here. I'm going to put you on speaker so he can hear all this delicious gossip.'

"Hi Roberto."

"Hey Noah. What's got Marcus all giddy."

"I met with Tiffany this morning." He paused for dramatic effect. "Seems there might be another Wainwright in the family in about eight months."

Marcus let out a yelp and Noah could hear Roberto calming him down.

When Marcus spoke, he was out of breath. "My God. She's pregnant?"

"So she says. Not sure if I believe her or not."

"Well, she can't fake it, so time will tell."

"I asked her for proof. And I need to figure out how to find out who the father is."

Roberto spoke up. "You should be able to get Atticus' medical records. At his age, a lot of things could leave him less than fertile. It'll at least give you a place to start. Other than a medical reason, you need to wait for the baby to arrive to do a DNA test."

"Thanks Roberto, that's very helpful advice."

Marcus said, "He's so smart. That's why I love him so much."

"You love me for my big brain?" Roberto asked.

"Well, not just your big brain."

Noah cleared his throat. "Okay, you too. Enough of that."

"Well, you enjoy your burger," Marcus said.

"I will. And you go back to your egg whites or whatever."

Chapter Twenty-Nine

Even though he was supposed to wait for Charlie to call him, Noah couldn't wait any longer. He used the excuse of having a key to give her and letting her know he was staying at the house for a few days.

He dialed. It rang six times, before going to voice mail.

"Hey so, yeah, I know I wasn't supposed to call you, but I wanted to let you know there's a key for you at the house. And also, I've decided to stay there for a few days. Not sure what I'm going to do in that big house all by myself, but I'll figure something out. Anyway, come by if you want. If I'm not there, Simms will have your key. Okay, bye."

He dropped his phone on the couch next to him. "Well, that was possibly the most pathetic phone message ever sent." He leaned back against the couch and closed his eyes.

After a few minutes, his phone rang, and he was happy, though a bit apprehensive, when he saw it was Charlie.

"Good evening."

"Noah. Why so formal?"

"Because I shouldn't have called, and I didn't know if it was going to make you more mad at me."

"I was never mad at you. I just thought we should end the evening before I did get mad at you." She was quiet for a moment. "So, you're going to stay at the house?"

"I thought I should take your advice and give the house a chance to prove to me it's not destined to be eternally evil."

"You should look on it as an adventure. There's so much to explore. You should take one room at a time and dig deep. Who knows what you might find."

"You make it sound almost fun."

"It will be fun. You just need to approach it with the right attitude."

"I'll try to do that." He got up from the couch and walked to the kitchen. "I don't suppose you'd like to do some exploring with me?"

"I'll think about it. When are you going to be there?"

"I've got two private lessons in the morning. Tennis lessons, at the club. Then I'll go there after." He felt the need to make that distinction.

"So, I can come get the key from you tomorrow afternoon?"

"Yes. Sounds good."

"Tiffany actually moved out?"

"She did. Of course I had to bribe her by offering to put her up in a hotel for a week, then help her get into an apartment."

"She's a manipulator, Noah. You need to watch out."

"I know what she is." He considered telling Charlie about the possible baby, but decided against it for now. He'd wait and see how she was tomorrow.

"Okay, be careful, and I'll see you tomorrow afternoon."

*****

Noah finished his second lesson, then headed to the house, arriving a little after noon. Martha was there again, and he sent her home early. Three days seemed excessive. How clean can the house be? But for now, he'd leave it alone. Today, though, he wanted the place to himself. Of course, there was no sending Simms home. This was his home. Noah felt a twinge of guilt at the thought of Simms losing not only his job but his home for the last forty years.

The bedroom he'd asked Martha to prepare was the one his mother always stayed in. It was a corner room with lots of light, and much preferred over the master bedroom that belonged to his father. Noah didn't think he'd ever want to sleep in the room Atticus died in.

He only brought one bag with some essentials and a couple changes of clothing. He could always get more from his condo, if he needed to. He didn't want to commit too much, too soon.

He sat on the edge of the freshly made bed and looked around. It was a little dainty for his taste, with an abundance of floral designs and pastel colors. He might have to change a few things. But the room itself was great and was bigger than his room at the condo. The view from the corner windows looking over the garden and the tennis court was certainly better than the condo view of his back patio and its ten square feet of dying grass.

Charlie said he should explore, so that's what he'd do. He went downstairs and headed for the library, the room that intrigued him the most. It was a room he and Marcus weren't allowed in as children, but he remembered peeking in the big double doors and seeing his father working at the desk. If there were treasures in the house, the library is where they'd be.

*****

He started with the desk and was still sitting in his father's big leather chair, when Charlie walked into the room, two hours later.

He leaned back in the chair and smiled at her. "I guess you don't need a key after all."

"The kitchen door was unlocked." She came up to the desk and looked at the piles of paper work. "What're you doing?"

"Well, I thought the desk would be a good place to start my exploring, but I got buried under all the paperwork in the desk. Seems my dad kept every letter he ever received, along with faxes, printed out emails, current invoices and bills."

"So, nothing interesting?"

Noah smiled. "Just these." He opened a drawer and retrieved a stack of letters bound in purple ribbon, and set them on the desk. "Apparently, he was sentimental, as well. At least he was thirty years ago." He looked at Charlie. "They're from my mother."

Charlie sat in a chair and picked up the stack of letters. "Oh my goodness. Did you read them?"

"No, I couldn't, not when I saw who they were from. It'd be like reading her diary."

"I wonder if she knows he still has them?"

Noah shrugged. "I don't know, but I'm going to give them to her. She can do what she wants with them."

"Did you find anything else juicy?"

"Well, my father owned racehorses, two of them, and a boat he keeps in Florida." He shuffled through some papers. "And it looks like he was planning to send Libby and an escort, aka her mother, to Europe when she graduated from high school next year."

"Did he send you to Europe when you graduated from high school?"

Noah shook his head. "No. He sent me a check for $200.00, though."

"How sweet."

"Marcus and I were the first two kids, he was still learning the ropes."

"Until you were eighteen?"

"He's a slow learner." He pulled a safety deposit key out of the drawer and held it up. "I wonder what he keeps in the bank."

She looked around the room. "Do you suppose there's a safe somewhere?"

"I thought about that. I know he has one. I just never knew where. So, my guess is in here or in his room."

Charlie smiled. "Can we look for it?"

"Yes. But I'm going to need a beer first."

She stood up. "I'll go get two beers and be right back." She stopped at the door. "Don't start without me."

Noah waited for her, but spent the time looking around the room and trying to figure out where it might be. He got up when she came back in the room and handed him a beer.

She took a sip of her beer, then looked around. "So, what do you think?"

"The most obvious would be behind a picture, right? I've never had a safe, so I'm just going by books and movies."

"Let's start there then."

They checked behind every picture and tried to find a hidden compartment in the massive bookcase. Thirty minutes later, they concurred there wasn't a safe in the library.

Charlie plopped down in a chair. "Do you think it's in the bedroom, then?"

Noah sat behind the desk. "Maybe, but I'm not ready to go exploring in there, yet."

"Of course. So you're not sleeping in that room?"

"No, I'm going to use my mom's room. The one on the corner with all the windows."

"Next to the dumb waiter. I love that room." She drank some beer. "And if you get hungry in the middle of the night, you can hop in the dumb waiter to get to the kitchen."

Noah shook his head. "That's probably not going to happen." He started straightening piles of papers and returning them to the desk. "You probably spent more time in this house than I did as a kid."

"I'd hang out with my dad once a month or so. So, I guess I did. That's kind of sad, really."

Noah shrugged. "Well, we lived 3000 miles away. So, a few weeks during the summer until I turned eighteen."

"Weird we only crossed paths that last summer."

"Your dad was probably trying to keep you away from the two wild Wainwright boys. Or, one, I guess. Marcus was never wild. I think your dad liked him."

She tilted her head at him. "Dad never once said anything bad about either of you. I think he felt sorry for you, because he knew what Atticus was like, but he didn't dislike you."

"Hmm, well good. Because I liked him. He was always nice to me." He cleared the desk of the last stack of papers, then looked at Charlie. "I wonder if it still works?"

"If what still works?"

"The dumb waiter."

"Why wouldn't it?"

"Because it probably hasn't been used since we rode on it twelve years ago."

"Things don't stop working just because they don't get used." She stood up and tugged on his arm.

He stood up. "So use it or lose it is just a myth?"

"Come on. Let's go check it out."

During the summer they spent together, they thoroughly explored the house. And one of their finds was a dumb waiter installed at the end of the hall and covered up with a painting. Finding themselves alone one day, they had to find out if it still worked. With Noah and Charlie upstairs and Marcus at the bottom in the kitchen, they sent it up and down a few times filled with odd objects of varying weight to make sure it worked. On the final trip down, Charlie and Noah got in it together and rode it down, surprising Marcus. That's when they got caught by Simms and were sent outside.

At the end of the hall, Noah took down the picture. The door to the dumb waiter was still there. He opened it and looked down the shaft. The cables all seemed to be intact. He pushed the button, and with a creak and a groan, the small cargo elevator started to rise.

When it reached them Charlie stood back. "Okay, you first."

"Why me? You go first."

"Because it's your house."

"That's a terrible reason. Why don't we just send down a book or something."

She shook her head at him. "What's the fun in that?" She nudge his shoulder. "But if you're too scared?" She started to walk away down the hall.

"Wait, hold on." He studied the space for a moment. "Fine, I'll go." He pushed on the bottom of it a couple times, then gingerly climbed inside. He looked out at her. "There's room for two." He held a hand out to her.

"Not going to happen, mister."

"You didn't have a problem riding in it with me the last time."

"Number one, we were stupid kids, and B, you weren't…the flinger of lonely women back then." She gave him a wave, then pushed the button.

He let out a yelp, and disappeared.

On the way down, he realized he had no idea what was waiting for him at the other end. It very well could've been sealed off. He wondered how long it'd take her to bring him back up if that was the case. He wasn't claustrophobic, but it was a very small space.

He hit the bottom and pushed on the door. To his relief it swung open. Charlie was waiting for him on the other side.

"What the hell?"

"I wasn't about to get in that thing."

She offered a hand to him, but he ignored it and climbed out by himself. "I know I broke your heart and all, but that was just mean."

"I'm sorry. I'll make it up to you with something delicious to eat."

"Like what?"

"Cold cuts, salad, a fruit platter. Basically whatever I can find in the refrigerator."

"Any of that works for me. I'll eat anything."

"Okay." She went to the refrigerator and took out a beer. "Start with this. Unless you want me to go liberate an expensive bottle of wine."

He took the beer from her. "No, this is perfect." He watched her set up a plate with slices of ham, turkey, salami, and three types of cheese. She then dished up some salad from a bigger container and put it next to the meat. She stood back and looked at it, then glanced at him.

"How's that?"

"Perfect."

She set it down in front of him, with a fork and a napkin. She then sat down on a stool across from him.

He picked up a piece of turkey and a slice of cheese and rolled them together before taking a bite.

"So, I got some interesting news yesterday about Tiffany."

"What's that?"

"She claims she's pregnant."

Charlie laughed. "You can't believe her. They were married for like a minute. And he was theoretically sick most of that time."

Noah shrugged. "I told her I needed proof."

"For sure. But even if she is, it doesn't mean it's Atticus' baby."

"I thought it was wrong when he fathered Libby at fifty-three. Of course now, that doesn't seem that old, but to a twelve-year-old, it was ancient."

"But seventy is pushing it."

"Definitely. Which leads me to believe she's lying."

Charlie studied the floor for a moment, then glanced at Noah. "At his age, if he did, you know. He probably needed some…pharmaceutical help."

Noah stood up. "Oh, Jesus. I didn't need that image in my head."

"Sorry."

He sat back down and sighed. "Now I need to go check his bathroom. It wouldn't be proof of anything, other than…" He moaned. "I really hate all this."

Charlie stood up. "I'll do it."

He looked at her.

"Seriously. I'll go look." She headed out of the library without waiting for Noah to either agree or stop her.

When she returned in fifteen minutes, Noah was still at the counter, but his plate was empty. She went to the stool across from him and sat down. With a shrug, she said, "No luck. But, he could've hid it in his sock drawer, which, I'm not going to go through."

Noah picked up his cell phone and punched in a number.

"Dr. Beals?"

"Yes."

"This is Noah Wainwright."

"Of course, what can I do for you?"

"I had a quick question about my father's medication. Not the red pills. More interested in little blue pills."

"Ah, yes."

"Did you prescribe them to him?"

"Umm."

"It's a little late to worry about doctor patient privilege. Seeing as he's dead."

Noah heard him sigh. "Yes, I refilled his prescription about three months ago."

"Thank you, Dr. Beals."

Noah ended the call and looked at Charlie. "So gross."

Chapter Thirty

Noah was waiting for Buddy at the club snack bar. He got a call from his brother-in-law that morning, something that had never happened before, not without Dell being present. But Buddy insisted it was urgent, so Noah arranged to meet him at the club after his last lesson. It was 2:00 and Buddy was late.

When someone came up behind him and squeezed his shoulders, he looked back to find a smiling Missy.

She sat in the chair across from him. "Hi stranger."

"Missy. How're you?"

She leaned forward. "Missing my private lessons."

"We have a new pro. Started a few days ago." He leaned towards her and spoke quietly. "He's younger and better looking, and I've heard he's given a private lesson or two."

She patted his hand. "That's impossible."

"That he doesn't give private lessons?"

"No, that he's better looking than you."

He pulled his hand away and sat back. "Okay, not better looking, but he's more than willing to take the torch from me."

"Maybe you could introduce us."

"I'll do better than that. I'll ask him to take your lesson tomorrow morning."

"You're too good to me."

"It's the least I can do."

He spotted Buddy at the door, looking a bit lost. "Oh, there's my date."

Missy looked over her shoulder. "Who's that?"

"My brother-in-law." Noah stood up and waved at him.

"Are you going to introduce me?"

"Trust me, you don't want to meet Buddy."

She shrugged and patted his cheek before standing up and walking off towards the order counter.

Buddy crossed the room and sat opposite Noah. "Who was that?"

"One of my clients."

Buddy winked. "One of your special clients?"

"You said it was urgent."

"Oh, right, thanks for meeting me." Buddy looked around. "Can I get a beer or something?"

"It's a tennis club, a juice bar, no alcohol." Noah took a sip of his mixed fruit smoothie. "I'll buy you a smoothie, though."

Buddy shook his head. "No, thanks. That sounds disgusting."

Noah gave him a minute before he asked, "So, what's up? You look like you're about to jump out of your skin." Buddy was possibly the most laid back person Noah had ever met, but today he was sweaty and fidgety. Something was up.

Buddy spoke quietly. "I have something to tell you." He looked around the room again as though he was being listened to. "And I don't want you to judge me. It's not like I've done this before. It was one time, and well, I was tricked. And you're the last person who should judge someone for something like this."

Noah tried to remain patient. "What'd you do? I promise I'll reserve judgement."

Buddy rested his clasped hands on the table and leaned forward. "It's about Tiffany. I met her, before that weekend."

"But you pretended you hadn't."

"I had to. She told me to."

Noah pushed his drink aside and handed Buddy the napkin it'd been sitting on. "Just tell me what happened."

Buddy patted his forehead with the napkin, then folded it in half and set it on the table. "She showed up at my work one day, introduced herself, and asked me to go to lunch with her. We'd heard about her, but hadn't seen her. She was…well, you know. Could you say no to her?"

"What happened at lunch?"

He unclasped his hands and tapped the table with his fingertips, then fidgeted with his shirt before going on. "We just talked. Nothing happened."

Noah was having trouble staying patient. "So…?"

Buddy looked around the room again. "It was the next day when she showed up after work and wanted me to come have a drink with her…at the bar…at the Plaza." He picked up the napkin again, folded it several times, then unfolded it and set it down.

Noah leaned back in his chair and crossed his arms over his chest. "Did you make a fool of yourself, Buddy?"

"No, it wasn't me. It was her. She was all over me."

Noah found that hard to believe. "Did you sleep with her, Buddy?"

Buddy rubbed his face and the back of his neck, then leaned forward again. "She wanted me to do something for her."

Now it was getting more interesting. Noah sat up straight in his chair. "What'd she want you to do?"

Buddy leaned halfway across the table and whispered. "She wanted me to kill Atticus."

Noah put a hand on Buddy's arm and gripped it tighter than he should. "What did you do?"

He pulled away from Noah. "I didn't kill him." He looked at the table. "But I told her I would, so she'd, you know."

"She offered to sleep with you in exchange for killing my father?" He said it a little too loud and got a look from the lady at the table next to them.

Buddy shushed him. "That and $50,000.00," he whispered.

Noah leaned back in his chair again and rubbed his chin. "Good God." This was proof Tiffany was responsible for Atticus' death.

He looked closely at Buddy. "You're not lying about this?"

"No, I swear."

"Did she pay you, aside from the sex?"

"No. She was going to pay me afterwards. After…you know…I killed him. But after the sex, I told her I couldn't do it." He rubbed his arm where Noah had squeezed it. "Man, was she pissed."

Noah couldn't help but smile. "Sorry. I can picture her face when she found out she had sex with you for no reason."

"Hey."

Noah needed to find out just how much Buddy knew. "So, how'd she want you to do it?"

Buddy shrugged. "She never said. We didn't get that far into the conversation once I told her I wouldn't do it. She yelled at me for a while, then told me to leave."

"So, why'd she trust you not to say anything?"

"Because she said she'd tell Dell I came on to her. She knew that'd keep me from talking."

"Why are you telling me now? You know Dell's going to find out." The whole family was going to find out, along with the whole world, or at least anyone who cared about the death of Atticus Wainwright III.

"Well, I was afraid for a while, because Dell's going to for sure kill me. But, once Atticus turned up dead, I had to say something. Because she obviously found someone else to do it for her."

Noah reached for his arm again and patted it. "Buddy, I'm proud of you. Not for caving and having sex with her, but for coming forward now and doing the right thing despite the consequences. Even though you waited a week to do it. And probably should've said something when she tried to hire you. Atticus might be alive right now."

This was now the second person who could've intervened.

Buddy studied him for a moment. "I could've saved his life. Oh God, I'm partially responsible. I never thought she'd actually go through with it. How many people could she possibly know who'd even consider doing that for her?"

"It only took one to say yes."

"So, what now?"

"So now we call Detective Reece."

"Who's Detective Reece?"

"We already knew someone poisoned my father. And we were pretty sure it was Tiffany. This little confession of yours, gives them the proof they need to question her."

"Mmm." He sighed. "Do you think there's any chance Dell won't find out?"

Noah shook his head. "Not a chance in hell, Buddy." He pulled out his cell phone.

"You're going to call him right now?"

"Yes, before you change your mind."

Noah dialed the detective and was glad he answered. He wasn't sure how long Buddy would be so cooperative. He told Reece he had some explosive new evidence, and he needed to come right away.

While they waited for Reece, Buddy looked worried. "So, am I going to be in trouble. I didn't do anything."

"Well, you should've come forward right away, but no, I don't think there's anything they can charge you with, except maybe stupidity."

Buddy looked at him for a moment. "I bet you couldn't resist her if she came onto you."

"She was married to my father. She could've crawled into my bed naked and I would've told her to take a hike."

"Yeah, sure. Like I believe that."

Noah took a sip of his melted smoothie. "So, when was this coup d'un soir?"

"The what?"

"When did you sleep with Tiffany?"

Buddy thought for a moment. "About two months ago."

Chapter Thirty-One

By the time Detective Reece showed up fifteen minutes later, Buddy was a wreck. Noah had to convince him to stay twice. The second time, he restrained him with an arm around his shoulder and a quiet, "Sit the hell down, Buddy."

Reece dragged a third chair to the table and sat down. "So, gentlemen, what's up?"

Buddy didn't seem capable of talking, so Noah spoke for him. "Buddy here, just told me Tiffany tried to hire him to kill my father."

Reece put his hand up. "Hold up." He studied Buddy for a moment. "Is this true?"

Buddy nodded.

The detective stood up and took hold of Buddy's arm. "Let's go to the station and get this all down on paper. I Don't want to make any mistakes or overlook anything."

Buddy looked up at him. "Are you arresting me?"

"No, that's not what this is."

Buddy looked at Noah, who tried to give him a reassuring smile. "It's okay, you're doing the right thing. Detective Reece will take care of you." He looked at the detective. "Do you need me for this?"

"Not yet. But stay available and don't talk to anyone about this. We don't want to give Tiffany a heads up."

As Buddy stood, his phone went off. He pulled it out of his pocket and turned white when he saw who the caller was. "It's her?"

"Tiffany?" Noah asked.

"No, Dell." He looked at Reece. "If I don't answer it, she'll go nuts."

"If you answer it in the state you're in, she'll know something's up." Noah held out his hand. Buddy hesitated a moment before handing him the phone. "Dell."

"Who is this?"

"It's Noah. I took Buddy to lunch, and he's got a touch of food poisoning. He's in the bathroom right now...well, you know. Not pretty."

"Where are you? Should I come down?"

"No, I got this. I think he'd be a bit embarrassed. I'll take care of him."

"Okay, whatever." She was quiet for a moment. "Since when do you and he get lunch?"

"Thought it was about time we did some brother-n-law bonding."

"Fine. Weird, but fine."

"I'll send him home soon."

Buddy looked at Noah. "There's no way she bought that."

Noah shrugged. "She seemed to."

Detective Reece left with Buddy in tow, and Noah hoped his brother-in-law would continue to be cooperative. He almost wished he insisted on going with him, but was also relieved he didn't have to.

He took out his phone and sent a text to Marcus.

Humongous break in the case. Call me when you get home tonight.

He stashed his phone and took a sip of his now warm smoothie. He frowned and pushed it aside. When a new one was set on the table in front of him, he looked up to see a smiling Missy.

She sat down. "You want to tell me what that was all about?"

Noah shook his head. "You wouldn't believe it if I did. And I really don't want to think about it anymore." He rubbed his face, took a drink, then held the glass up and looked at it. "What'd you put in this?" There was something in the mix besides strawberries and bananas.

She smiled. "Well, for the right people, under the right circumstances, you can get a little extra boost added."

"But what is it?" He took another sip and realized what it was. He leaned towards her and whispered. "Vodka?"

She nodded. "You looked like you could use it."

He took another sip. "Well, I wish it'd fix everything."

"It's not meant to fix everything, it's just meant to fix this moment right now." She stroked his hand with her pinky finger, then looked around the room. "So, what else can I do for you?"

Noah shook his head. "Missy, Missy, Missy. What am I going to do with you?"

She smiled. "You know exactly what to do with me. You always have."

He rubbed his face, then took another drink. "I'm going to finish this smoothie, then I'm going to go home." He checked his watch. "Probably be there in about thirty minutes."

She stood up. "Enjoy your drink, Noah."

He watched her leave. He wanted to forget everything for a couple hours. Was that so bad? He finished his drink, then headed for his car. He made it to the condo in twenty minutes.

Ten minutes later, there was a knock on his door. He opened it and stepped aside to let Missy in. She had her arms around his neck before he got the door closed.

"So, let's go distract you for a while."

Missy distracted him for quite a while, and it was dark when he stumbled out of bed and headed to the kitchen to get something to drink. He grabbed a bottle of water, then picked up his phone, which he discarded on the table along with his keys and his jacket. He checked his text messages.

"Oh shit."

There were ten texts from Marcus, starting out curious and ending with threats of death and dismemberment if Noah didn't answer him. The last message said,

I'm on my way over.

Noah checked the time, and said, "Crap," as he headed for the bedroom to find his pants. As he returned to the living room, there was a knock on the door, an extremely loud and urgent, knock.

Noah opened the door and Marcus burst into the room. "What the hell, Noah? I sent you twenty text messages."

Noah didn't dare correct him on the number of messages sent. "I was in the bedroom and I didn't have my phone with me. And how'd you know I was here and not at the house?"

"I took a chance. But believe me, I would've driven up to the house if you weren't here. You were in the bedroom all evening?" He went and plopped down on the couch. Then looked at Noah, who saw realization cross his face. "You weren't *alone* in the bedroom."

Noah shook his head.

Marcus glanced towards the closed door and whispered. "She's still in there?"

Noah nodded.

Marcus' eyes grew wide, and he whispered again. "Is it Charlie?"

Noah went to the couch and sat next to Marcus. "No. It's not Charlie."

Marcus squinted at him. "I thought you gave up the gigolo profession."

Noah stood up. "And I told you that's not what I am." He took a deep breath. "I…couldn't help myself. These last few days… and then today. I needed something to take my mind off for a few hours."

"Did it work?"

"Yes. Quite well, actually."

"Then no judgement here. God knows you needed a break." He gave him a little smile. "But if Charlie calls, don't answer the phone."

"Right, gotcha." He sat in the chair. "So, you ready for the biggest scoop of the year?"

"Bigger than the old man naming you executor of his estate?"

"Um… close tie."

Marcus leaned forward. "So, tell me, damn it."

"I had lunch with Buddy." He waited for that information to sink in, then continued. "Guess who had sex with Tiffany besides our father?"

"Well, possibly quite a few men, but if you're about to tell me Buddy, I'm saying no way in hell."

Noah nodded. "He swears it's true."

"Over the weekend?"

"No, but oh brother, there's so much more." He leaned back and crossed his legs. "You ready for this?"

"I swear, Noah."

"Okay, Tiffany offered Buddy sex and $50,000.00 to kill our father."

Marcus sat for a moment as if frozen in time, then jumped to his feet and shouted, "Shut the front door."

Noah stood and shushed him as he glanced towards the bedroom.

Marcus took a turn around the room then looked at Noah. "Did he do it?"

"No, of course not, this is Buddy we're talking about. He took the sex, then begged off on the rest."

Marcus started laughing and got shushed again. He held up his hands. "Sorry, I can just picture Tiffany's face when she realized she had sex with him for no reason."

Noah started laughing too. "Okay, quiet. I don't want to wake up my guest."

Marcus sat back down. "So, Tiffany really did it. She killed him or had him killed."

"She probably found someone else to do it for her."

"The little bitch. Too bad she's going to spend the next twenty or so years in prison."

Noah leaned forward in his chair. "So, I saved the best part for last." He stood up.

"Where're you going?"

"Water, I'll be right back."

When Noah returned, he stopped dead in his tracks when he saw Missy, naked as the day she was born, standing behind Marcus, who was turned around and smiling at her.

Missy, totally comfortable in her nakedness, smiled and said, "I'm so sorry, I didn't know you had company."

Marcus stood up and glanced at Noah, still frozen in place. "Since my brother is doing a perfect imitation of a deer caught in the headlights of a speeding car, I'll introduce myself." He offered his hand to Missy. "I'm Marcus."

She took his hand. "Noah's brother. How nice to meet you."

Noah could finally move, and he grabbed a throw off the end of the couch and wrapped it around Missy's shoulders. "Go back to bed, Missy. I'll be in soon."

"Okay, handsome." She wrapped herself in the blanket and headed to the bedroom.

When the door closed behind her, Noah looked at Marcus who was grinning at him.

They both sat and Noah said, "Please stop."

"My whole interpretation of your lifestyle just changed. All this time I thought you were *stchupping* sexagenarians."

"Okay, *shiksa*, you can get in trouble for cultural appropriation these days."

"But now I see you're...enjoying the company of...a little bit older, but very attractive women, who may be unhappily married, but will never walk away from the money. Aka, unavailable, no commitment needed, and safe."

"You thought I was *stchupping* sexagenarians? I'm very insulted by that."

"Our father has totally scared you off from embarking on a committed relationship."

"This whole new psychiatric analyzing of me has got to stop."

Marcus leaned forward in his seat. "Noah, this is devastating to me. I just might cry."

"If you start crying, I'm going to bed and you can see yourself out."

Marcus held his arms out. "How about a hug, then?"

"No."

Marcus leaned back in his chair and nodded his head towards the bedroom door. "So, how old is she?"

Noah shrugged. "Forty something."

"Well, she's exquisite."

"Her husband's money well spent."

Marcus leaned forward again. "So, you left me hanging, you saved the best part for last... How is there anything better than what you've already told me. Buddy had sex with a beautiful woman and Dad's newest wife killed him for his money."

Noah smiled. "Buddy had sex with Tiffany about *two* months ago."

"Jesus, Mary, and Joseph, I didn't think the little bastard was capable of procreating."

*****

Marcus stayed another half hour, then left Noah to go get distracted again if that was his desire. Noah finished his water bottle, then went back into the bedroom. He could tell Missy was asleep by her steady breathing, so he eased his way into the bed, trying not to wake her.

She let out a tiny moan, then mumbled something Noah didn't understand. He laid next to her, and she turned onto her side and threw an arm across his chest.

He should've been tired, but he wasn't. The distraction was good while it lasted, but now events of the last week bounced around his head. He stared at the ceiling and wished Missy were awake. He didn't want another round of sex, he wanted to talk. But if he was honest with himself, it wasn't Missy he wanted to talk to. It was Charlie. Charlie who wanted to be friends. Charlie, who he'd probably never have sleepy middle of the night conversations with.

He heard a change in Missy's breathing and he knew she was awake. She started moving her hand down his stomach, but he put his hand on hers and stopped her.

"Can I ask you something?"

"Sure, anything."

"Did you ever love Mr. Steinberger?"

"Of course. I still do."

He looked at her. "Then why are you here with me?"

She was quiet for a moment before she answered him. "I was twenty-two when I married my husband, and he was forty-nine. Like your father, his type, is younger women. When I hit thirty, I could tell he was losing interest. I knew he still loved me, but I didn't really interest him physically anymore. So, before he was tempted to wander, we sat down and made a pact, with discretion being at the top of the list."

"So, technically, you're not cheating on him, and I'm not the rogue sleeping with his wife."

She kissed him on the cheek. "This is a blame-free relationship. No strings, no guilt."

He sighed. As much as he wanted that to make him feel better about his lifestyle choices, it didn't. Marcus' words bounced around inside his head. *Unavailable, no commitment needed, and safe.*

She rubbed a hand along his forehead. "But that answer didn't remove the furrow from your handsome brow." She sat up and wrapped a blanket around her shoulders. "The question you really want an answer to is why you're here with me?"

Chapter Thirty-Two

When Noah woke up, Missy was gone. He couldn't remember any other time when she snuck out without waking him. But he was glad to find himself alone. He checked his watch and was surprised to find it was nearly ten. He was due at the club in an hour for Missy's lesson. He reached for his phone and called the new pro. Michael would jump at the chance to take on one of Noah's clients.

Last night was nice, and he needed the break from his current reality, but he needed to put a stop to it. Not just Missy, but anyone else as well. Missy was right. He didn't know how to answer her question. And until he did, he'd go to bed alone for a while.

He had a cancelation on one of his afternoon appointments, and he rescheduled the other one, so he had a free day ahead of him. The only decision to make was whether to stay at the condo or go back to the house. It was nice being home, and he wondered if his father's house would ever feel like home to him. Maybe if it wasn't so big and empty. Perhaps his father kept Simms on all these years to have another body in the house. He dismissed the thought. Atticus Wainwright's favorite person to be with was himself.

After another thirty minutes of contemplation, which consisted mostly of staring at the wall, he decided to get himself showered and shaved and go spend another afternoon and evening at the house.

*****

Noah was lounging by the pool. He came intending to swim laps again, but hadn't yet convinced himself to get off the chaise and get into the water. When he heard someone come up behind him, he glanced back to see Charlie approaching.

"Enjoying the perks of the Wainwright Manor, I see." Charlie sat in a chair next to the chaise.

Noah linked his fingers behind his head and crossed his ankles. "It's not the community pool at my condo, but it'll do. I kinda miss the screaming kids, though."

She smiled at him. "Are you not a kid, guy?"

"A kid guy? Oh, no. I don't have a problem with kids. Haven't been around them much." He sat up straighter on the chaise. "Speaking of kids, guess who may be in the running for Tiffany's baby daddy."

She slid her chair closer. "What'd you find out?"

Even though Reece told him not to talk to anyone about the new development, he'd told Marcus, which meant Roberto knew too, and soon, Charlie would be in on it, as well. He told her the whole story, without too many embellishments, and she remained quiet aside from a gasp here and there.

When he finished he asked, "So, what do you think about that?"

"Wow, you had lunch with Buddy?"

"What?"

She laughed. "I'm kidding. That's an unbelievable story."

"True, none the less."

She reached for his arm. "I'm sorry. I know you wanted to get to the bottom of this, but it's quite shocking. Are you okay?"

"I am. Thanks for asking."

"So, what happens now?"

"I got a quick call from Reece this morning. He said he'd get into it more with me tomorrow after they put together a plan. And in the meantime, keep it to myself."

"Whoops."

"Yeah, whoops times three. I think what bothers me the most, is I offered to pay to put her up in the hotel for a week."

"Well, at least you know where she is."

Noah sat up, putting his legs on either side of the chaise. He removed his t-shirt, then stood up. "I'm going to swim a few laps, then you're going to have some of my famous spaghetti. The sauce has been cooking all afternoon. Sound good?"

She took a moment to think about it. "Sounds excellent."

He went to the edge of the pool and dove in.

*****

Charlie watched as Noah swam his laps. *It'd be a lot easier to remain in the friend zone if you weren't so damn good looking.* When they spent the summer together twelve years ago, she had the biggest crush on him, but as hard as she tried, she couldn't get him to show any interest beyond friends. There were several moments when she thought something was going to happen, but he always seemed to check himself and back off. She never figured out whether it was because he didn't really like her beyond friendship, or whether he was afraid of what it'd mean if he let himself go there.

Now that they were adults, she was even more confused. He seemed to be a bit lost and stuck in a rut. She wasn't sure if she wanted to take on a project relationship. That's what it'd be. Something she'd have to work at, along with a lot of backtracking from him. She knew that, yet she was tempted. There was something about him beyond his attractiveness. But then there was the whole older woman fixation he had going on. *What was that all about?*

He came up to the edge of the pool and smiled at her, which didn't help her self-reflection at all. Then he pushed himself up out of the water and she looked away to prevent him from seeing what she was thinking.

Apparently, she didn't look away soon enough. He laughed. "I think you just forgot for a second you wanted to keep me in the friend zone."

She tried to fain surprise. "What're you talking about?"

He grabbed his towel and dried off.

She rolled her eyes. "Okay, fine. You aren't *too* bad to look at. But we both already knew that. And just because I admire a…piece of…art, doesn't mean I'm going to put in a bid on it." She shook her head and smiled. "Okay, I know, that was a terrible metaphor. Stop grinning at me and put on your shirt."

He dropped the towel on the end of the chaise, then put on his t-shirt. "I think it's only fair I get to see your…artwork now."

"Can we please end this conversation? And…never going to happen."

He sighed. "So, spaghetti?"

"Please. Anything to move onto a new subject."

They headed for the house and he glanced at her. "So, you think I'm a piece of art, huh?"

She swung an arm at him and hit him in the shoulder. "Shut up."

When they went in through the kitchen entrance, Noah said, "Okay, I'm going to go upstairs and get dressed. Will you go to the wine cellar and pick out a nice wine to go with our spaghetti?"

She breathed deep. "My gosh, that smells wonderful. I'd love to pick out the perfect wine."

"Thanks and thanks." He headed upstairs, taking two steps at a time. When he got to the top he looked down to find her watching him and he called to her. "I may never have to go to the gym again."

*****

He took a quick shower to rinse off the chlorine and as he was getting dressed, his phone rang. If it hadn't been Marcus, he wouldn't have answered it.

"I'm about to have dinner with Charlie, so make it quick."

"Hello, Noah. Yes, I'm fine, how are you?"

"Okay, blah, blah, I'm fine, you're fine. What's up?"

"You're having dinner with Charlie? Where at?"

"At the house. Why are you calling?"

Marcus sighed into the phone. "I'm headed in to work, but I wanted to let you know I ran into Laura today."

"Where?"

"At that coffee place on Third. She says if you don't call her soon, she's going to come knocking on your door."

Noah sat on the edge of the bed. "I'll call her tomorrow."

"Thank you. Now, is this dinner still a friend dinner?"

"Yes, Marcus. But maybe once she tastes my spaghetti, she'll change her mind."

"Your spaghetti is pretty damn good. Well, good luck with that. I'm off to serve the masses."

"I'll talk to you tomorrow."

Noah headed downstairs and found Charlie opening the wine. She had two glasses ready to be filled and smiled at him when he came into the kitchen. He went to the stove and tasted the sauce. Then filled a large pot with water for the pasta. He set it to heat, then went to sit at the counter across from Charlie.

"Should we eat in the dining room?"

She shook her head. "This is cozier."

"You really do love my kitchen."

When the water started boiling, Noah put the pasta into the pot, and put a loaf of French bread into the oven to warm.

He glanced over his shoulder at Charlie. "I'm not a baker. This is from that place on Stanford."

"Stephan's? I love that place. They have the best bagels."

Noah held up a plastic bag with six bagels in it. "I know."

When the pasta was ready, Noah served up two plates and set one in front of Charlie.

"Okay, I know you're a professional and all, but I think you're going to like this." He held up his wine glass in a toast. "To old friends."

Charlie took a drink, then took a bite of her spaghetti as Noah watched her. She closed her eyes for a moment and savored the taste. When she opened them, she smiled.

"Wow. Fantastic." She took another bite. "What is that…what am I tasting?"

"That'd be the Noah Wainwright secret ingredient."

"Which is?"

"It wouldn't be a secret if I told you." He cut into the bread and handed her a slice. "But, if you guess it, I'll tell you."

She took several more bites, drank some wine, and took one more taste. She studied him for a moment. "It's alcohol. But not wine."

He smiled and took a bite of bread dipped in some sauce.

"Whiskey?" she asked.

"Damn, you're good."

"How'd you come up with that?"

"Well, it'd be really cool if I could tell you it was my grandmother's recipe passed down, but I never met my grandmother, and my mom didn't cook."

"So, it's a Noah Wainwright original recipe?"

"Yes, but totally accidental. I was making sauce while I was drinking, and it was an embarrassing incident, I'm not going to tell you about, but the whiskey ended up in the sauce and *Voilà*."

"Now you need to tell me the embarrassing incident."

Noah shook his head and smiled. "Not going to happen."

They both cleaned their plates, and Noah took them to the sink. He returned to the counter as Charlie poured the last two glasses of wine.

She took a sip, then looked at him for a long moment. "So, I believe I've changed my mind."

"About?"

"The friend thing."

Noah straightened in his seat. "Seriously." He took a moment. "Really?"

Charlie shook her head. "No."

"What? I'm very confused."

"I haven't changed my mind because of the look on your face. Pure panic. It's exactly what I thought was going to happen."

Noah stood up. "What're you talking about? I'm not panicked." He took a few steps back from the counter. "And that was really cruel of you. Why would you do that to me?"

Charlie stood up too. "I wanted to call your bluff," she said quietly.

Noah sighed. "You thought I was just a dog after a bone, and once I got it, I wouldn't know what to do with it?"

"Something like that," she whispered as she reached out for him. "It was stupid and wrong. I'm sorry."

He pulled his arm away from her touch. "If you saw any doubt cross my face, it was a lack of confidence. The fear I wasn't good enough for you. I guess I didn't need to worry about that." He headed for the door. "Lock the door when you leave, please."

He went up to his room and closed the door, then sat on the bed and rubbed his face. He'd kill for a cigarette right about now. He checked his watch. Too early to call Marcus, his go to person when he was feeling overwhelmed and frustrated beyond reason. *Why would she tease me like that?* He thought she'd be the last person to play games. "I want to be more than friends. Oh, never mind, I was just kidding. I wanted to see how you'd react. Jesus."

He laid on the bed. Was he over reacting? Probably. But for now, he wanted to hold on to his anger. He expected more from her. He pulled his phone out of his pocket and stared at it for a moment, before he made a call. The voice on the other end was a welcome sound.

"Hey handsome, I didn't think I'd be hearing from you again. At least away from the club."

"Hi, Missy. It's not that kind of call." He sat up, arranged the pillows, then leaned against them as he put his feet up on the bed. "I wanted to talk with the one woman in my life who has never tried to manipulate me."

"Hold on a second." She was quiet for a few moments before she came back on. "Okay, I'm out on my patio. How can I help?"

"I don't even know where to begin. So much has happened in such a short period of time. I feel like I'm holding up this crumbling brick wall, and if part of it starts to go, I won't be able to stop the whole thing from falling."

"Your father's death."

"That's part of it. That's definitely what started everything snowballing out of control. I was happy, dammit. In my unmotivated, uninspired life. Why'd he have to die and ruin everything? And why am I mourning him? I never loved him, and he never loved me."

"I'm so sorry, Noah, that you didn't have a father growing up." She took a moment. "And I think that's what you're mourning. The idea of a father and the fact you never had one."

"Maybe. Do you have any children, Missy?"

"I do. I have a daughter who started college this year."

"Is Mr. Steinberger a good father?"

"Yes, he is."

"Then she's a lucky girl."

"Are you sure you don't want me to come over? You sound like you could use some distraction."

"It's tempting, but no. I made a vow."

"Of celibacy?"

He laughed. "No. I just need to figure out what I really want."

"Good for you. So, are you having problems with that woman who isn't a girlfriend yet?"

Noah sat up and took off his shoes, then unbuckled his belt and let his pants drop to the floor. He laid back on the bed. "I'm not sure she's who I thought she was. Or maybe I'm not who she thought I was. It's all very confusing."

"Most love stories are."

"I'm not sure this is a love story, or ever will be."

"Give it time. If she's the one, it'll work out."

He sighed. "I'm not sure I want it to."

"If you didn't, you wouldn't be telling me about her."

"Missy, will you and Mr. Steinberger adopt me?"

She laughed. "Oh my, that'd be quite awkward, wouldn't it?"

He smiled. "Scandalous."

Chapter Thirty-Three

After Noah finished his conversation with Missy, he stared at the ceiling and continued to sulk. She helped him a bit, but left him with yet another question to answer. Was this thing with Charlie the beginning of a love story? He had trouble believing it. She certainly didn't seem willing to go down that road, and he was having his doubts at this point.

When he heard a light tap on his door, he knew it could only be one person. He wondered if he ignored her, if she'd go away. Of course, that'd be incredibly rude of him. He pulled a fleece throw over his lower half and said, "Yes?"

"It's me, can I come in?"

Of course it's you. Who else would it be? "Sure."

She opened the door a couple of inches and peered in. "Are you sure?"

He waved her in. "Of course." He frowned at her. At least she looked guilty as she came in and moved towards the end of the bed.

He tilted his head and said, "So, what's up?"

"I wanted to apologize. You're right, that was mean of me and uncalled for."

He relaxed his clenched jaw, but wasn't quite ready to let her off the hook.

She continued. "After some self-reflection, I believe the fear I thought I saw on your face, was actually a reflection of what I was feeling. That summer we spent together. I thought you were very cute, and you and Marcus were so funny and a blast to be with. It was probably the best summer I ever had. And I spent most of it hoping you'd reciprocate the crush I had on you. Well, that didn't happen. Which was fine, since you went back to California. It would've been a doomed relationship, anyway." She ventured another step closer to the end of the bed and put her hands on the black metal bed frame that curled up and away from the mattress. "When I saw you at dinner that night, and later when you walked into the kitchen, it all came back to me. And I was really excited to see you again."

"You didn't seem that excited."

"Everything that has happened since has been me protecting that girl who had a crush on the cute boy who only wanted to be friends with me."

"So, you've been punishing me for rebuffing you twelve years ago, even though I had no idea you even felt that way back then?"

"No I'm not punishing you."

"Well, it sure feels like punishment."

"I've handled it all badly, I'm sorry."

Noah rearranged the pillow behind his head and straightened the throw over his legs. "It shouldn't be this hard, you know."

"I know."

"Either you want to spend time with me or you don't. If you don't, that's fine. I can take it. What I can't take is the back and forth, does she or doesn't she."

She looked at the wood floor for a moment. "Well, if it's not too late, she does. And if I can make this all up to you, somehow, I'll do it." Noah smiled, and she pointed a finger at him. "Not that."

"But that, someday?"

She studied him for a moment, then nodded her head. "I wouldn't rule it out."

He sat up a little straighter. "So let me get this straight, so there's no misunderstanding. Down the line, if things go better than they have, there's a possibility you might make a bid on the artwork you were trying not to admire a few hours ago."

She picked up a pink flowered pillow and threw it at him. "Well, now, maybe not." She noticed his pants on the floor. "You're not wearing pants."

"My house, my room, my bed. You came knocking at my door. I didn't ask you to come up here."

"Fair enough," she said with a small smile.

"Okay, So, are we good now? Anything else you want to confess to or make me feel guilty about?"

"That wasn't my intention. But there's one thing that concerns me."

"The flinging?"

She nodded. "That can't continue if the plan is to creep slowly out of the friend zone."

"It's already stopped."

"Okay can we start over?"

"Let's just continue on."

"Perfect. I still want to know how many, though."

Noah shook his head. "No, you don't."

*****

After a good night's sleep, Noah showered and dressed before making the dreaded phone call to Laura. He almost talked himself out of calling with the excuse she was probably working and he didn't want to bother her. But guilt overtook the dread, and he punched her number into his cell phone. She answered right away.

"Hello?"

"Laura, this is Noah."

"Well it's about time. How patient do you expect me to be?"

"Sorry. I'm trying to figure this all out. Can we get together for lunch or something?"

"Today at one, Manchester's Deli. They have decent food and they aren't so busy we can't hold a conversation."

"Okay."

She said, "See you then," and disconnected.

Noah looked at his phone for a moment. "I already lost control of this situation."

His next call was to Marcus, who didn't answer quite as quickly. In fact Noah was ready to hang up, when he got a frustrated, "Good morning, Noah."

"Did I catch you whipping egg whites again?"

"Oh, if only it was that trivial."

"Should I call back later?"

"No, no. What can I do for you?"

"I'm having lunch with Laura today. Any last minute insight from Roberto on the option of holding on to the business?"

"Okay, you win the having a bad day contest. My day seems so much better now in comparison. Hold on, let me go check with him."

He was gone for several minutes, then returned and said, "He thinks it's probably more info than you want to pass on to her. So, if she's interested, he'd be glad to sit down with both of you and go over it. Is that the way you're leaning?"

"I don't know. Maybe. I'll see how she is."

"You know how she is. It's a matter of if you want to deal with her on a long term basis."

"Wish me luck."

"Good luck, brother."

*****

When Noah got to the restaurant ten minutes early, Laura was already there. She was sitting at a table by a window overlooking the parking lot. So she was watching the door when he walked in, crossed the room, and sat across from her.

"Hi."

"Hello, Noah." She appeared to be dressed for work, so he assumed she was on her lunch break.

"So, what's good here?"

"I already ordered for us. Ham and cheese, mustard, onion, tomatoes, peppers, salt and pepper, right?"

"Um, yes."

"I was your stepmother, briefly."

"Apparently long enough to know what kind of deli sandwich I like."

"Didn't know what you wanted to drink, though. They have beer if you want."

Noah picked up the glass of water in front of him. "Water's fine." He took a drink. She was making him feel like he was twelve again.

A waitress dropped two baskets in front of them with their sandwiches, chips, and a cup of coleslaw. Laura had ordered a tuna sandwich, and he had a flash of memory. She loved fish of all kinds, and when he spent time at his father's while she was the wife, they ate fish often.

He took a bite and tried to get his mindset back to twenty-nine-year-old Noah. He set his sandwich down and wiped his mouth with the paper napkin.

"So, I haven't decided exactly what I'm going to do, but I've looked into Dad's finances, and he still has some business holdings to deal with."

"I thought he sold everything off a few years ago. That's what he told me, anyway. Said he wanted to retire."

"Well, he didn't. So, I'm trying to decide whether to keep the little he held on to, or to sell it all off."

"Shut everything down. You wouldn't know how to keep it going, and you can't trust it to any of the people he has working for him."

"You know them?"

"Well, unless he's been working with other people now, but I doubt that. He's pretty loyal to his business associates. Unfortunately, he never felt the need to be loyal to anyone else in his life."

"Would you be willing to sit down with Roberto and go over the business stuff? I didn't realize you might be able to provide some insight."

"Sure, if it'll help get this all resolved."

"If I kept the business part going, would you be interested in being CEO?"

"She stared at him for a moment. Are you asking me to run Atticus' business?"

"If I keep it going, yes. But if you and Roberto decide it's more trouble than it's worth, I'll sell it all and add it to the pot."

"How big is the pot, anyway?"

"Pretty damn big."

"You're going to take care of Libby, right?"

Noah pulled an envelope out of his jacket pocket and handed it to her. "He set aside money for college, and an account she can access after she's married. There'll be more, of course, but he designated this specifically."

Laura looked over the document and almost seemed emotional. But it quickly passed. "Well, that was the least he could do." She stuck it in her purse and took a bite of her sandwich.

"So who else have you met with? I imagine everyone is eager for you to get this all settled."

"I've talked to Dakota and Dell. So everyone but my mother. I'm seeing her this week."

"I heard you got the house."

"I did, yes."

"Are you staying there?"

"Some of the time. Not sure what I want to do with it, either."

She gave him a long, withering look. "All I hear from you is I don't know, I haven't decided, I'm working on it. I still don't think you're the right person for this job, Noah. Perhaps you should step aside and let someone who knows what they're doing, take over."

Noah studied her for a moment. "Someone like you?"

"I've been working in the business world for quite some time. I'm certainly better qualified than you."

"A piddling tennis bum?"

"That's not what I meant."

Noah took one last bite of sandwich, then pushed his chair away from the table. "I believe my father put me in charge of his estate because of my lack of business prowess. He knew I'd be fair and do the right thing." He stood up. "And since you're so much more professionally established, you can buy lunch. I'll get back to you when I have something to tell you. Don't call Marcus again. And don't call me, I won't answer."

"Noah, what about the business aspect?"

"You've helped me decide about that. I'm going to sell it all off." He walked away and left the restaurant. Laura had made one thing clear for him. He didn't want to deal with any of the Wainwright women on a long term basis. He'd figure out who gets what and be done with the lot of them.

He texted Marcus and told him he was headed over.

*****

Noah walked up the stairs to the flat and Marcus met him at the door with a beer in each hand, giving one to Noah as he came in through the doorway.

"Sit, drink, and them tell me what's up." Marcus sat in an overstuffed leather chair while Noah dropped onto the matching couch.

He took a drink. "Okay, I think I've made a decision today."

"Tell me."

"I'm going to give a small amount, a few million," he rolled his eyes at the absurdity of the statement he just made. "A few million to each wife and divide the rest up between the heirs."

"Even Dell?"

"Even Dell, but with the same stipulation Dad put on it, that she get and stay sober. Maybe hers would be an allowance of some sort that she'd only get if she remained sober." He took another drink. "Does that sound right? I don't think any of the women deserve more than that. And I know mom would be fine with a couple million. Right? She's not like the others."

"You want to split fifty plus million between you, me, Dell, and Libby?"

Noah took a moment before he answered. "Sounds weird when you lay it out like that, but yes."

"I thought you didn't want any of it."

"I didn't. But I might have kids someday, and—"

Marcus held up a hand. "Hold the phone. I've never heard you make that statement before."

"What, I have nothing against kids."

"Kids in general, no. But your kids, that's a first." Marcus smiled. "So, she is the one, isn't she?"

"Well, it seems it changes daily. But maybe someday. Time will tell."

"So, are we giving up the hobby, then?" Marcus asked.

"Yes."

"You sound so confident."

Noah folded his arms across his chest. "If I can give up smoking, I can give up, the hobby."

"Yes, but how long did it take you to give up smoking?"

"That's beside the point. And it's not the same thing. Ideally, I wouldn't be giving up the main idea of the hobby. I'd just be changing the person I hobbied with."

"How do we keep having these weird conversations? If someone overheard us, they'd think we were crazy. So, extracurricular sex out, hot girlfriend sex in."

"Correct."

"Okay. Got it."

"So you think she's hot?" Noah asked with a smile.

"Of course, I'm gay, not blind. She's quite attractive and spunky as hell. We had a blast that summer we spent together. Of course we were kids then, but she doesn't seem to have changed much. So you're going to split fifty mil four ways?"

"Depending on how much the business is worth, I figure two million per wife, excluding Tiffany of course, seeing as she'll be in prison. That's six million. So divide the rest, probably sixty when it's all said and done, four ways."

"Sixteen million dollars? And we fantasized about getting ten and never thought it'd ever happen."

"I guess you'll be writing gay porn sooner than you thought."

"Not porn."

Noah laughed. "I know. Spicy gay romance. And I'm sure you'll be great at it."

Noah looked around the apartment. "Are you sure you want to give this place up and move to the Hamptons?"

"Hell, with sixteen million, I don't need to give it up. We can keep it for when we want to spend a weekend in the city and see some shows."

"And visit your brother."

"Of course. But there'll be a room for you in our new, unapologetically ostentatious home, as well." He finished his beer. "What about Tiffany's baby? Assuming there is one and also assuming it's a Wainwright."

"We'll deal with that if it becomes an issue."

"That sounds like a good move." He smiled at Noah. "Seems the old man knew what he was doing when he put you in charge."

Chapter Thirty-Four

After the events of the last two weeks caught up to Noah, he decided to take a leave of absence from the club. He needed time to figure out what he was going to do with the rest of his life, and who he might do it with. Was Charlie the one? He wasn't sure yet, but since he was about to become a millionaire, he didn't need to teach middle-aged women to play tennis anymore. He was pretty sure his leave of absence would turn into a permanent situation. But just because he'd soon have more money than he could ever spend, didn't mean he wanted to sit around and do nothing. He needed a plan. But one step at a time.

First, he needed to set the legal wheels in motion and get the terms of the will written to hold up in court. He knew at least Laura was going to protest. Maybe Dakota, though two million would get her club up and running with some left over. So, she might not cause too much trouble. Both women should be happy their children were being taken care of. Time would tell.

After taking the weekend to regroup and contemplate his future, he set up dinner with his mother on Monday to fill her in on his decision. If she agreed with it, he'd call Ms. Schmidt on Tuesday morning and have her set it up.

*****

Noah and Ruth met for an early dinner at Callahan's. Marcus would be in at five, so they could see him, too.

Noah waited for his mother outside the restaurant, and when she showed up in a taxi, he opened the door for her and gave her a kiss on the cheek. She looked good as always, modestly dressed and minimally coifed.

She smiled and put a hand on his cheek. "You look tired."

"I haven't been sleeping too soundly lately."

"I can imagine."

He held the door for her, and the host sat them at one of the best tables in the house. Marcus had called ahead and told his staff to take care of his mother and brother.

They sat, and ordered some wine and spent a few minutes on small talk, but Ruth was eager to find out what Noah decided, and he was equally anxious to tell her.

She reached for his hand and clasped it. "So, tell me what's been keeping you up at night."

Noah took a sip of his wine. "Well, I believe I've made a decision, and I'd like your opinion."

"Okay. Tell me what you want to do with your father's money,"

"I want to give each wife two million and split the rest between the heirs."

"Interesting."

"Do you think that's fair?"

She squeezed his hand. "I think it's more than fair, I'm not sure I would've given the wives anything,"

"Even yourself?"

"Even myself. I think it's very generous. So, even Tiffany, bride of two months?"

Noah sighed. "Tiffany is another story. She won't be getting any inheritance."

"She won't take that lightly."

He leaned forward in his seat and spoke quietly, even though there was no need. "She won't be in a position to argue the fact,"

Ruth leaned back in her chair. "What haven't you told me?"

"Well, I was doing a bit a sleuthing and discovered, accidentally, and with the help of a Pharmacist, that Dad was poisoned."

Ruth took a drink and waved at the waiter to bring her another. "I knew he was too stubborn to die of old age." She shook her head. "The little bitch. She poisoned him?"

He wanted to tell her more. She'd absolutely love the part about Buddy and the baby, but he couldn't. Not yet. "Well, everything points to that, yes. They're still at the gathering evidence stage."

A waiter came to take their order and returned with a basket of bread and two more glasses of wine. Ruth buttered a slice of bread and took a bite, then looked at Noah.

"So, tell me about the girl in the kitchen."

"How do you know about the girl in the kitchen?"

"You spent an awful lot of time in there during that weekend."

Noah smiled and drank some wine. "I guess I did. Her dad used to work as the on call chef for special occasions."

"Frank Rosemont?"

"Yes, she's his daughter, Charlie."

"Oh my gosh, I remember her when she was a child. But how'd you meet her?"

"That last summer Marcus and I spent with dad. I was seventeen and Marcus was eighteen. We were free after that, she was there spending the summer helping her dad. He was working full time at that point."

"The girl who had a crush on you?"

"How does everyone know that but me?"

"Marcus came home and told me all about it."

Noah leaned out of the way as the waiter set a steak and lobster meal in front of him. "I don't understand how I didn't see it. She says I broke her heart."

"I'm sure you did."

"Well, we're tiptoeing towards a possible relationship."

"Sounds overly cautious."

"We've hit a road block or two. I've made a couple of course corrections, and changed a few things in my life, and we'll see how it goes."

She smiled. "That makes me very happy. I'm going to need some grandchildren soon before I get too old to enjoy them."

"Hold on, not so fast. We haven't even officially gone out on a date. Although, I made her spaghetti the other night. Of course it didn't go too well, but we worked some things out, So, it's onward and upward, I hope. We'll see."

"Whatever happened to boy meets girl and they live happily ever after."

"That'd be a fairy tale you read, Mom. It's never that easy."

"Oh, I don't know. I think if you're in love, all the other stuff resolves itself."

Noah set his fork down and held up a finger. "Speaking of being in love." He reached into his pocket, but paused before pulling out the stack of letters he brought. "If you don't want these, I'll get rid of them. I thought it should be your decision." He pulled out the letters and handed them to her.

She gasped when she saw what it was, and looked up at him with tears in her eyes, which he didn't expect. He reached for her hand. "Should I not have brought them?"

"Oh Noah, I didn't know he still had them. Where'd you find them?"

"They were in the desk."

He let go of her hand and she ran her fingers over the top envelope. "I loved that ornery man, even though everyone told me he was trouble." She looked at him. "Did you read them?"

"No, of course not."

She tucked them into her purse. "Thank you," she whispered, before taking another sip of wine. She looked at him over the rim of her glass then set it down. "You look confused."

"I just don't see how three women, who are smart and capable, could fall in love with a man like him. Tiffany obviously married him for his money, but you didn't. And I don't think the others did either."

"He was a gorgeous man."

"I know you're not that shallow, Mom."

"Charming, cultured, generous to a point. He had a way of making a woman feel like she was the most important thing in the world to him."

"Until she wasn't."

"Well, yes. Until he met someone else who filled that space."

"Bastard."

"He was definitely that. But, for a couple years, we were happy."

"Can I confess something to you?"

"Of course, darling, anything."

"I think deep down, I'm afraid I'm going to turn into him. I don't want to leave four ex-wives behind when I die."

She reached across the table and took his hand again. "You're nothing like your father. You have compassion, which he lacked. And you aren't obsessed with money. You, my beautiful boy, will be fine, and any woman would be lucky to be loved by you."

"You're just saying that because you're my mother."

"No, I'm saying it because it's true."

Chapter Thirty-Five

On Saturday, Noah pulled up in front of Charlie's house a few minutes after noon. As he was opening his door, she came out with a smile. He reached across the seat and opened the car door for her. When she got in, she looked around the interior of the BMW.

"Wow, this is really nice."

"Thanks." He started the car and pulled out into the street. "Now that I'm going to be filthy rich, maybe I'll get you one for your birthday."

"Oh, nice. But my birthday's in March. That's a long time to wait for something this nice."

"Hmm, Christmas? Or perhaps Halloween."

"A little better." She smiled at him. "Labor Day is coming up."

He glanced at her. "Nobody gets gifts on Labor Day."

"We could start a new tradition."

He turned onto a busier street that led to a freeway. "So, should I hop on the interstate?"

"I usually take this all the way to Madison. It'll take us straight to the market district."

"Madison it is."

Twenty minutes later they were at the little coastal fish market. Noah found a space to park, and when they got out of the car, the air was an interesting blend of fish, salt water, and diesel fuel from the fishing boats. It was cooler on the coast, and Noah helped Charlie into the jacket she'd brought before putting on his own. The market was always busy, but since it was later in the day, they missed the hectic morning shoppers.

Noah took Charlie's hand, as they meandered down the rows of booths selling a wide variety of fish. But since they were after crab, their destination was along the edge of the pier where the crab boats tied up and sold right off their decks. They ended up at a boat called The Albatross and looked into a tank of crabs, freshly caught that morning.

When someone called out Noah's name, he turned to see one of his clients from the club. She came up to him and smiled. "Noah, I missed you at the club yesterday. They said you took a leave of absence. Are you okay? You're not sick are you?"

"No, I'm fine. Just some family stuff to deal with." He glanced at Charlie. "This is Charlie Rosemont. Charlie, this is Mrs. Timothy from the club."

The women shook hands and Mrs. Timothy smiled. "So nice to meet you. Take care of this guy, he's sorely missed at the club."

"I will."

The woman left and Charlie glanced at Noah.

Noah shook his head. "No."

"Just checking."

"You need to stop obsessing about that. It's over and done with."

"Sorry."

Noah looked in the tank again and tried not to get agitated by Charlie's constant referrals to his hobby, as he and Marcus called it.

She put a hand on his arm. "I'm sorry. I won't do it again."

He looked at her. "Well, you probably will, but as long as I know you're trying not to, I'll overlook it. I just want to move on. And we can't do that if you're constantly looking back."

She turned to the tank. "So, which one do you want?"

Noah looked them all over. "The big one in the corner with the broken claw."

She looked at the merchant. "We'll take the two in the back left corner, please. And can you blanch them for us?"

"Sure thing." The man pulled the crabs out and walked towards the large pot of boiling water a few feet away.

Charlie turned her back and Noah looked at her. "What're you doing?"

"I can't watch. It seems so cruel."

He put his hands on her shoulders. "That is possibly one of the most adorable things I've ever seen. May I kiss you?"

She glanced around at the people milling about. "Right here? In the middle of the fish market?"

"Sure." He put his arms around her waist. "Why not? The crabs won't mind."

She smiled, then hugged his neck. "I suppose it's strangely romantic."

He leaned in and kissed her lightly on the lips, pulled back and looked at her, then kissed her more intensely. When the merchant cleared his throat behind them, Noah let go of her and stepped back. He pulled out his wallet and paid the man, then took the bag with their crabs and grabbed Charlie's hand.

"Where to now?"

"The Farmer's Market down the block."

They walked in silence for a few minutes while they people watched and enjoyed the market atmosphere.

When Charlie glanced at him, he asked, "What?"

"So much for easing our way into a relationship."

He stopped and turned to face her. "Should we go back to pretending we want to be friends?"

She took his free hand, then smiled and kissed him on the cheek. "No, this is good." She started walking and tugged on his arm to get him moving again.

They reached the farmer's market and Charlie started filling the cloth tote she brought with fresh greens, carrots, tomatoes, and peppers. As she was heading for the fruit vendors, Noah put a hand on her arm and stopped her.

He pulled her behind a table of flower arrangements and turned his back to the walkway. "Hold up."

"What's going on?"

"I just saw Tiffany."

Charlie raised up onto her tiptoes and peered over Noah's shoulder. "Where?"

"Don't let her see you."

Charlie spotted Tiffany, and watched her using Noah for cover. "She's with someone." She switched shoulders. "Oh my God. It's Richard." She pulled out her phone and took a picture.

Noah risked a glance over his shoulder. "Who?"

"Richard the food prep and dishwasher guy."

"You've worked with him?"

"At your house. On that weekend. You borrowed cigarettes from him."

"That guy? She's with that guy?"

Charlie nodded as she took another picture, then stashed her phone.

"Is he your guy?"

"No, he was there when I showed up for Thursday night dinner."

Noah grabbed Charlie's shoulders. "He's Tiffany's guy."

She looked at him. "He's the guy? You think he's the guy who…"

Noah nodded, as he glanced over his shoulder again. "Son of a bitch." He grabbed Charlie's hand and led her through the tents until they were safe from being spotted by Tiffany and Richard.

Charlie asked, "What should we do?"

Noah took out his cell phone and dialed Detective Reece, who again surprised him by answering after two rings.

"Reece here."

"Detective Reece, this is Noah Wainwright. I believe I just discovered who Tiffany's accomplice is."

"Who? And how do you know? You're not off playing private eye, are you?"

"No, totally accidental. I spotted her and a guy named Richard who was working in the kitchen that weekend. She treated him like hired help and Charlie didn't know him. Tiffany hired him. And by that I mean, give Dad the final lethal dose."

"Sounds promising. Where are you?"

"At a farmer's market. And they aren't here buying vegetables. And he's not hired help. They're rather chummy."

Charlie motioned to Noah she wanted the phone and he handed it to her.

"Detective Reece, this is Charlie Rosemont. When I showed up to work Thursday afternoon, Tiffany told me she hired him through a temp agency. And she spent the rest of the weekend ignoring him. Now, well, she's not ignoring him anymore."

She handed the phone to Noah. "What do you think? What do you want us to do? Should we keep an eye on them?"

"No. Don't do anything. Walk away and enjoy your day. We'll find out who this Richard is. Do you have a last name?"

Charlie who had her ear up to the phone glanced at Noah and shook her head.

Noah answered, "No, afraid not."

"Okay. Be cool and don't let her see you."

"Gotcha. We'll leave out the other exit."

"Call me tomorrow and I'll let you know if I found out anything."

Noah stashed his phone and took Charlie's hand again. "Let's go."

Charlie smiled. "This is so exciting."

Noah looked at her. "We may have just spotted the man who killed my father."

"Oh, right. I'm sorry. I wasn't thinking."

"You seem to do that a lot." They walked a few steps before he said, "But I agree, if my father wasn't the victim, it'd be hella exciting."

Chapter Thirty-Six

On the drive to Noah's house, they talked about the possibility of Richard being a murderer for hire. And the fact he too, could be the father of Tiffany's child. The whole conversation was surreal to Noah and brought him back to the feelings he had when his father summoned him to what was soon to be his deathbed. If he hadn't witnessed firsthand the state his father was in, he probably wouldn't believe Atticus was dead, and that he was just playing a game to weed out the worthy from the sponges.

When they got to the house, Noah parked under the canopy next to the kitchen entrance and they exited the vehicle with their market fresh items in hand.

In the kitchen, Charlie fell into boss mode and instructed Noah to get a large pot of water boiling for the crab and then fetch a bottle of wine, preferably a Chablis or a white burgundy.

Noah filled the pot and set it over a burner, before he headed to the wine cellar. The access was an unassuming door next to the kitchen. It opened up to a set of stairs leading to an impressive collection of wine. A collection that was now his.

Noah knew nothing about wine. So, when Charlie asked for a white burgundy, he had no idea what she meant. He worked his way down the aisles, lifting a bottle now and then to read a label.

"So white burgundy is a bit of an oxymoron." He found a row of Chablis and he touched a bottle. "I might be back for you." At the end of the row of Chablis, he found what she asked for, a Puligny-Montrachet. He looked at the bottle. "And I wonder how expensive you are."

He returned to the kitchen, and she took the bottle from him and looked at it. "Perfect choice. You know your wines."

"No. I don't. Not at all. But I seem to have inherited a very nice collection."

While he was gone, she threw together a salad with everything they got at the market, and the water was boiling.

"So, do you want to drop these poor things into the water, or open the wine?"

"Knowing how you feel about the little critters, I'll handle the crab."

She handed him the iced seafood, then took two wine glasses out of the cupboard and retrieved a cork screw from one of the drawers.

Noah dropped the crab into the water, then watched her move about his kitchen. "You know your way around better than I do."

"You want to grab a couple of plates?" She nodded toward a cupboard. "And some silverware and napkins. Lots of napkins." She looked at him. "Are we eating in here, again?"

"Fine with me."

She pulled the cork from the bottle and set it on the butcher block counter to breathe while the crab finished cooking.

When it was ready, they sat on either side of the counter and Noah raised his glass. "Cheers to an interesting day."

She smiled and touched her glass to his. "It was an interesting day, wasn't it?" She watched him over the rim of her glass, then set it down. "And you kissed me."

Noah picked up a crab leg and pulled the meat out of it. "I did. And I believe you kissed me back."

"I did." She watched him dip his crab into melted butter. "So, the creeping slowly out of the friend zone—"

"That was a bad plan. This is a much better plan."

"Okay, just as long as it doesn't turn into a mad dash to the finish line."

Noah set the empty shell down and licked his fingers. "The finish line?"

"You know what I mean."

"Can we jog to the finish line?"

She contemplated for a moment. "How about a power walk to the finish line?"

Noah picked up his fork and stabbed at his salad. "I can live with that."

Charlie took a couple bites of crab and sip of wine, then asked, "So are you getting used to living here?"

"It's growing on me. I'm not quite ready to give up my condo, though."

"Have you found the safe yet?"

"I haven't looked since you and I did. It has to be in my dad's room, though."

"Can't go in there yet?"

Noah shook his head. "I guess it's kind of dumb."

She reached across the table and took his hand. "It's not dumb."

He shrugged. "How's your dad doing?"

She squeezed his hand, then let go and took another sip of wine. "He's doing okay. He's decided to stop all treatment. Just wants to spend the time he has left without medication making him sick."

"I'm sorry. How long does he have?"

"Six months or so."

Noah studied her for a moment. "I brought this up before, and you got annoyed with me, but, if there's anything I can do, please ask. A medical trial or new treatment you can't afford or insurance won't cover. I'd like to help, if I can."

She stood up and leaned across the counter to kiss him on his forehead. "You're a sweet man. Thank you. I'll talk to him, but I don't know that he'll accept."

She picked up her plate and walked by him on the way to the sink. He took her arm and smiled. "You missed."

"What?"

"My lips." He pointed at his mouth.

She gave him a quick kiss, then continued on to the sink. He turned in his seat and watched her for a moment. "You call that a power walk?"

"Bring me your plate."

He got up and brought his plate to her, and stayed right next to her.

She took a step back. "You need to go to your stool and sit down."

He moved close again and put a hand on her back. "You don't trust me?"

"I don't trust me."

He pulled her in and kissed her, then let go and returned to his seat. "You sure this is far enough away? I can go in the other room if you want."

"Don't get cocky. Just drink your wine."

"Trying to get me drunk?"

"Stop. Change the subject."

"So, we should probably start going out on an actual date now and then. Isn't that how this works?"

"Have you not dated before?"

"Not too much, no."

"Oh my."

"I'd love to take you somewhere Thursday night. I'm meeting with the Wainwright's in the afternoon, and will probably need something to look forward to."

"I can do Thursday night. Will you take me to Callahan's? I've never been."

"Well, I know the Maitre d', so I could probably get us in."

"Then it's a date." She came to the counter and sat down. "So, how much is 'not too much'?"

"Umm, I dated a girl during college for about a month."

"Why haven't you dated?"

"I guess, I've been waiting for you."

She smiled and sighed, then stood up. "And I need to go."

"What? Why?"

"Because, like I said before, I don't trust myself and the finish line is lurking dangerously close."

"I personally don't see that as a problem."

She kissed him on the cheek. "Come on. Time to take me home."

He got up slowly and followed her to the door. "You really need to work on your aim. You missed again."

Chapter Thirty-Seven

Marcus came into the kitchen to find Charlie removing a large pan of pastries out of the oven. "Oh, hey. I didn't expect to find you here."

"Just using the oven for a luncheon I have today."

Marcus checked out the pastries. "Those look too good to eat. Where's my brother?"

"I haven't seen him. I thought he was with you getting breakfast or something."

"Damn it. He overslept." He left the kitchen and headed up the stairs with Charlie on his tail.

*****

Noah grumbled when Marcus shook him, then squinted up at him. "What the hell?"

"It's eleven. They'll be here in an hour. Why are you still sleeping?"

"It's eleven?"

"Get up. Shower. Wear something nice. I'll go put some coffee on. Charlie make sure he gets up, please."

Noah looked past Marcus to see Charlie standing in the doorway. "Hey, Charlie."

"Good morning."

He rolled onto his back and put a second pillow behind his head, then covered his mouth as a loud yawn escaped.

"What're you doing here?"

"I was using your oven. I'll be gone before everyone gets here." She moved to the end of the bed. "Rough night?"

"I got to bed around three. I ventured into my dad's room and I found the safe in the closet."

"You did. What's inside?"

Noah shrugged. "I couldn't get it open. That's why I was up so late, trying every combination of numbers I could think of, birthdays, anniversaries, his social security number. You name it, I tried it."

"And no luck?"

"No luck."

"Maybe your mom knows what it is."

"Maybe. I'll ask her." He yawned again. He'd love to stay in bed all day and talk to Charlie. But, in less than an hour, he'd have a houseful of expectant Wainwrights to deal with.

Charlie smiled at him. "You better get up before Marcus comes back up here."

"Yeah, you're right." He started to get up and Charlie backed up towards the door.

"I need to go pack up my pastries."

"So, are we never going to get within ten feet of each other again?"

"Go take your shower and we'll talk about it tonight."

When Noah made it downstairs and into the kitchen, Charlie was gone. Marcus handed him a cup of coffee and a freshly baked cinnamon roll. He sat on a stool and took a sip of coffee.

He asked, "So, how do you think this is going to go?"

"A total bloodbath."

"Well thanks for that."

Marcus smiled and squeezed his shoulder. "Just kidding. It'll be fine. Just lay it out for them. There's not a lot they can do at this point."

"Dell is going to freak out and Laura is going to make me feel like an unqualified imbecile."

"Probably. But I've got your back. And so does Mom." He checked his watch. "And it's time."

Fifteen minutes later, everyone had arrived, and either grabbed a coffee or a drink from the bar. They all sat down and it took Noah back to the day he found out he was executor. Everyone was sitting in the same seats they had that day. Marcus stayed in the back of the room while Noah went to the desk and faced the family.

He cleared his throat and leaned on the desk, but then stood back up. He felt like he was in grade school giving an essay in front of the class. Only this time the classroom was filled with hostile people.

He cleared his throat again. "Okay, so I'm sure you've noticed Tiffany isn't here. I didn't tell her about it because she's about to be arrested and won't be getting any inheritance."

He waited for the noise to settle. Everyone wanted details. "I can't tell you anything right now. But it'll all come out soon."

Dakota stood up. "You can't drop that on us and not tell us anything."

He glanced at Marcus, who gave him a slight nod of approval. "Okay, I can give you a little information. Apparently, Atticus was being poisoned over a period of time and it slowly killed him."

Laura looked appalled and put a protective arm around Libby's shoulders. "That's horrendous, even for him."

Dell held up her glass. "I knew she was only after his money." Buddy patted her arm and glanced at Noah.

Dakota stood up. "How do you know this and why are we just hearing about it?"

"We had to keep it quiet until there was enough evidence to arrest Tiffany. If she found out we were on to her, she might've taken off. So, the fewer people who knew, the better. And I hope you'll all keep it to yourself for now until she's in custody." He avoided looking at Buddy when he added, "Seems she had an accomplice who did the dirty work. They're still trying to locate him."

Dakota sat down. "Well, isn't this just typical Wainwright family drama? Of course he couldn't die a normal death."

This caused another fervor, and Noah waited a few moments before holding up his hands. "Today isn't about that. Today is about the will." He glanced at Marcus, who gave him a thumbs up. "I know most of you wonder what the hell Dad was thinking by making me executor, believe me, I'm right there with you. But the fact is, he did. The will has been written and filed with the court. And if you have a problem with my decisions, get a lawyer and fight it in court."

Dell held up her glass again, which was now empty. "Get on with it."

"Dad left instructions for a few disbursements he felt were important. I've already discussed those with the recipients. Basically a token amount for each of his children."

Dell spoke up again. "This house isn't a token amount, Noah. What I got was a joke, compared to this."

Marcus spoke from the back of the room. "Let him finish, Dell."

Noah nodded a thank you to his brother, then went on. "Each wife, the three of you, will get two million dollars. You all received a settlement when you divorced and you got child support and spousal support. You've all lived comfortably off of Atticus' money. So, I believe that's a fair amount." He waited for the grumbling to start, but the room remained quiet. He went on. "The rest of the estate, once I've liquidated the business assets, will be divided evenly among myself, Marcus, Dell, and Libby." He looked at Dell. "The same stipulations will apply."

She glowered at him but didn't say anything.

Noah turned to Laura and Libby. "Libby's money will be set up in a trust she can access when she's twenty-one." He looked at Libby. "I'll talk to you about this in depth later, but get someone you trust to help you with investing and such."

Libby glanced at her mother, then nodded.

"So, that's basically it. There's a sailboat in Florida if anyone is interested in it as part of your inheritance. Also, two racehorses. Otherwise, I'll sell them and add the money to the heir's inheritance."

Noah expected an explosion of dissent, but the room was silent. He glanced at Marcus who shrugged.

"Any questions?"

Ruth stood up. "I want to thank you for taking this on. You've been fair, and I for one, think you did a damn good job."

"Thank you, Mom." He looked around the room. "Anyone else have anything to say?" No one spoke up, so he said, "Okay, then I guess that's it."

He went to the bar and poured himself a drink as Marcus joined him.

"I'll take one of those." He glanced around at the Wainwright women. "It can't be that easy."

Noah shook his head, then spotted Laura headed his way. "And here it comes." He smiled at her. "Laura."

"While I appreciate you taking care of Libby, don't you think two million out of fifty plus is a little insufficient?"

"Like I said, you've been getting money for several years. I consider this a bonus, actually. I could've given it all to the four of us."

"Well, don't go spending it yet. I plan to take this to court."

"I assumed you would."

"And I didn't like your veiled comment to Libby, that she should get someone she trusts to manage her money."

"She'll be twenty-one. It'll be her decision. If she wants your help, I'm sure she'll ask for it."

Laura hmphed and walked away, and Marcus grinned at Noah.

"Damn, look at you. All bad ass. I'm loving the new Noah Wainwright."

Noah took a drink of his scotch, then saw Dell approaching with Buddy on her tail.

"You're going to withhold $10,000,000.00 plus from me because of some stupid stipulation our father put in a letter to you?"

"Yes, I am. It's for your own good. And if you want it bad enough, you'll comply."

Buddy stepped up to the bar and poured two drinks. He handed one to Dell, then took a sip from the other. "So, racehorses, huh? That might be cool."

Dell took his arm. "Don't be ridiculous. What would you do with racehorses?" She stalked off, dragging Buddy behind her.

Marcus watched them go. "So, with the money, and when she finds out he slept with Tiffany, how long do you think he's got as her husband?"

"Not long, he's doomed." He put a hand on Marcus' shoulder. "I need to get some air. I'll be back in a few."

"Go ahead. I've got this."

Noah went out into the foyer, then through the dining room and out the French doors to the patio. He took a few deep breaths of fresh air and tried to release the tension he built up since he woke up. When he heard the door open, he turned around prepared to be annoyed, but it was Libby, and he smiled instead.

She closed the doors and stood in front of them. "Sorry to bother you."

"You're not." He pointed to a chair. "Have a seat." She perched on the edge of a chair and Noah sat in another. "So, what's up?"

"It's a lot of money, isn't it?"

"Yes, it is."

She thought about it for a moment. "And my mom can't get to it?"

"No, she can't. But like I said, you'll need someone to help manage it. It'll be tempting to go out and blow a bunch. But you'll do better in the long run if you use some restraint and spend it wisely."

"Can you manage it for me?"

"Me, no. I'm not the right person for that. But Roberto would be a good choice. He's good with those things. And he'll do what's best for you while listening to what you want. You've met him, right?"

"Yes, at the wedding."

"That's right, you came with my mom." He finished his drink and set his glass aside. "He's a good guy. He'd be a good choice. So, your mom told you about the rest, right?"

"College and something on my wedding?"

"Yes. He was also planning on sending you to Europe after you graduate. If that's something you want to do, I can make it happen."

"That'd be awesome." She looked at the ground for a moment. "Would I need to take my mother?"

Noah laughed. "Well, you'll need to take someone. But your choice. She'll need to agree, of course, since you won't quite be free to make that decision on your own."

She sighed. "I guess I'll be going to Europe with my mom, then."

"You've got a whole school year to get through first. We'll see how things stand at the end of the year."

She nodded as she stood up and kissed Noah on the cheek. "Thank you."

"It's not my money. I'm just the middle man."

"Not for the money. For being nice to me."

"That's what brothers are for."

She got up and headed for the door, but stopped and looked back at him. "I still want to take tennis lessons from you."

"I'd like that. Just so happens I have a tennis court."

She went inside and Noah remained on the patio. He hated to admit it to himself, but the place was growing on him. It might still take a while, but he could see a time, not too far in the future, when he could call it home.

A few minutes after Libby left, the doors opened again and Simms stepped out. "Will the ladies be staying for dinner, Sir?"

Noah shook his head. "No, no way. They'll be gone soon."

"Would you like Martha to put something together for you before she goes home?"

"No, I've got a date tonight."

"Very good, Sir." He bowed slightly. "Give Miss Charlie my best."

Noah smiled at him. "Nothing gets past you, does it, Simms?"

"I'm the fly on the wall, Sir." He turned for the door.

"Simms, unless you're set on going to your sister in California, I'd like for you to stay on. I really don't need a butler, but I can't imagine living here without you doing what you do. It wouldn't be the same."

He bowed again. "It would be my honor, Sir."

Chapter Thirty-Eight

Noah pulled into the parking structure a few blocks from Callahan's and found a spot. He turned off the motor, then turned in his seat and smiled at Charlie. "So, our first official date."

"Yes, I'm officially dating Noah Wainwright."

"Ex tennis pro and heir to a small fortune."

"I'd say it's more of a medium-sized fortune."

He opened his door and stepped out of the car. When she got out of her side, he smiled at her over the hood of the car. "Still having trouble wrapping my head around that."

He took her hand, and they started walking towards the restaurant.

"So," she said as she pulled her jacket tighter across her chest. "What're you going to do with yourself now?"

He put his arm around her. The breeze was chilly and neither of them were dressed appropriately for it.

"I have no idea."

"Well, I suppose you don't need to do anything. You can still play tennis in the summer and ski in the winter. Only now you can play tennis and ski anywhere in the world."

They reached the restaurant and stepped through the door when the doorman opened it for them. Marcus approached them and kissed Charlie on the cheek, then shook Noah's hand.

"You don't know how long I've waited for Noah to bring a date here."

He motioned for them to follow him, and he led them to a table in a quiet corner of the room. "This is our best table. Edward will be your waiter, and if he doesn't give you excellent service. I want to know about it." He took the menus tucked under his arm and set them on the table.

Charlie smiled at him. "This is perfect, thank you, Marcus."

"I'll check in on you from time to time if I get the chance. But I won't hover, of course. I don't want to interfere."

"Go back to work, Marcus," Noah said. "We'll be fine."

Marcus left and Edward showed up with a bottle of champagne. "Compliments of the house," he said as he expertly opened the bottle and filled two glasses. "I'll be back for your order, shortly."

They each picked up a glass and Noah held his up in a toast. "To the beginning."

"Of?"

"Whatever lies ahead."

They both drank, then Charlie said, "I believe you're becoming an optimist, Mr. Wainwright."

"Well, I can afford to be one, now. And I'll tell you this. Whatever the future holds, it won't be tennis in the summer and skiing in the winter."

She took another sip and cocked her head at him. "Perhaps tigers can change their stripes."

"I'm completely stripeless at this point."

"Good to know." She picked up her menu. "So, what's good?"

"Everything."

*****

Halfway through dinner, which was steak for Noah and salmon for Charlie, his phone rang. He didn't recognize the number and put it back in his pocket.

"Go ahead and answer it." Charlie said.

"Really?"

"Yes, please."

With a shrug, he said, "Hello."

"Mr. Wainwright, this it Detective Reece."

"Oh, hey. I hope you have some news for me."

"I do. We tracked down Richard and brought him in for questioning. He broke after an hour and confessed to everything."

"And implicated Tiffany?"

"Yes."

"So, you can arrest her?" Noah gave Charlie a thumbs up.

"Yes. But Richard said she was getting a little edgy, so in order to avoid too much of a scene, was wondering if you'd like to help us out?"

Noah pushed his plate aside. "How so?"

"I thought perhaps you could invite her to lunch, and when she's least expecting it, we'll come arrest her."

Charlie was leaning forward trying to hear the conversation, so Noah put the phone on speaker and set it on the table between them. "You don't think she'll make a scene in a public place?"

"Hoping so."

Charlie shook her head and Noah nodded. "Don't count on it. But, I'd love to have a front-row seat."

"Okay, can you meet with her tomorrow?"

"I'll call her tonight or in the morning and set something up."

Noah hung up and stashed his phone. "You got most of that, right?"

"They're going to arrest her."

"This is going to be fun. You want to come?"

"I wish I could, but I have a full day tomorrow. I'll expect a play-by-play though, tomorrow night."

They finished their meal, along with most of the champagne, but when Edward offered dessert, they declined.

Charlie looked across the table at Noah. "So, are you sober enough to drive?"

Noah thought about it for a moment. "I will be after we take a walk."

"Sounds good, except we'd probably freeze."

Noah caught Marcus' eye and motioned for him to come over. Marcus finished the conversation he was having, then came to their table.

"How was everything?"

"Excellent, as always. So, do you have a lost and found?"

"Um, sure. People leave stuff behind occasionally."

Chapter Thirty-Nine

Noah was in the kitchen scrambling a pan of eggs wearing nothing but an apron. It was early, and the house was empty, and he was beginning to feel at home. He added a dash of salt and pepper to the eggs.

"You know you're getting comfortable when you do some naked cooking."

Marcus always said if you're not naked cooking with a friend, then what's the point, and Noah wondered if Charlie would cook with him sans clothing. *You can barely get her to kiss you. I think naked cooking is pretty much out of the question at this point.*

"Excuse me, Sir."

The sound of Simms' voice surprised him, and he glanced over his shoulder.

"Morning, Simms."

Simms did a quick glance at Noah's bare backside.

"Oh, right, sorry." Noah turned his back to the stove. "I'm just making some breakfast. And sometimes, I feel clothes are optional."

"It's fine, Sir. It's nothing I haven't seen before."

Noah wasn't sure how to react to the statement, and Simms looked like he wanted to retract it.

Noah nodded at the coffee machine. "Just made a fresh pot of coffee."

"Thank you. I believe I'll have a cup." Simms opened a cupboard above the coffeemaker and retrieved a cup. He filled it, then stirred in some sugar.

Noah turned halfway toward the frying pan, keeping the view of his backside from Simms' line of site, and attended to the eggs.

After a moment, Simms seemed to regain his composure. "Are you cooking for two, Sir?"

Noah sighed. "I'm afraid not." He looked down at his apron. "That'd better explain my attire though, wouldn't it?"

"I'm glad you're feeling at home, Sir." He moved towards the door. "If you don't need anything, I'll leave you to your breakfast."

"Thank you, Simms."

"You're welcome, Mr. Wainwright."

"I'm Mr. Wainwright, now?"

"Of course, Sir. You're the new master of the house." He bowed and went out the door.

"Huh. I guess I am."

Noah dumped the eggs onto a plate and set it on the counter, then went to the landline phone, mounted on the wall, and dialed Marcus. The cord was long enough to reach the counter, so he sat and took a bite of egg.

"You're calling me at eight in the morning?"

"You didn't need to answer." Noah took a sip of coffee and scooped up a forkful of eggs.

"Why are you using the house phone?"

"I don't have a pocket for my cell, at the moment."

"Are you naked cooking?"

"Scrambled eggs and coffee." He ate the eggs on his fork.

"Seems you've acclimated to the big house."

"I guess so. Simms even called me Mr. Wainwright."

"Simms? Did he catch you in your birthday suit?"

"I'm wearing an apron, but yes."

"Poor Simms. He probably had a day or two where he thought he was done with crazy Wainwrights."

"So, I have a question."

"What?"

"Is it possible Simms is gay?"

"Of course he's gay."

"How do you know?"

Marcus sighed loudly. "If you're a member of the club, you can spot other members."

"So, what? You have a secret signal or something?"

"Actually, it's a secret handshake."

"Okay, whatever."

"I can show it to you sometime."

"I get it."

"Of course you can never use it. It's strictly forbidden to anyone outside the club."

"I'm hanging up now." Noah stood and hung up the receiver, then returned to his breakfast.

*****

Noah got home too late after his dinner with Charlie to call Tiffany, but after he ate, showered, and dressed, it was late enough to call her. Even though it was ten. She sounded like he woke her when she answered.

"What do you want?"

"Good morning, Tiffany."

She yawned into the phone. "Why are you calling me? Have you come to your senses?"

"Well, a little bit, yes."

"Really?"

"Don't get too excited. But I'd like to meet you for lunch today. Are you free?"

"Well, since I don't have a job, or a house to run, I think I'm free."

Noah refrained from responding on the 'house to run' comment, but said, "Talking about houses, any luck finding an apartment? You've been at the hotel, well past your allotted week." Of course, after this afternoon, that would be a moot point.

"It's so hard."

"Well, we'll talk about that today, too. Any luck getting that pregnancy proof I asked for?"

"I'm going to see my doctor next week. I don't see why you won't believe me. It's not like I'd lie about something like that."

"Okay, so about lunch. There's a café on Carson and 10th Ave. Can you meet me there?"

"Why don't we go somewhere nice?"

Detective Reece instructed him to take her there. Apparently it was his go to place for arresting people and he'd have undercover help there in case things went south. Noah couldn't imagine Tiffany getting too crazy, but you never know. She surprised him several times already.

"They've got great food, and it's not too busy." He hoped it would convince her.

"Fine, whatever. What time?"

"How about one?"

"Okay, I'll see you at one."

Noah hung up with her and called Detective Reece. Once the arrangements were made and finalized, Noah started getting nervous. He decided to go give the tennis backboard a workout before he had to get ready to go into town.

He spent an hour on the wall, then thirty minutes working on his serve. When he was worn out, he sat on a chair with a bottle of water and contemplated the empty tennis court. "You need to find someone to play tennis with." He had friends at the club he could play with, but he needed to separate himself from the club. He needed a clean break. Which left him playing tennis with a wall and serving to no one.

He sighed as he got to his feet. "Poor little rich boy has no one to play with." He headed for the house.

*****

Tiffany was late. Noah checked his watch. Twenty minutes late. He glanced around the room and tried to figure out which of the patrons were undercover cops. He hadn't come to any conclusions when Tiffany walked in through the door. He waved at her and she came to the table.

Without sitting down, she looked around the average, boarder line sketchy, café.

She looked at him. "Really? Good food or not, this is—"

"Just sit, Tiffany. Please, it's not that bad." The waitress who showed up at the table didn't help his case. She was middle-aged, unkempt, and had a red stain on her apron. Noah studied it, hoping it was catsup.

Tiffany gave him another look, but sat down with a sigh and frowned at the waitress.

"Coffee?" the server asked with something resembling a smile.

"Yes, please," Noah said with an actual smile, which seemed to perk the waitress up. She put a hand to her cheek, then said, "Coming right up."

Tiffany looked at him. "That smile of yours can light up even a place like this."

For once, Noah felt like she actually meant it and wasn't just flirting with him. For a second he had a flash of regret for what was about to happen. But then he remembered she orchestrated the murder of his father, and it quickly disappeared.

She rested her arms on the table. "So, what'd you want to talk to me about?"

He wasn't sure how long he was supposed to engage her. Reece said they'd come in before they delivered the food, though. So wouldn't be too long.

"Well, I've been thinking about the will, and I feel you should get something, even though you were married for such a short time. The other wives all got settlements when they divorce Atticus, so you should at least get that."

"It's a start. But hardly sufficient seeing as how much he was worth."

Noah spotted Reece coming in through the door and the detective gave him a look that translated to, 'don't react'.

Noah smiled at Tiffany. "So, what do you think is fair?"

Before she answered, Reece came up behind her and sat at one of the two empty chairs at their table.

"Mrs. Wainwright."

"Who the hell are you?" She looked at Noah. "Who is this?"

Reece pulled his badge out of his pocket and showed it to her. "I'm Detective Reece. I'm the detective in charge of your husband's case."

She looked at Noah, again, then back at Reece, and Noah wondered how long she'd try to play innocent.

"What case?" she finally asked.

"It appears your husband was murdered."

Tiffany put a hand to her mouth. "Murdered?"

Noah had to admit, she was a damn good actress.

Tiffany looked at him again. "What is he talking about, Noah?"

Reece put a hand on her arm and when she tried to pull away from him, he tightened his grip. "I'd like you to come with me, Mrs. Wainwright. Nice and quiet."

She tried to pull away from him again. "Why? What are you suggesting?" She looked at Noah. "Do something."

Noah leaned back in his chair. "Just go with him, Tiffany. Don't make a scene."

Suddenly, the innocent widow disappeared. "You bastard. You brought me here. You knew this was going to happen."

"Please, Tiffany, don't," Noah said as he leaned forward and put his hands on the table.

Reece's tone changed. "You can either go quiet, or you can go in cuffs. Your choice."

Noah studied her face. He truly couldn't decipher what she was thinking. But he was relieved when she slowly stood up.

The relief only lasted for a second. When Reece took her arm, she pulled away from him and turned to make a run for it. The unassuming man at the table next to them rose, and stood in her way. She looked at him, then glared at Noah again. Then she suddenly pulled a one-eighty and slumped down to her chair. The tears started, and she buried her face in her hands.

"I didn't do anything. It was him. It was all his idea."

"Him, who?" Reece asked.

"Richard." She glanced up at Noah. "That kitchen helper guy."

Noah pulled out his phone and showed her the pictures from the Farmer's Market. "You mean this guy?" It earned him another glare from Tiffany.

"You still need to come with us," Reece said, taking her arm again. "Are we done trying to run?"

She looked at him. "I didn't do it."

"We'll work that all out. I need you to come with me now and let these folks get back to their meals."

Tiffany looked around the café. All eyes were on her. She stood up to her full 5'6'', and smiled at the detective. "Of course. Whatever I can do to help."

He took her arm again and nodded at Noah. "I'll be in touch."

"Okay, good luck."

Tiffany shot him an evil scowl as Reece led her away from the table and out the door. He watched them put her in the car before he took a breath. Then he took out his phone and called Marcus.

*****

He met Marcus at a bar a few miles from the café. They each ordered a scotch, then Noah relayed the whole story.

Marcus took the last sip of scotch and set the glass down. "I can't believe she tried to run."

"Doesn't surprise me at all, actually."

Marcus studied him for a moment. "So, a month ago, you were innocently going about your life, playing games for a living, without a care in the world. Now, you're participating in sting operations with homicide detectives."

"How the hell did I get here?"

The bartender brought them two more drinks and Noah studied the ice in his glass for a moment. "At least one good thing came out of all of this."

Marcus took a drink. "Charlie?"

Noah nodded. "Yeah."

"Well, you waited a long time for the right one to come along. So what base are you on?"

"First."

Marcus chuckled. "Wow, you really are turning over a new leaf." He patted him on the shoulder. "I'm proud of you."

"Well, if it was up to me, the fans would be doing the wave."

"Follow her lead. You'll get there."

"I don't know how to deal with the frustration. I'm not fond of cold showers."

"You need a hobby. And by that, I mean an actual hobby, not—"

"I know what you mean." He took a drink. "Maybe I'll learn to play the piano."

*****

After spending a few hours with Marcus, which included dinner, Noah returned to the house. He came in through the kitchen and instantly missed Charlie. It was still early, but not knowing what else to do, he headed for the stairs. Simms intercepted him.

"Good evening, Sir. Did you need anything before I retire for the night?"

"No, I'm good. I'm going to go read a book or something."

"Very good. Have a good evening, Sir." He started to leave, but Noah spoke up.

"Simms, I wanted to ask about the piano."

"The piano, Sir?"

"The big white instrument in the otherwise empty room next to the library." At the look on Simms' face, Noah smiled. "Too sarcastic?"

"Just a bit, Sir."

"Sorry. So is it tuned?"

"Is what tuned, Sir? The piano in the otherwise empty room?"

Noah laughed. "I believe you're developing a sense of humor, Simms."

"Only took me sixty-seven years, Sir."

"So, is it in tune?"

"Mr. Kwan's granddaughter plays occasionally and it's cleaned and tuned if necessary every six months."

"Awesome."

"Do you play, Sir?"

"No, but I thought I might learn. Maybe Mr. Kwan's daughter can give me lessons."

"She's five, Sir."

"Okay, I'll need to come up with another plan. Thank you, Simms."

"You're welcome, Mr. Wainwright."

Chapter Forty

As Simms navigated the stairs down to his room, Noah considered going down and tapping aimlessly on the piano, but decided it'd be a waste of time at this point. Instead, he went to his father's room and went into the closet to the safe.

He stared at it for a moment, then took out his phone. It was a bit late, but his mother would probably still be up. He dialed her number.

"Everything okay, Noah?"

"I guess I should call more often. Everything's fine. I just have a question. Do you know the combination to the safe?"

She was quiet for a moment. "I used to know it. But he probably changed it. It was over thirty years ago when he put it in."

"I might as well try it."

"12, 13, 88."

Noah tried the combination, and held his breath as he tried the handle on the old safe. It moved, made an encouraging click, then open up. "That's it. It worked."

"That man," Ruth said, quietly.

"Mom, do those number have a significance?"

"It was the date we met. Friday the thirteenth. He was quite superstitious. We had a quick cup of coffee in the late afternoon. Then he asked me to meet him at midnight for a drink, so he could say we met on the fourteenth."

Noah didn't respond right away, but finally said, "Mom, I really wish I'd known some of these things while I was growing up. It might've changed how I felt about him."

"I've often thought about that, but I don't think it would've made much of a difference. He was still never a father to you and Marcus. And he certainly wasn't much of a husband to any of the wives. I just choose to hang onto the few good memories I have of him."

"Well, I'm glad you have them."

They talked for a few more moments, then ended the call. Noah looked at the safe door, still open only a few inches. "Okay, let's see what you have in here, Dad."

Noah opened the safe and looked inside. On one side was two stacks of cash. He pulled them out and flipped through the end of one. The bills were all hundreds and each stack was about ten inches thick. He didn't know exactly how much was there, but it had to be over $200,000.00. He set it aside. On the other side of the safe was a rack with silver dollars. There were fifty of them. They were old and seemed to be uncirculated. He set them next to the cash.

The next item he retrieved was a black velvet box that was about five by five inches. He opened it and found a gold pocket watch and a string of pearls. He opened the watch and read the inscription on the inside of the cover. *To my love, Atticus. Yours always, Carlotta.*

Noah never met any of his grandparents, but he did know that Carlotta was married to Atticus I. This watch belong to his great grandfather.

The last thing in the safe was an envelope. Noah opened it up and pulled out the papers inside. It was the original deed to the house and the property it was built on. There was also a picture of the house taken right after it was built. On the porch was Noah's grandfather, Atticus II, his grandmother, wife number two, Patrice. She held a baby on her lap, Atticus III.

Noah was surprised by the reaction he had to the picture. There'd been few pictures taken of him and Marcus growing up. He'd seen only a couple pictures of his father and mother. He'd never seen a picture of his grandparents. He stuck it back in the envelope. Those were feelings he'd deal with another time.

He studied the treasure from the safe. Nothing really surprising. Not knowing what else to do with it at the moment, he returned everything and closed it up, then he went to his room and called Marcus to tell him what he found.

*****

Noah slept restlessly, and when Detective Reece called at nine, he was still asleep.

"You have news already?" Noah asked as he sat up and leaned against the headboard.

"Tiffany stuck to her story of innocence for a while, trying to blame Richard. But when we told her we had Buddy's story, she clammed up, asked for a lawyer, and hasn't said a word since."

"Has she said anything about the baby?"

"Baby?"

"She claims she's pregnant with my father's baby. But I have my doubts."

"Hold on a minute."

Noah listened to music for several minutes until Reece came back on the line. "Okay, so I just went through Richard's confession. He says, and I quote, 'She said she loved me. We were going to get married. And with the baby and all, I didn't want to screw that up. I wasn't going to let someone else raise my kid.' So, he thinks it's his."

Noah sighed. "Well, I hope it's his. It'll make my life so much easier. So what happens now?"

"Her court appointed lawyer is coming this afternoon. It's a pretty tight case. I doubt she'll talk her way out of it."

"And what happens with Buddy and Dr. Beals?"

"That's up to the DA. They both withheld evidence that could've prevented a murder. But, I don't know that they'll pursue it, since they have Tiffany and Richard."

"Okay. I'll let Buddy know he might be off the hook. Seems he's at least not the baby daddy."

"The odds are against it."

Noah hung up and stared at the wall in front of him. It seemed like things were starting to fall into place. Everyone was getting what they deserved. He sat up. Not quite everyone. He got up and dressed, then went down the hall to his father's room.

He emptied another shoe box, then opened the safe and took out the cash. He stashed it in the box, closed the safe, and went downstairs. He found Simms in the library dusting the first editions. They were stored in a glass case, and couldn't be that dusty, but Noah assumed Simms did it on a regular basis.

Noah cleared his throat and Simms turned to face him.

"May I help you, Sir?"

Noah looked at the box in his hand, then held it out to Simms. "I found this in my father's safe. I want you to pass it out, as you see fit to the employees. I think it's only fair that they get compensated for all the years they put up with Atticus."

Simms took the box and looked inside. "But Sir."

"And make sure you include yourself in the distribution." Noah headed for the door. "I'm going to eat some breakfast then hit the tennis court."

"Very good, Sir."

As Noah went through the doorway, Simms called out after him.

"Sir?" When Noah turned back, he said, "Thank you. I believe things are going to be different around here from now on."

Noah smiled. "It's a new beginning for all of us."

Chapter Forty-One

Noah kept up a continuous volley with the wall for thirty minutes. He slammed one last ball than caught it in his left hand as it flew back at him.

"Impressive."

He turned to see Charlie watching him. He held up a finger to her as he bent over and rested his hands on his knees for a minute to catch his breath. He stood up and smiled at her.

"How long have you been there?"

"Long enough to be mesmerized by your tenacity." She followed him to a bench where he had a towel and a water bottle. "I thought you were taking a break from tennis."

He wiped his face with the towel and took a long drink of water. "I'm taking a break from the club, not from tennis." He drank some more water. "I have to say, I'm not hating having my own court. Of course, having someone other than a wall to play with would be nice." He took another drink. "Are you here to use the kitchen?"

"You already forgot about fitting me into your schedule for a Wainwright sandwich?"

"Oh right, no. I didn't forget."

She tilted her head at him.

"Well, a lot has happened since Thursday night."

"Okay, I'll give you that. But, you know, your kitchen isn't the only thing that interests me at the Wainwright manor."

"Well, if you're here for Simms, you might be disappointed."

"What have you discovered about poor old Simms?"

Noah glanced over his shoulder. Logic told him Simms wouldn't be standing behind him, but the man had the odd habit of appearing out of thin air.

"I believe I discovered he's gay."

"Really. I always figured he was asexual."

"Like a salamander?"

Charlie laughed. "Yeah, something like that. So what brought you to this conclusion?"

"Well, I was cooking some breakfast yesterday morning…" He looked at her for a moment. "Now, try not to judge me here, but sometimes I like to spend time not wearing clothes."

Charlie turned in her chair. "Wait a minute. Are you telling me you were cooking breakfast in the nude?"

"Well, I had an apron on."

"Still! Eww."

"Why eww? It's not like I was rolling around on the counter tops."

"Still."

"Okay, so that answers that question."

"What question?"

"Well, at the time, I pondered whether you'd ever naked cook with me."

She stood up. "No. Never. So did he make a pass at you or something when he saw you in all your…nakedness?"

Noah laughed. "No, of course not. Now that would be eww." He took a drink of water. "It was something he said. And then I confirmed it with Marcus."

"How would Marcus know?"

"Apparently, if you're in the club, you can see the hidden neon sign that flashes 'I'm gay'."

"Interesting."

He stood up and walked to her, stopping a foot away. "So, if it isn't Simms you came to see, it must be me."

"Well, it was, but now the whole naked cooking thing has me reconsidering."

He took her hand. "I knew I shouldn't have told you."

"Are you done beating up the wall?"

"I am. I was going to take a dip in the pool. You want to join me?"

They started walking towards the pool.

She glanced at him. "I don't have a swimsuit with me."

"That's fine. Suits aren't required."

"But you're wearing one, right?"

He squeezed her hand. "If you insist."

They arrived at the pool and Noah pulled off his t-shirt, then removed his shoes and socks. "What do you say?"

"I'll watch from here."

She sat in a chaise and put her feet up as Noah dove into the pool. He swam underwater to the far side of the pool, then swam back to her. "It feels really nice. I know you want to come in."

She shook her head. "Do your laps, or whatever. I'm fine. The view is pretty good from here."

He floated on his back for a minute, before he stood up and brushed his hair out of his eyes. "At least come put your feet in. The water is a constant 85 degrees. It's perfect."

She sighed, then sat up and slipped off her sandals. She sat on the edge of the pool and dangled her legs in the water. "Happy?"

"Ecstatic." He swam over to her and grabbed hold of her ankles. "Come join me."

"I'm dressed."

"I don't care." He pulled on her legs. "Voluntarily or involuntarily, you're coming in."

"Don't. Noah, I swear. Don't pull me in. I spent an hour picking out the perfect outfit. I washed my hair…"

"Excuses, excuses, excuses." He pulled a little harder and smiled at her. Then he let go, stood up and grabbed her around the waist. He lifted her up, and she squealed as she wrapped her legs around him and hugged his neck, trying to stay dry, but her lower half was already wet.

"Oh my God, I'm going to kill you." She untangled herself from him and he set her down in the water that came up a few inches above her waist. She gave him a shove and stepped away from him and pulled her cell phone out of her back pocket. She held it up to him and glared. "My phone."

He laughed, but stopped when she continued to scowl. "I'm sorry. I'll buy you a new one." He took a step towards her. "Seriously though, it feels good, right? The water."

She splashed water at him. "Why'd you do that? I told you I didn't want to get wet."

"Because I'm immature and I really wanted you to swim with me."

She started making her way to the edge of the pool. He caught up to her and put a hand on her arm, then took the phone from her and tossed it over his shoulder into the deep end of the pool. He put his arms around her and pulled her in close. She resisted for a moment, then gave in and let him kiss her.

"I want a really, really nice phone."

"I'll buy you the best phone on the market. Whichever one you want." He kissed her again. "And for the record, your outfit was perfect."

"Was, being the operative word." She put her arms around his neck. "I should be really mad at you."

"Well, you seem to be mad at me about half the time, so, I figured I'd go for it." He kissed her. "Your hair's still dry."

"So far."

He tucked a strand of her hair behind her ear. "It's been at least a couple weeks since we decided to take our friendship to the next level."

"Yes, I guess it has."

"Don't you think It's about time to take our relationship to the next, next level?"

She looked around. "Right here in the pool?"

"Well, it's my pool, and there's nobody around."

"Not true. Martha's still here until four. And there's probably a grounds man or two wandering around. And of course, Simms is everywhere."

Noah glanced towards the house. "Dammit. Considering I live alone, this house is pretty damn crowded." He kissed her again. "Well, I do have a rather nice bed upstairs."

She stepped away from him and started making her way through the water to the built in steps. "You have between the pool and the bedroom to convince me."

He smiled as he went to the side of the pool and hoisted himself up onto the decking. He held a towel open for her as she came up, then wrapped it around her. He grabbed another towel and wrapped it around his waist. He took her hand as she glanced over her shoulder at her phone in the bottom of the pool.

"Goodbye phone."

They headed for the house at a brisk pace and by the time they got to the door, they were running. They burst through the kitchen door to find Martha standing with her hands on her hips.

"I just mopped this floor."

Noah looked at the puddle forming at his feet.

"Skedaddle," she said with a small smile.

They hurried through the kitchen, across the foyer, and up the stairs, leaving wet footprints behind. At the top of the stairs, Noah looked down to see Martha shaking her head.

He called to her. "Sorry."

She looked up at him and waved. "Go on, then."

They continued down the hall until Simms came out of a room and intercepted them. Noah stopped short.

"Simms."

"Sir."

"Um, we're just…"

"Very good, Sir." He bowed and headed for the stairs. "I expect I'll be busy in the library for quite some time."

"Thank you, Simms."

They continued on to Noah's room, which was still decorated in pastel flowers. Charlie looked around. "You haven't redecorated yet?"

"You seriously want to discuss my room décor?"

"It's so pretty. I think you should leave it like this."

He dropped his towel on the floor. "We'll talk about it in the morning."

"In the morning? It's only one."

"You don't think I'm finally going to get you up here, just to let you go in an hour, do you?"

"I still need to be convinced."

He put his arms around her and kissed her long and hard, then slid her towel off her shoulders. He tucked a lock of hair behind her ear and whispered, "What do you want me to say?"

She smiled. "I'm convinced."

"Tell me you want me."

"Noah Wainwright, I've wanted you since we were seventeen."

*****

Noah dozed happily next to Charlie. He opened his eyes and could tell it was now late afternoon because the sun was streaming in through the west-facing window. He rolled over and put his arms around her with a loud sigh.

"What was that for?" she asked.

"I just realized what I've been missing all these years."

She kissed his neck. "Me?"

"Well, yes. Of course. But also…cuddling."

"Cuddling is the icing on the cupcake. You've never cuddled?"

"No, not really."

"That's quite sad." She sat up and pulled a blanket around her shoulders.

"Well, possibly. But the silver lining is, I can spend the rest of my life overcompensating for all the cuddles I've missed."

She smiled at him. "Well you have my permission to overcompensate all you want."

"You know, before you can add icing, you need to make the cupcake."

"That's very true. I'm a cook, I can completely verify that that's true."

"So, does the overcompensating permission apply to making the cupcake, too?"

Before she could answer, there was a light tap on the door. He said, "What the hell?" as he rose onto an elbow.

Martha spoke through the door. "Mr. Noah, a package was delivered. I didn't want to disturb you, but it says open immediately, so…" She was quiet for a moment. "I'll leave it by the door and go back to my vacuuming."

Charlie giggled. "You're going to have the cleanest rugs. She's been vacuuming for a couple hours now."

Noah laughed as he got out of bed and retrieved the package Martha left in the hall. He shook his head when he saw it was from Marcus. In big red letters, it said, 'Open Immediately'. He brought it to the bed.

"What is it?"

"It's from Marcus."

"He had something delivered to you?"

"He knows I have a slight issue with checking my mailbox."

"So…what is it?" She asked again.

Noah shrugged as he ripped open the brown paper wrapping. He pulled out a paperback book and showed it to Charlie.

She studied it for a moment. "That looks remarkably like you." The cover, with the title, *The Reluctant Heir*, had a chiseled blond man on the front holding a tennis racket.

Noah looked at it. "It certainly does. Maybe a little embellished here and there."

Charlie put a hand on his chest. "Oh, I don't know. I think it's a pretty good likeness."

Noah opened the book and glanced at a few pages. "Oh, you're in it too." He read from the book. "*Charles,*" He glanced at Charlie, *"pushed through the swinging kitchen doors with a large pot of steaming lobster bisque as Neil watched him from a nearby table, enthralled by the way he moved about the room, resembling a cougar sauntering through the jungle".*

Charlie laughed. "Oh my."

Noah closed the book. "Seems my brother has used our relationship as material for his first spicy gay romance novel."

She reached for the book. "Oh, let's get to the spicy part."

Noah pulled the book away from her. "You do realize both Neil and Charles are men?"

"Oh, right."

He tossed the book on the floor. "I'd rather write our own spicy romance novel."

She laid down and pulled him down next to her. "Chapter one, Noah kissed Charlie, while the romantic sound of the vacuum cleaner hummed in the background like a swarm of honey bees, settling into the hive for the night."

Noah shook his head. "Needs a little work."

"Shut up, Neil."

ABOUT THE AUTHOR

Leigh is a writer and the author of The Boy In The Yellow Wellies, The Man Without A Heart, Out Of Focus, and The Last Will And Testament Of Atticus Wainwright III. Leigh writes contemporary fiction that is character driven and delves into family dynamics and relationships. Leigh has published several short stories, but her first love is novel writing. She lives in and is inspired by beautiful rural northern California.

BOOKS BY THIS AUTHOR

THE BOY IN THE YELLOW WELLIES

John O'Leary never expected to fall in love.

He was happy as a single father, successful at his job, and financially secure. Uprooting his life with the complications a relationship brings, wasn't on his agenda. But when a building came crashing down on his head, everything changed as a beautiful copper-haired woman opened his heart to the possibility of love.

But fate wasn't done interfering in John's life, and the opportunity for love faded, along with his lost memories. Can John find his way back to his life, and to the woman who uprooted it and changed his agenda?

Follow this charming man as he navigates through love, loss, and self-discovery.

THE MAN WITHOUT A HEART

John O'Leary has learned to live without his past.

He started his life over at the age of thirty after a devastating head injury.

He's made peace with the loss and has created new memories with the love of his life, centered around the delightful chaos of being the father of nine children. When tragedy strikes and shatters John's heart, along with his world, he is forced to come to terms with a new normal.

John lives without a past, can he live without a heart?

Discover how John builds new memories with his family in this second book of the two book series.

OUT OF FOCUS

Barrett Cavanaugh has seen better days.

Once a highly sought after cinematographer, it only took an untrustworthy partner and a few bad business deals, to turn the tables. When a telegram reaches Barrett in a Mexican bar, he dares to hope his luck has changed.

Barrett and his friend Rhys, head to a South Pacific island along with a dysfunctional film crew, as the allure of the money drowns out the voice of caution in Barrett's head. The only possible upside, is the unexpected addition of an intriguing female archeologist. Can Dr. Rowena Abernathy save the otherwise doomed project?

Once on the island, things go from bad to worse as little progress is made on the documentary. But when life-threatening incidents begin to occur, and they question whether they're alone on the island, it's up to Barrett to save the day.

Will they be able to put their differences aside in order to get off the island alive?

Made in the USA
Columbia, SC
19 April 2021